A REUNION TO REMEMBER

Visit us at www.boldstrokesbooks.com

A Reunion to Remember

by

TJ Thomas

2016

A REUNION TO REMEMBER
© 2016 BY TJ THOMAS. ALL RIGHTS RESERVED.

ISBN 13: 978-1-62639-534-3

THIS TRADE PAPERBACK ORIGINAL IS PUBLISHED BY
BOLD STROKES BOOKS, INC.
P.O. BOX 249
VALLEY FALLS, NY 12185

FIRST EDITION: APRIL 2016

CREDITS
EDITOR: CINDY CRESAP
PRODUCTION DESIGN: SUSAN RAMUNDO
COVER DESIGN BY JEANINE HENNING

Acknowledgments

My enduring thanks go to Len Barot and Sandy Lowe for giving me the opportunity to publish with Bold Strokes Books. I would also like to thank all of the hardworking people at BSB for helping to market and release quality books year after year. My fellow BSB authors are a welcoming and inspirational community. I learn so much from you and am proud to count you as friends.

To all my family and friends who have humored me as I express my exuberance at having a novel published, thank you for listening. Thank you to my sister, Ginny, who helped foster my imagination by insisting we play all those make-believe games as children. My brother, Paul, probably isn't even aware he helped inspire me to be a writer, by being one himself, when we were young. If it was cool enough for him, it was certainly something I wanted to try. This would be a much longer list if I tried to thank everyone in my family individually, but to all of you, both my family of birth and my family of choice, thank you for always being there.

From inception to submission, this book was more than six years in the making. I had the help of a long list of readers throughout this process, and each one helped me inch closer to a story worthy of these characters. If I forget to mention anyone by name, please know you are not forgotten from my heart. From those who read the first draft—Alex, Diana Stephens, Heather T, KT, Sue Gonda, and Susan E. Cayleff. ...To those who read the version I deemed appropriate to submit for publication—Edwina Trentham, Jackie Katz, JM, and Amy "Teeps" Teeple, and to Elle, who read every version—I am forever grateful for your constructive critiques of early drafts of this story and your encouragement along the way.

Special thanks go to my editor, Cindy Cresap, who taught me a great deal about the craft of storytelling. Her helpful and humorous feedback was instrumental in making this book what it is today.

Most importantly, thank you to my wyf, Elle, for her inspiration, patience, and love. She endured countless hours of conversation about fake people, gave insightful feedback every time she touched the story, and above all, believed in me from the very start. Our love propels me every day to be and do better.

Dedication

Elle, I love you this much

(..)!

PROLOGUE

Jo was riding high on her team's latest victory. She was thrilled because it had been a tough win. She worked hard to become a starter on varsity as a sophomore, and today she felt like she'd proven herself. Her teammates congratulated her on the awesome save she'd made in the final twenty seconds of the game that helped seal the victory. She couldn't wait to recount the win to her mom.

She pulled the screen door open. Several things assaulted her senses at once. The smell of her dad's favorite whiskey stung her nose. The blaring TV made her cringe, and at the sight of her father's jacket hanging by the door, her stomach dropped. In the next second, she turned and tried to catch the door before it slammed shut. She was too late. The loud bang stilled the blood in her veins, and she froze in place. Things had been okay for a while. Jo couldn't believe she'd forgotten, even for a moment, and let her guard down as she entered the house.

"Joanna Elizabeth Adams, come here!"

Jo thought fleetingly about ignoring her father and going right back out the door. But she knew it would be worse if she did. She let her bag drop to the floor with a soft thud and walked into the living room. She glanced briefly at her dad to see where he was. He stood by his recliner. *This is going to be bad.* Jo looked down at the floor and waited.

"How many fucking times have I told you to keep it down while I'm watching a game?"

"A lot."

"And still you come running into the house slamming the door."

"It was an accident. I didn't know you were home." Jo knew as soon as she spoke she'd said too much.

"Where else would I be? This is my fucking house. Do you mean to tell me when I'm not home you run around slamming the goddamn doors?"

Jo didn't answer. There was nothing she could say that would prevent the inevitable.

Tension filled the room. The volume still blared on the TV, but the silence between them grew. Finally, her dad spoke again. "What do you have to say for yourself?"

"I'm sorry."

"For what?"

A steady stream of ideas ran through her head. Jo thought about saying she was sorry for slamming the door. She considered apologizing for interrupting his game. But she said nothing. She heard her mother step into the room, but she didn't turn to look her way. She looked up, directly at her father who now stood only two feet from her, and said, "I'm sorry you're home."

Jo tried to relax her body as she knew from experience it made it hurt a little less, but she was not prepared for what came next. She saw a flash of light glint off her father's ring just before the back of his hand made contact with her cheek. Then she felt the sting as it sliced her lip. She heard her mom gasp as she stumbled backward. As she struggled to find her balance, her mom said, "Jo, please go upstairs."

Jo turned. She saw the sadness and apologies that wouldn't be uttered in her father's presence on her mother's face. As much as she wanted to stand up to her father for once, her mother had asked her to do something, and she knew if she stayed, it would be worse for both of them. Turning her back on her dad was another mistake. Jo felt her dad shove her. As she fell at her mom's feet, she heard him say, "Get out of my sight, you little bitch."

She grabbed the bag she'd dropped, ran up the stairs to her room, and shut the door behind her. Closing the door wouldn't block out the sounds completely, but it would help. She lay motionless on the bed. She could hear her father's angry rant and her mom's muffled pleas.

Eventually, the noise downstairs subsided, and an eerie quiet took its place. Since the TV was off now, Jo guessed her dad left to finish watching the game at the bar, where he spent most of his time. She briefly considered going to check on her mom, but if somehow her dad were still home, she'd just make it worse. She had already caused enough trouble for her mom for one day, she wouldn't add to it now.

She stayed put and thought about how she'd explain the swollen lip Monday morning. Every time her father had hit her before, he was careful to do it somewhere that wasn't visible. She figured if she hadn't provoked him, he probably would have done the same this time. Deep down she knew it wasn't her fault. But that didn't make it any better. Sometimes it didn't matter what she did or didn't do. She didn't always know what exactly would set him off. He was erratic, and his mood changed in an instant sometimes. She was tired of all the lies, so tired of hiding what he was. She refused to cry. She learned a long time ago that wouldn't help anything.

Sometime later, Jo heard a soft knock on her door and watched as it opened slightly. Her mom leaned in and asked, "Is it okay if I come in?"

"Sure." Jo scooted up on the bed to give her mom somewhere to sit.

She lifted Jo's chin, turning her face to both sides as though she was evaluating the damage. "I bet that hurts," she said.

Jo shrugged. "It stings." Jo didn't see the point of telling her mom that her face hurt like hell. There was nothing she could do about it anyway. Besides, even though she couldn't see her mom's injuries, she was certain they were there, given how carefully she was moving.

"Here, this will help some." She held out an ice pack wrapped in a thin towel.

Jo took it and held it to her cheek. She was certain she grimaced as the pain intensified with the cold, but she quickly schooled her features. "It does. Thanks."

Her mom studied her like she was having some internal debate. Finally, she said, "Jo, is there anywhere you feel safe?"

"What do you mean?"

"Someplace you are comfortable. Safe."

Jo thought for a moment. "Yes, one place."

"Where?"

"Why?"

"Because I don't want you around him when he's like this."

"He's always like this. What about you?"

She shrugged. "I don't have any other choice, but it's better for me when you're not here because I don't have to worry about you too."

Jo surged forward. "Yes, you do have a choice. There are shelters. We could get away from him."

She shook her head. "I can't leave him. But I can try to get you out of here when he's like this."

Jo studied her for several moments, wishing she could convince her to leave. Finally, she relented. Her mom had to make that decision for herself. "Christie's. I feel safe at Christie and Julie's house."

"Okay. I want you to pack enough clothes for a couple of weeks and get all your school and soccer things together. Let me know when you're done and we'll go over."

"Okay. I love you, Mom."

"I love you too, Jo.

❖

Most of the car ride to Christie's house was quiet. Jo wasn't sure there was anything left to say. When they were almost there, her mom spoke. "I'd like you to go up to Christie's room so I can talk to her parents."

"Okay."

Jo had told her mom the truth. Christie's house was the one place she felt completely safe, but that didn't mean she relished the idea of showing up on the doorstep with her face looking the way it did. When they stepped onto the porch, Jo adjusted the ball cap she was wearing so most of her face would be in shadow.

Mr. Black answered the door. Jo let her mom do the talking.

"Hi, Bill. I need some help. Can I talk with you and Rhonda?"

Clearly surprised, he opened the door and stepped aside. "Sure, Patty, come on in." Mr. B opened the door wide to let them in. "Jo, Christie and Julie are up in their room if you want to go see them."

"Thanks."

As Jo escaped up the stairs, she heard Mr. B say, "Rhonda's in the kitchen. Let's talk in there."

Rhonda looked up from the grocery list she was making at the kitchen table, surprised to see a visitor. "Hello, Patty. How are you?"

"Not so good, actually. I need to talk to you both if that's okay."

"Of course it is. Have a seat."

Patty clasped her hands on the table and appeared to be biting the inside of her lip. "So…there's no easy way to say this, so I'm just going to say it fast. Keith has a temper, especially when he's been drinking."

Rhonda felt herself tense. "Does he hit you?"

"Sometimes."

"And Jo?"

"Yes. In fact, that's why we're here tonight. Jo didn't realize Keith was going to be home when she got home from the game today and she let the screen door slam while he was watching football. Sometimes it's something really small like that that sets him off. He's never hit her in the face before. I'm afraid it's going to get worse for her. When I asked Jo if there was anywhere she felt safe, she said here. I know I should leave Keith and get Jo out of that environment, but I can't do that yet. I'm working on that. But I can't watch him hurt her anymore. She shouldn't have to be around when Keith's showing his temper. I was wondering if it'd be okay if I sent Jo over here when things get bad at our house."

Rhonda and Bill exchanged glances.

"Absolutely," Rhonda said. In her mind it wasn't even a question. Rhonda had wondered once or twice about Jo's injuries, the bruises she occasionally saw on her arms or legs, but Jo had always brushed them off as having happened on the soccer field. Now she knew she should have asked more questions.

"Of course," Bill said. "Jo's welcome here any time, all the time." Rhonda was grateful she and Bill were on the same page.

"You are too. We have a spare bedroom if you need to get away."

Tears slid down Patty's face. "I appreciate that very much."

Bill asked, "Does Jo have clothes with her?"

"Yes. I told her to pack for two weeks. I thought it would be a good idea for her to have extra clothes here in case she has to head this way on short notice."

"Smart thinking," Rhonda said. "Bill, why don't you help Patty with Jo's bags? I'll go get her and the four of us can chat for a few minutes."

As Rhonda approached Christie and Julie's room, she heard giggling. It made her heart lighter that Jo could laugh at a time like this. Jo was Christie and Julie's best friend. She knew they would be over the moon when they found out Jo would be staying with them more often. She watched for a moment as they lounged on the beds, flipping through magazines and trading funny things they found on the pages. She knocked on the open door to get their attention.

"Hi, Mom," Julie said.

"Hi. Jo, would you come downstairs for a few minutes? Bill and I would like to talk with you and your mom."

"Sure." Jo pushed herself off the bed and walked into the hall.

As Jo came into the light, Rhonda saw her cut, swollen lip. She winced inwardly. The entire left side of Jo's face was red and puffy.

Jo met her gaze directly. "It's not that bad."

"I'm sorry, Jo. I wish I'd known sooner."

Jo shrugged. "Not your fault or your problem," she said without any hint of malice. She turned and trotted downstairs.

By the time Rhonda made it down to the living room, Jo sat on the sofa with Patty. Bill was in a chair nearby. Rhonda chose the opposite seat and faced Jo and Patty. Patty's face was puffy from crying and there were unshed tears waiting to fall. Jo sat stone-faced without a tear in sight, giving nothing away. Jo was unlike Christie and Julie in some fundamental ways. She did not bear the sheen of innocence that Rhonda's girls still had. But she remained friendly and seemed genuinely happy in their company. Jo wore the mantle of maturity that had been thrust upon her with confidence and grace. Sometimes it was hard to remember she was only fifteen like Christie and Julie. "Jo, do you know why your mom brought you here today?"

"My dad hit me again and I told her this is the place I feel safest." Jo said matter-of-factly.

"Your mom asked Bill and me if it would be okay for you to stay here when things are bad at your house. We told her you're welcome here any time. We also told her the spare room is open for her any time she needs it. How do you feel about that?"

Jo didn't look at her mom before she answered. "I have mixed feelings about it, actually. While I appreciate the offer, I feel like I should be at our house so I can protect my mom."

"Oh, Jo," Patty said, "It's not your job to protect me."

Jo turned to Patty. "Somebody needs to."

"No. It's my job to keep you safe and this is how I can do that right now. It will help me if I know you're out of harm's way."

Rhonda watched as Jo fought an internal struggle. Rhonda imagined she was weighing wanting to stand up for her mom and doing what her mom asked of her. Finally, she turned to Rhonda. "Okay."

"I'm sure we'll figure some of it out as we go along. But for right now, I'll bring you here after you and Christie finish soccer practice and you'll talk to your mom at some point every day to figure out the plan. If the coast seems clear, Bill or I will drive you home. While you're here, you'll contribute to the household chores just like our kids and you'll follow the same house rules. Any decisions about activities or trips, we'll run by your mom. Neither Bill nor I want to take the place of your parents. We're just a safe harbor when you need out of the storm. Fair enough?"

Jo looked at her mom and then between Bill and Rhonda. Then she nodded. "Sounds like a plan."

Rhonda watched Jo hug her mom good-bye. Tears streamed down Patty's face and Jo murmured reassurances. After the door closed, Jo turned to face them. "So, what now?"

"Are you hungry?" Rhonda asked.

Jo thought for a moment. "Starving."

"Why don't you run up and take a shower. When you're done, meet me in the kitchen."

"Okay."

When Jo came into the kitchen ten minutes later, Rhonda was at the table. Across from her, on the table, was a plate with a sandwich and chips. "Hi."

Rhonda looked up. "Hi. I didn't know what you'd want to drink. You can help yourself."

"Thanks." Jo took the glass from the table and filled it with milk before sitting down in front of the plate. Jo took a couple bites of her sandwich and washed it down with a swallow of milk before looking back at Rhonda. "Can I ask you a question?"

"Yes, and for the record, you never have to ask to ask a question."

"Why are you doing this?"

Rhonda stopped and looked up at Jo. She put her papers aside. "First, because your mom asked me to, but also because this is how I can help."

"Why do you want to?" Jo asked.

"Because you're a special young woman, and it never hurts to have support in your corner. You're a great friend to Christie and Julie, and I hope they are to you too. But you have gone through a lot in your life and if you ever feel like there's something you can't talk to them about, I hope you'll talk to me."

Jo looked as though she wanted to say something but seemed to catch herself. "Thanks." A few minutes later, Jo stood, cleared her dishes, and loaded them into the dishwasher. "Thank you for the sandwich. Good night, Rhonda."

"Good night, Jo."

Chapter One

Jo strolled down University Avenue in the heart of Hillcrest, a trendy neighborhood in San Diego. With only a hint of breeze in the warm air, the late summer evening was perfect. She contemplated her life, something she'd been doing a lot lately. The invitation to Amy's wedding had made her start thinking about where she wanted to be, what direction she wanted her life to take. Perhaps after she returned from Massachusetts she would need to take a long hard look at things.

She shook off the mood and walked through the gates at Gossip Grill, ready to put her heavy thoughts aside and have some fun. She handed over the small cover charge and made her way inside. It was late enough that the DJ already had the crowd into the music. She glanced around the room as she walked to the bar. She was happy to see her friend Cam dancing.

It was great to see her out having fun. After Cam lost Melanie nearly eighteen months ago, she'd lost herself for a while too. If Cam was here, then likely…yep, she saw the rest of them too. Kate and June danced together, in their own little love cocoon. The three of them had been practically inseparable since they were freshmen in college.

Once she had her beer in hand, Jo meandered around the room. She stopped and kissed her friend Laura Jane on the cheek. Laura Jane wrapped her in a hug. "Hey, stranger, will I see you this week?" Laura Jane was the Karaoke Maestro for the Gossip Grill on Tuesday nights.

"I'm going to try, but I have a crazy week. Then I'm headed out of town."

"Well, I hope you can make it. Save a dance for me later?"

"You got it."

By the time she made a circuit of the room, her friends were taking a break away from the dance floor. She received hugs all around when she made it to their table. She joined them and talk quickly turned to Amy's pending nuptials.

Cam said, "I still can't wrap my head around Amy getting married. The only thing stranger would be you taking the plunge, Jo."

"Ha, ha. Very funny, don't even joke about that." Jo used to think there would never be a day she would be willing to be with just one woman for the rest of her life. But lately, she'd been thinking a lot more about that. The majority of the past decade had been a series of one-night stands, with a few long weekends thrown in for good measure. The closest she got to anything serious was the two-year thing she had with Aideen. *Relationship* seemed like too tame a word for what they'd had, but it was the closest she'd come to one. They had lived together briefly, but in the end, decided they were better as friends. She wasn't sure she was built for a long-term relationship, but she had started to ponder the wonder of having someone to come home to at the end of the day, someone to share her time with, beyond the bedroom. Sex had always been easy to come by. She never had to look far for a willing partner. But it no longer felt like enough and that scared her more than a little. Luckily, her friends pulled her back from the precipice direction of her thoughts.

"So, when do you head out?" Kate asked.

"Friday, I'm going to help Amy with last-minute details. How about all of you?"

"A week from Friday," June answered for all of them. "Did you find someone to watch Kona?"

"Yes, Aideen's going to stay with her." Jo ignored the raised eyebrows of her friends.

"It will be fun to have the gang back together again," Cam said.

"Yes, it will. Now enough wedding talk. I need to dance." Jo joined the throng of women moving to the fast beat. She was soon surrounded by lovely, luscious ladies, and she let all her deep thoughts drift away.

After she said good night to her friends, she walked home alone. Her thoughts returned in full force. Why was this on her mind so much these days? She knew the answer though. Thinking about Amy getting married, actually getting the invitation in the mail, it made her yearn for something beyond her reach.

She let herself into her condo and greeted Kona, who sat by the door wagging her tail. "Hiya, Kona girl, how was your evening? Did you throw a rager? If so, you cleaned up nicely." Kona followed her to the bedroom where she shed her clothes and showered quickly to wash away her night. Then she slid between the sheets. She gave Kona permission to join her on the bed. Once they both settled in, her mind wandered in a different direction.

She had been reliving memories from high school ever since she received the formal invitation to the wedding. When she thought about that time in her life, she couldn't help but think of her parents. Her father's tyranny had impacted her life in many ways. Fortunately, she also had fond memories of her time with the Blacks. She tried to focus on those remnants in her mind.

As she lay in bed, her mind played like an old projector screen showing home movies. Wobbly and slightly grainy, she watched snippets of her childhood. Dancing to the latest pop sensation with Christie and Julie in the kitchen while they were supposed to be doing the dinner dishes. Late night talks with Rhonda. Running with Mike, the youngest sibling in the Black family. Learning how to change the oil and tires on a car from Bill. Listening to Christie and Julie fawn over boys. Telling them she preferred girls and their easy acceptance.

So many good memories. Sometimes it was hard to remember why she'd never gone back. She'd thought about letting them know she was headed their way, but she didn't know how busy she'd be with wedding details, and she didn't want to disappoint them if it turned out she didn't have time to see them. Her focus this trip had to be the wedding. But maybe one day soon, she'd need to take another trip to see the people who had helped her survive her teenage years.

Chapter Two

Tying up loose ends at work the rest of the week took all of Jo's energy and focus. She barely had a spare moment to think about her trip until she was on the plane. She was going home. Strange that it still felt like home to her even though she hadn't been there for over ten years. Every time she spent time with Amy since college, Amy had come to San Diego, where most of her family still lived. There hadn't been any reason for Jo to return to Massachusetts until now, but with her best friend getting married, and as her maid of honor, Jo had duties to perform. She wouldn't miss it for anything.

The last time Jo spoke with Amy, she mentioned that Rhonda was going to the wedding. Jo was still trying to decide why that made her a little nervous as the plane touched down. Soon, she was wrapped in Amy's bear hug. "I can't believe you're finally here. This must be strange for you."

"It is, a bit. But you're getting married. I would have gone anywhere to see that. Where's the other blushing bride?"

"She stayed home. She wanted to give us a chance to catch up. You'll see her in the morning."

"Great, so what's the plan?"

"For tonight, I thought we would get you checked in and drop your bags at the Jeff and then head to Johnny's for drinks. If you need or want a car while you're here, you can either use mine or we'll swing over and get you a rental tomorrow. How's that sound?"

"Perfect. Lead the way."

❖

Jo had a wonderful time catching up with Amy. They picked up right where they left off, like she had seen her last week instead of last year.

"Thank you for coming, Jo. I'm glad we finally got you back in the Pioneer Valley."

"I couldn't miss your wedding. It's a 'gotta see it to believe it' sort of thing. Honestly, I'm not sure why I stayed away so long. I love this area. I had forgotten how much. It's just…complicated."

Amy nodded sympathetically. "Sure."

Wanting to shift the focus away from her, Jo asked, "Do you ever regret moving here after college?"

"Never. I never hoped things would turn out so well when I decided to explore the 'lesbian capital of the US' that is the Pioneer Valley. But I've loved it here since the day I arrived. Then to be able to build my dream in the restaurant and find the love of my life, it's amazing how life works out sometimes."

Jo raised her glass. "I'll drink to that."

"Cheers!"

Jo had met Randi last year when she came with Amy to San Diego, and she had known this was the last relationship for her friend.

"So, you said Rhonda is coming to the wedding?" Jo asked.

"That's what her RSVP said."

"Cool. I didn't realize you two knew each other that well."

Amy shrugged. "Well, after you recommended her to do the designs for the restaurant, we hit it off. Randi and I hang out with her occasionally. She's great."

Jo took a sip of her beer. "Yes, she is."

"How long has it been since you've seen her?"

Jo didn't have to think. "Ten years."

❖

The sun hadn't yet risen when Jo's alarm sounded the next morning at half past six. She wanted her body to adjust to the time change, and getting started early was the best way to make that happen. She pulled on her workout clothes, brushed her teeth, grabbed her room key and phone, and went to the inn's fitness center. She had the place to herself. There were definite advantages to getting a jump start on the day. She did a complete circuit on the weight machines. Her muscles were singing as she worked out what was left of her travel fatigue. When she was ready for cardio, she bypassed the treadmill and elliptical and headed for the street.

She was glad she warmed up before venturing into the cool, New England morning. Running this early back home was certainly warmer. She jogged south on Boltwood Avenue toward College Street. In just a few minutes, she was on the track at Amherst College. She wasn't alone. There were various athletes. Nobody questioned her being there. She fit right in.

Running on a track wasn't her preference, but the roads around downtown Amherst were not the most accommodating for a good run. So for now, she used what was at her disposal. She jogged for the first half mile and then ran harder once her legs felt warmed up.

Jo loved running. As a teenager, running was the one place she could be completely free from everything happening at home. It cleared her mind and calmed her. It always had. She ran for nearly an hour. Once she hit her seven miles, she slowed back down to a jog to cool down. After a couple more circuits on the track, she moved to the grass infield and stretched. Then, she headed back to the inn.

As she inserted her key card, her phone rang. She pulled it from her pocket and looked at the readout. Surprised, she answered. "I didn't expect you up this early on a Saturday."

"Times change, my friend. You ready for breakfast?" Amy asked.

"I just finished my run. I can be ready in twenty."

"Perfect, we'll see you then."

With an efficiency that was second nature to her, she washed and dressed with time to spare. She stood for a moment appreciating the view out the window. The peak of autumn was at least six weeks away. She was sorry she'd miss that. She loved fall in New England. She missed having seasons. San Diego was beautiful, but she was still a New England girl at heart. *No reason to stay away so long next time.*

As she exited the Lord Jeffery Inn, or the Jeff as the locals called it, she saw Amy's car pull up to the curb. It barely had time to stop before Randi jumped out. Jo opened her arms and Randi ran into them. She wrapped her in a warm embrace. "I missed you last night."

"I missed you too. But I thought the two of you could use some time, just the two of you, before things get crazy."

Jo nodded. "It was nice, thanks."

Amy walked up. "Where shall we eat?"

Jo shrugged. "No idea. That's up to the two of you."

"In that case," Randi declared, "It has to be Sylvester's."

"Sounds good."

"Perfect."

They headed from Amherst to Northampton on Route 9 toward the former home of Sylvester Graham of Graham Cracker fame. The home had been turned into a restaurant nearly thirty years before and was now the premier breakfast spot in the Pioneer Valley.

As Amy drove, Jo saw what she couldn't in the dark of night, and she started pointing out things that had changed since she moved away. Hampshire Mall was quite different. Most of the stores had not been there when Jo left for college. Dick's Sporting Goods and Target were new, as were many others. Hadley had come into its own while Jo was in California.

The line was already out the door when they arrived at the restaurant. Amy made her way inside to get coffee for the three of them in the coffee bar across the entryway from the restaurant. Randi took the opportunity to check in with Jo. "So, what's new?"

"Not much, same job, same condo, pretty much same everything."

"Who's staying with Kona?"

"Aideen."

Randi raised an eyebrow. "Oh?"

Jo shook her head. "We're still friends and I trust her with Kona. It's nothing more than that."

"Okay. So, are you seeing anyone?"

"Not at the moment."

"Well, there will be quite a few beautiful single women at the wedding. You could get lucky."

Jo didn't tell Randi she wasn't interested in a one-night stand. She shrugged. "We'll see." Jo deflected any additional attention. "So, what about you? Are you nervous? The big day is almost here."

Randi's brows drew together and she touched Jo on the arm. She seemed about to share some deep confidence, then her features lit up. She squeezed Jo's arm. "I can't wait. The day cannot get here soon enough."

Amy made her way down the ramp and passed out the coffees. "What can't get here soon enough?"

Randi stroked Amy's cheek with her free hand. "The day you become my wife."

Amy brushed her lips over Randi's. "For me either, my love."

Jo looked away, not in embarrassment but because she was a bit envious of what Amy and Randi had together. She was happy for them, but as much as she was becoming aware she wanted that with someone, she doubted that kind of love was in the cards for her. Jo shook off the feeling and enjoyed the morning with her best friend and the woman she would wed in a week.

Over breakfast, they went over last-minute details that needed to be tended to. This was one of the reasons she came out a week early, to help in any way she could. Being here for Amy and for Randi was very important to her. She was honored Amy had asked her to stand up with her, and she planned a heck of a send-off tonight. She thought it wise for Amy to have a chance to recover from her night of debauchery before the wedding.

Rather than drop Jo back at the Jeff, Amy drove half a mile farther and let her out at the rental car agency. Jo had decided having a vehicle at her disposal would be nice while she helped with preparations.

Jo hugged Amy. "I'll pick you up at seven." Then she embraced Randi. "I'll get her back to you safe and sound tomorrow."

Randi kissed Jo's cheek. "You better."

Once Jo was back in her room, she set about putting things in order. She quickly unpacked and found a place for everything. She placed her tux in the closet over the shoes she had polished to a shine back in San Diego. With that done, she walked to the window. Appreciating the view, she took out her phone and made a couple of calls to make sure things were all set for tonight. With all of her tasks checked off for now, Jo headed out to get reacquainted with the town where she'd grown up.

CHAPTER THREE

Jo meandered around the small college town. Even with a major university and two colleges in close proximity, Amherst managed to keep its small town feel. It felt familiar and not much different from when she left. Sure some restaurants and shops bore different names, but the character of the town remained the same. She stood on the sidewalk outside Amherst Books, perusing the titles in the front window, when she heard her name.

"Jo?"

She turned toward the voice.

"Jo Adams?" Before Jo could utter a word, her best friend from high school, Christie Black, grabbed her in a tight hug. "What are you doing here? Why didn't you let us know you were coming?"

A wash of emotion flushed over her. Jo hugged her fiercely. She had not realized until that moment how much she missed her, missed the connection she once had to her and her family. "Christie, oh my God!" Jo reluctantly stepped back. She stared in disbelief for a moment. "My best friend from college is getting married next week. I wasn't sure how much time I would have to see anyone since I'm helping with wedding stuff most of the week." Though technically true, what Jo didn't say was she had no idea how things stood between them since she lost touch and had not spoken to Christie in more than eight years.

Christie glanced at her watch. "Well, do you have time for a cup of coffee?"

Jo jumped at the chance to catch up. "Sure."

Christie pulled out her phone. "Let me just text Peter that I'll be later than I expected."

"Okay."

With that done, Christie dropped her phone back into her purse. She slipped her arm through Jo's. "How the heck are you?"

"I'm good, really good. You look great. Peter's your husband, I presume."

"Yes, he is. We have two wonderful children, Mary and Cody. I'm sorry you couldn't make it to the wedding."

They reached their destination and grabbed a table near the front of the café.

"I am too. I just couldn't get away right then. I was helping with the kids of a good friend going through chemo."

"You were where you needed to be. Your gifts were very thoughtful. I enjoyed having a joint ceremony with Julie. Growing up sharing everything wasn't always easy. But when we fell in love, for keeps, at the same time, it made perfect sense to have our weddings together."

"That's great."

Christie turned serious for a moment. "Your friend, how is she?"

"She's good. She's been in remission for years. I just saw her and her kids a couple of weeks ago. Everyone is well."

"I'm so glad."

Jo studied Christie. Her blue eyes bright, her cheeks flushed with pleasure, and her wavy, dirty blond hair fell just below her shoulders. "You look and sound happy."

Christie favored Jo with a brilliant smile. "Life is good."

"I'm glad to hear that."

As soon as the waitress left with their coffee order, Christie leaned toward Jo. "So tell me about you. I want to know everything."

"I doubt either of us have time for 'everything,' but the highlights, let's see, since I last saw you, I graduated from college, stayed in San Diego, have a career I enjoy very much as an independent consultant. I have a chocolate lab named Kona, and a great condo in Hillcrest." Jo shrugged. "Not much to tell."

"Oh, come on now, there has to be more. Are you in a relationship?"

"You were always the best at twenty questions," Jo said. "My last serious relationship ended about a year ago. We're good friends now and that works better for us. My turn. How is the rest of the family—Rhonda, Julie, Mike?"

"Julie's doing well. She married Ben. Their kids are Dylan and Jamie. Technically, Jamie is Julie's stepdaughter, but she's like her own. Ben's first wife passed away when Jamie was very young. Mike just started his third year of law school. Can you believe it?" Christie paused to take a sip of her coffee. "Mom is also good. Her business has taken off. She loves the fact we're all still close."

"I'm sure she does."

"Any chance you'll make it back out for the reunion?"

"I'm going to try, but it will depend on what's happening with work."

They talked for more than an hour catching up and reminiscing about their youth, but Christie had to get going. She reached across the table and laid her hand on Jo's arm. "Please tell me we can get together again before you leave. When's the wedding and when do you head back to San Diego?"

"The wedding is Saturday, but I don't head back until Monday."

"That settles it. You have to come over for dinner next Sunday. Please say yes."

"Yes. I wouldn't miss it. Just text me your address and tell me what time to show up."

After exchanging numbers, Christie hugged Jo tightly. "It's good to see you."

"Great to see you too. I'll see you Sunday."

Chapter Four

The rest of the week passed quickly. Jo kept busy with wedding chores. She made several trips to the airport fetching family and friends of the brides. There was little time to think about anything besides wedding preparations. With so much to do, the big day seemed to arrive quickly.

Randi prepared in the bridal suite while Amy and Jo got ready in Jo's room. Jo glanced over at her. They were watching a baseball game on TV to kill some time.

"Are you nervous?"

Amy shook her head and blew out a breath. "Not nervous, but I'm so excited I might crawl out of my skin. I have honestly never wanted anything more. I love her so much."

"You're a lucky woman," Jo said, wondering if she would ever experience that.

"I am."

❖

Right on time, Jo and Amy made their way to the front of the tent. The weather was perfect on this early September evening. The trees were full and the fragrant flower garden was at its peak. It set a beautiful scene. Rhonda sat in the middle of a row, in the middle of the room and studied Jo as she stood chatting with Amy. Jo made quite the picture in her tux. Her broad shoulders tapered to a trim waist. Her chestnut brown hair cut short, her deep blue eyes vibrant and focused. Her skin a golden tan from the San Diego sun, she stood several inches taller than Amy. There was a time she knew almost everything about Jo, but that was a very long time ago. The only information she had currently was what Christie told her after bumping into Jo the week before. Well, that and what she could now see for herself. Jo was stunningly handsome. She briefly wondered about her attraction to Jo. Then she was swept away in the romance of Amy and Randi pledging their love to one another.

Once the ceremony was over, the guests were ushered into the reception hall and tray-passed hors d'oeuvres were served while the bridal party took photos. In very short order, Amy and Randi were introduced to their guests and shared their first dance as a legally married couple. Then, service began on the plated dinner. When Jo got the signal from the head waiter that everyone had champagne, she stood to start the toasts.

After the toasts, the DJ started playing dance music. Jo set down her champagne flute and made her way through the tables.

Rhonda sat at the table with some of Jo and Amy's college friends. Jo approached the table with a wide smile. "Hello, everyone." She greeted her friends Cam, Kate, and June by name and exchanged hugs with each of them.

Rhonda was glued to her seat, her heart hammering in her chest, when Jo turned in her direction.

"Rhonda, I hope these crazy women are entertaining you."

"Very much."

Jo stepped closer. "Good, glad to hear that." She held out her hand. "May I have the pleasure of this dance?"

With only a moment of hesitation, Rhonda slipped her hand into the one Jo offered and looked up into Jo's deep blue eyes. "I'd be delighted."

The song was a bit too fast and loud for conversation, so Jo and Rhonda simply danced. When a slow song came on next, Rhonda turned to walk back to the table. Jo laid a hand on her arm to stop her. "Stay, please."

Rhonda hesitated briefly. Then she stepped back and wound her hands around Jo's neck. "Okay."

Jo was a bit disconcerted that she and Rhonda had barely said a word to one another, and she felt so connected to her, she didn't want the song to end. They silently moved in unison to the music, their bodies fit together perfectly. Holding Rhonda in her arms aroused her tremendously. It didn't surprise her, Rhonda was gorgeous, but she couldn't let it show. Once the song ended, she stepped away creating much needed space. She sighed and felt a sense of loss she didn't want to examine too closely. She swallowed and looked at Rhonda. "Thank you for the dance. I'm going to get some air." Jo turned quickly and walked toward the patio before Rhonda could utter a word.

The evening air had cooled significantly, and Jo tried to take some deep, cleansing breaths. It did nothing to ease the ache in her depths. She couldn't stop thinking about how good and right it felt to hold Rhonda in her arms. When she heard heels on the pavers behind her, she turned.

Rhonda stood a short distance away, slightly flushed, holding two glasses of wine. "I hope you didn't run off because of something I said." Rhonda was stunning, her wavy, silky blond hair hanging loose just past her shoulders. Her pale green gown brought out the vibrant green of her eyes to perfection. She was breathtaking.

Jo gripped the railing behind her, so she wouldn't reach out for Rhonda as she so urgently wanted to. "Of course not."

She held a glass of wine to Jo. "Do you like red?"

Jo realized she was staring at Rhonda's mouth, thinking about doing things she could never allow herself to do. "I do." She reached for the glass and resisted reaching for Rhonda.

"Are you going to tell me what's wrong?"

Jo sipped the wine, trying to calm herself and soothe her dry throat which was thick with desire. "Wrong? Nothing, you're a very beautiful woman."

Rhonda cocked her head slightly. "And that's a problem?"

"Seems to be."

Rhonda looked puzzled.

Jo considered brushing it off. She would be gone in two days anyway, and she would get over it. But she had nothing to lose, so she opted for the truth. "Dancing with you was…I have to confess, I had quite the crush on you back in the day. It seems I still do."

Rhonda laid her hand on Jo's arm. She smiled, but Jo couldn't tell if she was amused or flattered. The simple connection settled Jo somewhere deep inside and revved her up at the same time. No other woman had ever made her feel so much with such an innocent touch.

"Let's go back inside so we can catch up." This time, Rhonda held out her hand.

Jo took it and let herself be led back to the tent.

They talked and danced for hours. She wouldn't let Rhonda persuade her to slow dance again. When those songs came on, they returned to the table and chatted with Jo's friends.

When asked about what Jo had been like in high school, Rhonda thought about the younger version of the beautiful woman beside her. Finally she said, "I hate to disappoint you ladies, but I can't give away any of Jo's secrets."

Everyone laughed, including Jo.

As the party waned, Rhonda looked around the table and said, "Well, I should call a cab."

"I'll give you a ride," Jo said. "I stopped drinking hours ago."

"Thanks, I'll just grab my jacket."

After bidding farewell to their friends, they walked to Jo's car.

Jo climbed in, turned to Rhonda who had slid into the seat next to her, and asked, "Is it still the same house?"

"Yes, do you remember how to get there?"

"I think I can manage, but let me know if I take a wrong turn."

"Okay." Rhonda couldn't seem to shake the tension now that she and Jo were alone. She breathed deeply trying to relax. She was so focused, she almost missed Jo's question.

"How is your business doing?"

Rhonda relaxed then. She could easily talk about her passion. "It's wonderful. Sometimes I still can't believe that I started my own architecture firm out of my house while my kids were still in school. But it's been fantastic and it's been growing every year through word of mouth, mostly. I'm getting so many requests now that I'm even considering taking on a partner or expanding."

"That's great. I'm so glad to hear it's successful. Even when I was younger it was easy to see it was something you wanted with every fiber of your being."

"I guess I was pretty obsessed at first. But I love running my own company."

"I would imagine anyone starting a business from scratch would have to be pretty focused on it for a while to get it off the ground."

"I never really thought about that but it's probably true. My timing might have been better though, maybe I should have waited until everyone had finished high school."

"That sounds a lot like regret."

"Not regret, exactly, but I just wonder sometimes. Don't get me wrong, I wouldn't change what I've made my business into, but—"

"Are you still as close with Christie, Julie, and Mike as you always were?"

"Yes." Rhonda was a little thrown by Jo's abrupt question but she answered easily.

"Have they ever said anything about missing out on time with you when they were younger?"

"No."

"Do you think it's possible you're the only one looking back because you forget how much time you still managed to spend with them even though you were building your business? Because I remember you being at every soccer game, there to help them with homework, and whatever they needed. You were always there for all of us."

Rhonda met Jo's gaze until she had to turn back to the road. "I suppose that's possible. I don't even know why I started thinking about that just now."

"Okay. Well, believe me, you were and I imagine still are, a wonderful mother to your children, and now I bet you're an amazing grandma to their kids. You were also an excellent friend to me."

"Thanks, Jo. I hadn't realized I needed that reassurance. I appreciate it."

"You're welcome. You let me know if you ever need another reminder."

"Sounds like a plan."

They arrived at Rhonda's house. Jo walked Rhonda to the door. "Good night."

"Good night, it was good to see you."

"Great to see you too, Rhonda." Jo turned to leave.

"Oh, just one more thing."

Jo turned back.

Rhonda stepped to her and pulled her down for a sweet, gentle kiss.

Jo's hands went to Rhonda's hips and she responded to the kiss with no hesitation. After a few moments, she lifted her head. "Rhonda?" Jo's voice was a mixture of confusion and desire.

"Hmm, that was nice. Thank you for getting me home safely." Rhonda turned and went into the house.

Chapter Five

When the sun peeked through the window and woke her, Jo considered skipping her workout, but she needed somewhere to use her pent up energy, and a run seemed safest. Running usually cleared her mind, but this morning she found herself drifting back to Rhonda and the night before. *Nice*, that was the word Rhonda had used for the kiss. Jo would have used others, sizzling hot, amazing, and the list went on. But she had to stop thinking about it. As *nice* as it had been to kiss Rhonda, Jo spent a restless night convincing herself nothing more could happen between them. They lived three thousand miles apart and had completely separate lives.

Finally, Jo put it away and refocused on her friends as she attended the brunch for the bridal party and close family. After the meal, Amy pulled her aside. "You get Rhonda home okay?"

"Of course I did," Jo replied a bit defensively.

Amy held up her hands. "Whoa, okay. What's that about?"

Jo sighed and shrugged. "Sorry, just tired I guess. How was your wedding night?"

"Memorable."

Mercifully, Amy did not bring Rhonda up again.

❖

Rhonda was distracted most of Sunday thinking about Jo. She hadn't known she was going to kiss her until she was doing it. She didn't know exactly what had possessed her. When she saw Jo standing in the front of the tent, decked out in her tux, she felt tingling and pulsing in places no one had touched in a long time. Then dancing with her had made her head spin. By the end of the night, she had to know what that gorgeous mouth tasted like. It had been even better than she'd imagined. She didn't know why she'd left Jo on the doorstep when every part of her was screaming for her to invite her in, but she knew it was for the best.

When Christie called to invite her over for dinner with Jo, she almost begged off. But she thought it would be better to clear things up between them as soon as possible. Clearly, nothing more could happen between them and Rhonda didn't want things to be awkward. She was sure Jo would understand.

❖

Jo dressed casually in a charcoal shirt and black trousers. She arrived at Christie's promptly at five, wine in hand. Christie opened the door and greeted Jo with a big hug. Then she turned and introduced her husband. "Jo, this is Peter."

They shook hands.

"It's great to finally meet the legendary Jo Adams."

Jo looked at Christie.

She confessed, "I've been talking his ear off with high school memories since I saw you last week."

"Ah." Jo turned back to Peter. "In that case, don't believe a word she said."

Christie ushered Jo further into the house. "The kids are back in the kitchen with Mom."

The last words rang in Jo's ears. She was suddenly nervous about being there. She dutifully followed Christie and Peter to the back of the house and met their children. Then she walked to Rhonda and brushed her cheek with a kiss. "Rhonda, I didn't know you'd be here."

"I hope it's a pleasant surprise."

"Of course it is."

Rhonda look relieved.

Christie asked, "So, how was the wedding, Jo? All Mom will say is, it was lovely."

"Amy and Randi are perfect for each other. It was a beautiful ceremony and dancing at the reception was fun. It was definitely a night to remember."

Rhonda blushed. Christie didn't seem to notice.

"That's wonderful. So how did you spend today?"

Jo felt totally awkward talking to Christie about mundane details of her life when she could not stop thinking about how much she wanted to kiss Rhonda again. "Um." Jo tried to remember the question. "I went for a run. Then read and answered some emails. There was one from my boss that I found very interesting. Apparently, they need someone in this area for a three-month contract, and he asked if I was interested."

"That would be awesome. That would mean you'd definitely be here for our reunion too," Christie said.

"It certainly would be nice to get to see more of you," Rhonda said.

Jo's temperature rose. She couldn't decide if Rhonda was flirting or just being polite, but her words were exciting. But she could barely hold eye contact with Jo; her signals were definitely confusing.

"It's something to think about for sure. The contract would start in two weeks, and I'd have to find a place to stay. I wouldn't want to leave my dog, Kona, that long, so I'd need a place I could have her."

Christie said, "I have a great idea. Why don't you stay with Mom?"

"Oh, no, I couldn't. My company will put me up somewhere. I just have to find something." Jo realized it had quickly become something she was planning to do, not just thinking about.

"But why not? It's perfect. Don't you think so, Mom? Jo could keep you company in that big house. There's plenty of room. The dog would have lots of space in the backyard."

Rhonda finally met Jo's gaze. "You are always more than welcome to stay with me. Kona too.

"Thank you. I'll consider it."

With dinner done, Christie and Peter took the kids upstairs for their baths but only after promising Mary and Cody that they could come back down to spend more time with Rhonda and Jo.

Jo and Rhonda started clearing plates. In the kitchen, when she was sure she and Rhonda were alone, Jo asked, "Should we talk?"

"Let me start with an apology. I had a little too much to drink last night. I shouldn't have kissed you like that. I'm sorry. Can we possibly just forget it happened?"

"Sure." Jo knew she wouldn't be able to forget it for a long time, but she could pretend it didn't happen if that's what Rhonda wanted. "Now, about me staying with you, I know Christie just sprung that on you. I can find somewhere else."

"No, really, I would love to have you. It would be nice to have some company for a little while. I meant what I said."

"My company will pay for my lodging. If you want to write up receipts for rent, I'll give that money to you."

"That is certainly not necessary. How about you take me out for a nice dinner once a week or so and we'll call it even?"

"I can do that."

"It's settled then. Would you like to run over to the house with me tonight, so you can see it again?"

"I guess that makes sense, sure."

When Christie and the kids returned, Rhonda and Jo were loading the last of the dishes into the dishwasher. They filled Christie in on the plan. Jo and Rhonda played with the kids for a little while longer. Then they hugged everyone and said their good-byes. Jo followed Rhonda back to her house.

Rhonda opened the door with her key and let them into the house. Jo stood for a moment as the memories swamped her. She had spent so much time here as a teenager. She could almost hear the laughter echoing around her. This house, Rhonda, Christie, and Julie had been her safe harbor. She would never forget that. She would not do anything to ever disrespect those memories. So, she'd "forget" the kiss from the night before and ignore her attraction to Rhonda. She was certain staying here wasn't the best idea but she couldn't come up with a reason not to that wouldn't sound flippant or weak, and she certainly didn't want to hurt Rhonda's feelings either.

"You okay?"

"Yeah, I'm just a bit overwhelmed with memories."

"That makes sense."

Jo shrugged out of her brown bomber jacket and hung it over the stairwell. "Want to show me around?"

"Yes, of course. I don't think it's really changed all that much. Why don't we start with your room, so you get an idea of that space?"

"Sounds good." Jo followed her up the stairs. She fixed her stare on the middle of Rhonda's back, refusing to look lower.

Rhonda opened the door to the guest room. The furniture looked new, but it wasn't that different from a decade before. A queen-size bed took up the majority of space with nightstands on both sides. There was a nice amount of space on the far side of the bed, where Jo could picture putting Kona's bed. "And you're sure you're okay with me having my chocolate lab, Kona, here?"

"Yes, I'm sure. We've been over this. Do you not want to stay here?"

"Why would you ask that?" Jo mentally shook her head. She could have used that as an out. Instead she'd blown her chance.

"Because you keep making sure this or that will be okay."

Jo sighed. "I just…"

"What?"

"I don't want to be a burden to you."

"You have never, not once in your life, been a burden to me. I am looking forward to spending time with you, getting to know you again. I know that you feel like Christie just thrust this on me, but honestly, she only beat me to it. I was going to offer myself. I do have so much room here. It's conceivable we won't even see that much of each other. But I'm happy to share my home with you while you're in town."

"Okay."

"How about I give you a quick tour of the rest the house? I know you need to catch an early plane."

"Sounds like a plan."

By the time they made their way down to the lower level, Jo had relaxed a bit. She saw an empty room off the family room. "Do you use this room for anything?"

"Not really. Basically, it just sits here empty. I've been working on clearing out the clutter the last couple of years."

"Would it be okay if I brought my weights and fitness machines with me and set up a mini home gym in here? You're welcome to use the equipment too."

"Sure."

"Awesome."

CHAPTER SIX

Back in San Diego, Jo put things in order and packed her SUV. With her gym machines, her truck was so full that she needed to send Kona by air. However, it was still too hot in California for the airlines to allow animals to fly in the cargo area. In order to least disrupt Kona, Jo asked Aideen to take care of sending her once the weather cooled off. Aideen also agreed to stay at the condo until Jo returned.

Cam had convinced Jo to go out with her and June and Kate for a sort of last hurrah before she was gone for months on end. Jo was sitting with them at Amarin Thai when she got a text. She glanced briefly at her phone.

"Who is that?" Kate asked.

"Rhonda."

"Interesting."

"What?"

"When you saw who was texting you, you got a huge smile on your face."

Jo shrugged. "She's asking if there's anything I want at the house to make me feel more comfortable. I just thought it was really sweet."

June joined in. "Rhonda is very sweet from what I gathered at Amy's wedding."

"She is," Jo said.

"You two seemed to have a good time that night," Cam said.

"We had a lot to catch up on."

"Uh huh," Cam said in a playful tone.

"What are you implying?"

"It just looked to me like there was more going on than two friends catching up."

"There wasn't. There's not. She's just an old friend."

"Okay, if you say so."

"I do. I am going to respond though since it's so much later there."

"Tell her we say hello."

With that done, Jo redirected the conversation back to Kate and the dance classes she was thinking about teaching in the spring.

❖

Rhonda sat in her living room with a glass of wine when Jo's response came in.

"Anything you have is fine. Please don't go to any trouble on my account. We can shop together once I'm there. Btw, Cam, June, and Kate all say hello. They insisted on a good-bye dinner. They also wanted to know if you had any idea what you were getting into when you agreed to shelter me."

Rhonda studied her phone for several moments before typing her response. *"Sounds like a plan. Hello to all. My question to them would be: which time? Lol. I'm certain you're as much a handful now as you were as a teenager. Which, by the way, was not at all."*

"Thank you. See you in a few days."

"Have a safe trip. Good night."

"Good night, Rhonda."

❖

A few days later, Jo pulled into Rhonda's driveway. She was so happy to get out of the truck after four long days on the road, she did a little happy dance right there in the driveway. She turned when she heard clapping. Rhonda was standing by the front door, beaming. Jo did a quick little bow. "Thank you, thank you very much."

When Rhonda reached her she opened her arms and Jo stepped into them and returned the warm embrace. She stepped back as quickly as she could without being rude. She needed to remember to keep touching Rhonda to a minimum if she was going to retain her sanity.

"It's good to be here."

"Come on in and have something to drink. We'll worry about your stuff in a bit. How was the trip?"

Jo followed her inside. "Really good, actually, it's just a lot of driving."

"No doubt. I can offer you beer, wine, or anything you see on the bar."

"A woman after my own heart. Just a beer for now would be great. Thank you. It smells amazing in here."

"I have lasagna in the oven for later." Rhonda grabbed two beers out of the refrigerator. She handed one to Jo and then twisted her cap off. She took a long pull off it before settling on one of the bar stools.

Jo opted to stand to stretch her legs a bit. She sipped her beer. "Yum. So, how was your week?"

"Not bad. I finished up the designs on a project set to start next week. I made sure your room was ready for you. Put clean sheets on the bed yesterday."

"Thank you. I guess I should get my truck unloaded before it gets too dark."

"I'll help."

"I appreciate it."

The two of them worked together to get everything Jo brought with her into the house. Jo concentrated on getting all the weight equipment downstairs and Rhonda took her clothes and other personal items upstairs. Once they were done, Rhonda said, "Why don't you go grab a shower, wash off the trip, and then we'll have dinner?"

"That sounds wonderful."

Chapter Seven

Jo let herself quietly into the house after her run. When she smelled coffee, she changed course and headed for the kitchen. Rhonda sat on a stool at the breakfast bar sipping coffee and filling in a crossword puzzle. "Good morning, Rhonda."

Rhonda swiveled the stool to face Jo. She wore a silk robe that dipped low on her chest. Her smooth, tan skin showed over the top. The outline of her breasts made it obvious she wore very little beneath it. Jo's mouth went dry. *Holy crap! Pull it together. You cannot go there.* She hastily redirected her gaze to Rhonda's face in time to hear her response.

"Good morning. How was your run?"

"Good. Mind if I grab some coffee?"

"Help yourself. There are also bagels in the bread box if you're interested."

"Thank you." Jo pulled down a mug. Having something to concentrate on gave her the time she needed. "Actually, I think I'll grab a shower before I eat anything."

"Okay. Like always, as long as you're here, it's your home too. Help yourself to anything you like."

"Thanks." Jo fled, Rhonda's last words echoing in her head.

She stripped down and stepped into the shower. She let the hot water cascade over her. She had to get a grip. Her clit beat an insistent pulse between her legs. She usually had no problem taking care of that herself, but she absolutely refused to touch herself while thinking about Rhonda. That was out of the question. She took slow, deep breaths to bring her body back under control. Rhonda was her friend. Rhonda was straight. Rhonda was Christie and Julie's mom for Christ's sake. She could not think about Rhonda in that way. Once she reined in her hormones, she felt better. She might not be able to control her body's reaction to Rhonda, but she had complete control over any action she took. No way would she make any sort of move in that direction. It wasn't going to happen. After dressing, she made a quick phone call before heading back downstairs. While she made herself a bagel she chatted with Rhonda making sure to keep her gaze on her face. "How's your morning?"

"It's good. Do you have any plans for the day?"

"Yeah, I just talked to Amy. We're going to watch the game and then maybe have dinner with some people. She's convinced I need to meet people here. I think she's trying to launch a campaign to get me to stay."

"Would that be so bad?"

"Not necessarily. But I enjoy my life in California."

"I imagine this is a whole different world for you?"

"It is, yeah, but I'm having a nice time reconnecting with old friends, present company included."

"We're enjoying having you back in the area and will as long as you choose to stay."

"Thanks."

"I don't know if you have any interest, but Julie's oldest, Jamie, has a basketball game tomorrow. I'm going to watch. Want to tag along?"

"Sure, sounds like fun."

"Great, it's a date."

"Great." Jo looked at her watch. "I should get going. I don't know how late I'll be tonight. It depends what Amy gets me into."

"No worries. Although, I'd appreciate a text, if you stay somewhere else tonight."

Jo almost asked where else she might stay. Then she realized Rhonda assumed she might hook up with someone tonight. She couldn't decide how she felt about that. She opted to keep her response casual. "No problem."

❖

Jo made her way to the bar to get another round for the group. Amy and Randi had taken her out for dinner with a few of their friends. They'd moved from dinner to drinks at a nearby club. Amanda and Rachel seemed very much in love and had kept Jo laughing about some of Randi's college exploits. Laura had been subtly flirting with Jo all evening. She wasn't sure why it made her a bit uncomfortable. Usually, she would have spent an enjoyable evening flirting back. But she wasn't into it tonight. It was odd, but clearly she was having an off night.

Amy joined her at the bar to help carry drinks. "So, what do you think of Laura?"

"She seems nice."

"Nice? That's all you got?"

"I guess so."

"She seems pretty into you."

"Yeah, I picked up on that. I'm going to have to disappoint her though."

"Why? Have you gone blind?"

"No." Jo nudged Amy with her shoulder. "I can see that she's hot. She's just not doing it for me."

"Are you sick?" Amy lifted her hand to Jo's head as though to feel for a fever.

Jo knocked it away. "No. I've just developed more discriminating tastes."

"Since when?"

"Since I realized I want more than a bunch of one-night stands."

"She probably wouldn't mind something more than that."

"Not interested. Why don't you go pay attention to your wife and let me take care of my own love life?"

"Since when do you not want me to be your wing man?"

"Since I don't need one. I'm not going home with anyone tonight. I'm just out having a good time with friends. Can't we leave it at that?"

Amy looked at Jo as though she didn't know her anymore. "Sure, if that's what you want."

"It is."

They made their way back to the table. Jo decided she should tell Laura herself that she wasn't interested. But she didn't want to talk to her with everyone around.

"Laura, would you like to dance?"

"I'd love to."

Once they were out on the dance floor, Laura said, "I'm thrilled you asked me to dance. I got the idea you weren't interested in me."

"Actually, I'm not. I'm sorry. I didn't want to have this conversation in front of everyone. It's definitely not you. You're hot and seem great. I just…there's this other woman I can't get out of my head…it's complicated."

"Hey, we could have some fun. I'm not looking for any sort of commitment."

"I'm flattered, but it's not something I'd be into right now. A different time, who knows, but right now my head wouldn't be in the game."

"That's too bad. Well, if you change your mind and just want a night of uncomplicated fun, Randi has my number."

"I'll remember that. I think I'm going to take off."

"Any chance I could bum a ride off you? I don't want Amanda and Rachel to have to cut their night short."

"Sure. No problem."

❖

Rhonda and Barbara finished dinner and headed to a nearby club for a drink. After they got their cocktails at the bar, Rhonda turned to scan the room for somewhere to sit. When she spotted Amy and Randi at a table near the dance floor, she wasn't too surprised. There just weren't that many places in Amherst proper to go for drinks if you didn't want to be surrounded by coeds. She headed their way. "Good evening, ladies."

"Hi, Rhonda," Randi said. They both stood and hugged her.

"Please join us," Amy said.

"Thanks, this is my good friend, Barbara. Randi and Amy are the two who got married last month."

Barbara shook hands with the newlyweds. "It's nice to meet you both and congratulations!"

Rhonda looked around, trying not to be obvious. "Is Jo here somewhere? She said you were all hanging out tonight."

"She was here. She and Laura just left a few minutes ago."

"I see." Rhonda took a sip of her drink trying to cover her disappointment. Rhonda vaguely remembered Laura from the wedding. She was stunning. Luckily, before her thoughts went too far down that path, Amanda and Rachel returned to the table. She greeted them both warmly and introduced Barbara. Rhonda suddenly didn't feel like being around a lot of people and she and Barbara left once they finished their drinks.

After Rhonda dropped Barbara at her house, she checked her phone. No text from Jo. Maybe she wasn't planning on staying out all night. When she saw Jo's truck in the garage, she was confused. She was surprised to see the flickering light in the living room when she came into the house from the garage. She walked in to investigate. The flames in the fireplace were going strong, but what she saw on the couch drew her attention more. Jo slept on her back, and she was quite alone. Rhonda rarely had a chance to study Jo unawares, and she took advantage of the opportunity now. Fully clothed, Jo's lean muscles were obvious through her jeans and T-shirt. The subtle curves of her breasts enticed her. She felt the urge to run her fingers over Jo's firm arms. She focused mostly on her face, especially her sensual mouth. Rhonda remembered what that mouth felt like on hers and she wanted another taste.

It would be so easy. She knelt beside the sofa and lightly touched her lips to Jo's. Her hand landed in the center of Jo's chest and she felt when her breathing changed. Jo pulled her closer and deepened the kiss. She stroked her hand down Jo's shirt and heard her moan as she grazed her erect nipple through her shirt. She wanted more. She pulled the shirt free from Jo's jeans and slid her hand underneath. Rhonda gasped as she made contact with Jo's warm skin. She splayed her fingers across Jo's taut abs before moving further up and finding her nipple once more. As she fondled and squeezed Jo's breasts, Jo writhed on the couch. She slid her hand down and dipped her fingers beneath Jo's waistband. Jo lifted her hips as though searching for Rhonda's touch. When Rhonda reached what she was searching for, Jo was so hot and wet, Rhonda almost lost it right then. She stroked Jo until she crested and she felt the echoing flood soak her own panties.

It would be so easy and so complicated. She knelt beside the sofa and patted Jo's shoulder. "Jo, it's time to wake up and go up to bed."

Jo stretched. Rhonda licked her lips.

"Hi, when did you get home?"

"A few minutes ago. Did you have a nice night?"

"It was all right. How about you?"

"I had a nice dinner with Barbara. Seems I just missed you at the club. Amy said you and Laura had just left when we got there."

"Yeah, I made it an early night. Laura asked for a ride. Then I came home and was surprised you were out."

"It was a last minute thing."

As they walked upstairs to their bedrooms, Rhonda was glad she hadn't actually kissed Jo, as much as she'd wanted to at the time. She was soaking wet. If a simple fantasy had that kind of effect on her, she needed to be sure what she wanted before she acted.

Chapter Eight

Rhonda sat across the table from Barbara. She was glad they had lunch plans. She needed to tell someone what was going on in her head and Barbara would understand. "I have a confession to make."

Barbara sipped her iced tea. "Okay, I'm listening."

"I'm attracted to a woman."

Barbara leaned forward, and in a move uncharacteristic for her fifty-year-old self, she clapped. "Finally, tell me everything."

"She's completely wrong for me, and there's no way that anything can ever happen between us, but my God, she is gorgeous."

"You're stalling. Who is she?"

"Jo Adams."

Barbara sat back, her lips open in the form of an O, but no sound came out of her mouth.

"Say something."

"Wow."

"Not helpful."

"How old is she?"

"Twenty-eight, one of many reasons nothing can happen."

"So, start at the beginning. When did you first feel the attraction?"

"At the wedding last month, Jo was Amy's maid of honor. When she stood up at the front in her tux, I practically drooled. I mean I hadn't seen her in ten years and that's my first reaction, really? But it was—strong and fast. Then later she asked me to dance. We had a nice time, and at some point she confessed that she'd had a crush on me a decade ago."

"Well, who didn't?"

"Stop." Rhonda blushed.

"So, what happened after that?"

"She drove me home and I kissed her."

"Excuse me?"

"I know. I couldn't believe it either. When I saw her the next night at Christie's, I blamed it on too much to drink and she said we could forget it happened."

"But?"

"Now, I'm not sure I want to."

"What do you mean?"

"She's moved into my guest room and we're spending more time together, but the attraction hasn't gone away. It's growing."

"What are you going to do about it?"

"I have no idea. I'm not sure I should do anything about it. She's only here for a few months."

"Even better."

"What do you mean?"

"You can explore the feelings you're having and there's a built in exit ramp."

"That's never really been how I do things."

"You've never been attracted to a woman before either."

"This is true."

Chapter Nine

Rhonda didn't know why she was so nervous. Jo would be back with Kona any minute now. Rhonda liked dogs, but she so very much wanted this dog to like her. She was probably being ridiculous, but Kona was important to Jo, and Rhonda wanted her to like it here. She was sure she'd gone a bit overboard with the basket full of toys she'd gotten while Jo picked Kona up at the airport.

When she heard Jo's truck pull in, she took a deep breath. She watched Jo let Kona out of the truck. Jo walked in first. Kona didn't enter the house until Jo said, "Yes."

Rhonda walked over to say hello. Jo told Kona to sit and she did. Then she looked at Rhonda. "Ready?"

"Yes."

Jo looked at the sleek chocolate lab. "Kona, greet." Kona held out her right paw to shake hands with Rhonda.

Rhonda bent to take the offered hand. Then she let Kona smell her hand. Kona's tail wagged wildly. A hopeful sign, Rhonda thought. "Why don't we take her into the yard, so she can get familiar with it?"

"Good idea. Kona, come." They walked through the kitchen and out the back door. Jo looked at Kona as she sat on the back porch trembling with excitement, waiting for her command. "Go look."

After being released, Kona took off and sniffed everything around the large yard. She rubbed her face on the back fence and her sides against the house, marking the space as her own.

Rhonda stepped next to Jo as she watched Kona explore. "She's beautiful."

"Thanks. Don't think I didn't notice that massive pile of toys you stockpiled. You didn't have to get her anything."

"Are you kidding? Of course I did, but I might have gotten a little carried away. I want her to like it here, to feel like it's her home too."

"She will. Would you wait here with her while I go grab her stuff from the car?"

"Certainly."

Rhonda sat on the top step on the back deck and watched Kona explore the yard. Eventually, Kona headed her way. Rhonda stayed where she was. With no hesitation, Kona laid on the top step next to Rhonda and laid her chin on her leg. Rhonda put her hand on Kona's head and began stroking her softly. "Welcome home, little one. I hope you like it here."

❖

Two days later, Jo and Rhonda were in the kitchen with Kona. Rhonda said, "The kids are so excited to meet Kona, and their parents are dreading the puppy requests that will follow."

"I bet. Sounds like someone's here now."

"I'll go check." As Rhonda entered the living room, she saw Mike hanging Barbara's coat and then his own in the closet by the front door.

"Well, hello. I didn't expect you two to come together."

Barbara smiled and hugged her. "Mike was kind enough to offer to drive. How could I resist such a charming young man?"

Rhonda hugged him. "That was nice of you."

Mike's "Aw, shucks" had them laughing as they made their way into the kitchen.

Jo turned from the stove. Rhonda was flanked by Barbara and Mike.

Rhonda crossed the room first. "Jo, you remember Barbara and Mike?"

"Of course." Jo closed the distance between them and willingly stepped into Barbara's outstretched arms for a hug. "Barbara, you haven't changed a bit." Then she turned to Mike. There was a moment where the two of them seemed to size each other up. Then Jo held out her hand and Mike took it warmly. "Mike, you on the other hand have changed quite a lot."

Mike smiled. "You've changed some yourself. Still running?"

"Yeah, five or six times a week most of the time. Did you keep it up?"

"I did. We should go for a run one of these mornings."

"Let's do that. Tell me when and where."

"How about tomorrow at six in the morning? We'll leave from here."

"Sounds like a plan. See you then."

"Cool."

"I hear someone else coming in, I'm going to go say hello."

When Jo walked into the living room, she had only a moment to brace herself, as Julie ran toward her and launched herself into her arms. "Jo, I can't believe you're really here."

"Hey, Julie, I'm really here." Jo returned the affectionate embrace with equal fervor.

"I can't believe how much I've missed you."

"Right back at you. I'm sorry we lost touch."

"We can't let that happen again. I'm so glad you're here for a while. We can get all caught up."

"I'm looking forward to it. But in the meantime, can I meet your family?"

"Oh, yes, of course." Julie turned to where Ben, Jamie, and Dylan were waiting and introduced them all to Jo. "Jo was my best, best friend in high school."

Christie walked in at that moment and must have heard the comment. "I second that. She was both of our best friends."

Christie embraced Jo and then made way for Mary and Cody to greet her. Then Jo ushered everyone into the kitchen. She led Kona to the backyard where there was plenty of room for everyone to get acquainted. Kona's tail wagged fast, her excitement evident, but with Jo's quiet commands, she remained calm and greeted each person in turn.

The kids rubbed her down and petted her velvet soft ears. Her whole body shook in excitement. Once Kona had a chance to smell everyone and become familiar with their scents, Jo took the kids to the side. She showed each one how to use the ball launcher so Kona could fetch the ball back to them. She also showed them how to tell Kona to drop the ball at their feet, so the ball could be thrown again. Watching them closely, she let them take turns with the launcher. Kona and the kids were in heaven. The adults enjoyed watching from the deck.

"What a great dog," Ben said.

Rhonda turned to Ben. "She is great. I had no idea how well trained she'd be, but I guess if I'd thought about it, I should have known."

Dinner was soon ready and they all went back inside and sat in the dining room. With twelve people around the table, it was rather loud and boisterous, but it was wonderful.

After dessert was polished off, everyone helped clear the table. Then the crowd divided into small groups. Jo offered to take the kids into the backyard to play a game of nighttime soccer to burn off some of their energy. Peter and Ben helped her bundle up the kids, and the seven of them headed out into the backyard under bright lights. She had a bright orange soccer ball with her. Christie and Mike started to tackle the dishes while Barbara made coffee.

The group in the backyard kicked around the soccer ball. Julie and Rhonda strolled over to the back door to take in the action. The game outside quickly evolved into a friendly session of keep-away. The girls chased Ben and Peter around trying to get the ball away from them. Cody and Dylan mostly chased each other. Jo was a part of keep-away off and on, but she also kept an eye on the boys. When Dylan tripped and fell hard, she was the first one to reach him.

Julie reached for the door, but Rhonda stopped her. "Give them a minute. Let's see what happens."

Julie held her gaze, and by the time she turned back, Ben had reached them and Dylan was crying loudly.

Jo concentrated on Dylan for the moment. She lay on her stomach so she was face-to-face with him. "Ouch, I bet that hurt." Her approach slowed the crying almost as quickly as it started. "Can you sit up?" She helped Dylan into a sitting position facing her. Dylan still sniffled and tears threatened to spill over. "Peter, will you take the kids in and ask Rhonda to make some of her famous hot chocolate?"

"Sure. Cody, Mary, Jamie, let's go."

Jo looked up at Dylan's dad. "Ben? Do you have a spare set of clothes for Dylan in the car?"

"Sure do."

"I think he's going to need them."

Glad to have something to do he answered quickly, "Okay."

Without a crowd around them, Dylan's crying had almost stopped. Jo suspected the fall only scared him given how bundled up he was, but she wanted to be sure. "It's pretty cold sitting on the ground. Do you want to sit in my lap?"

Dylan looked at her with big eyes and nodded.

Jo picked him up and set him on her lap. "There, that's better. Now we can get down to business. I need to know something. Do you like yellow watermelons?"

The question made Dylan cock his head in thought. The tears stopped.

Feigning impatience, Jo asked again. "Well? Do you like yellow watermelons?"

"I never had a lellow watermelon, but I like the red ones."

Jo nodded her head solemnly. "Good to know. I've never eaten a yellow watermelon either, but I bet it would taste good. Does it hurt anywhere?"

Dylan thought about it for a moment before shaking his head.

"Good, that's good. I don't know about you, but it's getting pretty cold out here for me. Want to go in and get some of your grandma's hot chocolate with me?"

Dylan nodded and scrambled off Jo's lap.

Jo stood and asked Dylan, "Would you like me to fly you inside?"

"Okay."

Jo picked him up. Dylan held out his arms like an airplane and Jo made plane noises with Dylan as she took him to the house.

Once inside, Jo saw Julie's concerned expression. "He's okay. Aren't you, Dylan?"

"Yep."

Jo handed Dylan to her. "Dylan and I would love some hot chocolate."

Dylan laid his head on Julie's shoulder. "Yep."

"Thank you, Jo."

Jo shrugged. "No problem. The fall just scared him a little. I think he's fine."

Julie laid a hand on Jo's arm, stopping her.

Jo saw the sincerity on Julie's face and acknowledged it with a nod. "You're welcome. Now I'm going to go change out of these wet clothes. Dylan, I'll meet you back here for hot chocolate, extra whipped cream for me, please."

"Okay."

When Jo walked into the kitchen after changing into dry clothes, she discovered the older kids had already been released to play video games downstairs. Apparently, the men were also down there trying to get in on the fun. Barbara, Christie, and Julie sat at the table chatting. Dylan was there too, drawing a picture.

Jo walked over and rustled his hair. "Hey, buddy, you're a lot dryer than when I last saw you."

"You too. I waited to have hot chocolate with you."

"He was insistent," Julie said.

"Wow, thanks, buddy. Sorry I'm late."

"It's okay. I drew a picture."

"Very cool, who's it for?"

"You."

Jo was taken aback. "Me?"

"Yep."

"Can I see?"

"Okay."

Dylan turned the picture so Jo could see what he was drawing. "Wow, Dylan, that's really good." The picture was of two people playing soccer.

Dylan pointed to one figure and then the other. "That's me and that's you."

"Nice." Then Jo looked a little closer. "Are we playing with a yellow watermelon instead of a soccer ball?"

"Yep."

"Dylan this is the best picture anyone has ever made me, thank you."

"You're welcome. Can we have some hot chocolate now?"

"Absolutely."

Rhonda brought over the mugs.

Jo took a sip of the hot chocolate and leaned over to Dylan. "This is yummy. Is yours as good as mine?"

Dylan nodded, and licked his top lip. "Yep."

❖

As the sun rose, Jo quietly slipped out of bed for her morning run. She snapped on Kona's leash and closed the front door just as her running partner for the morning pulled up. Jo stretched as he climbed from his car. "Morning, Mike."

Mike started stretching. "Hey, Jo, how's your weekend going?"

"Good. It's nice to have a long one. How about you?"

"Good. I had a date last night."

"Must not have gone all that well if you're here with me this early."

"Actually, I let her know I had early plans, and she let me stay anyway. We're meeting up again later today to watch the game."

"That's great. You ready to go?"

"Sure."

Jo adjusted her pace to match Mike's. "It's good to see you kept up with your running, Mike."

Mike glanced over. "You were right. It's a great stress reliever. It got me through a lot of crap as a teenager. When things started to build up, I would remember what you told me and go for a run. Thanks for that."

"Don't thank me. Thank your mom."

"What do you mean?"

"Rhonda gave me that advice when I was having a hard time. I only passed it on to you. At the time, you were more willing to listen to me than either of your parents."

"Huh, I never knew. Mom never said anything."

"Does that surprise you?"

Mike shook his head. "I guess it shouldn't. She cares more about the result than getting credit for the idea."

Chapter Ten

When the work week returned, Rhonda and Jo went back to their easy routine. Most evenings after dinner, they sat on the couch and talked for hours. After the first time or two, Rhonda had said, "Jo, surely you'd rather be out with your friends instead of sitting here chatting with me."

Jo had responded, "Why would you think that? I'm having a wonderful time."

After that, Rhonda just went with it. She had purposely avoided one topic since reconnecting because Jo hadn't brought it up, but finally her curiosity won out. "Jo?"

"Hmmm?"

"You haven't mentioned Patty and Keith since you've been here. How are your parents?"

Jo took a moment before responding. "Mom's good. I just spoke with her recently. She says hello, by the way."

"Hello back." When Jo didn't volunteer any more information, Rhonda pressed, "And your dad?"

Jo's expression darkened. This had always been a tough topic for her and she gave her the time she needed.

"Six years ago, when he tried to crash Mom and John's wedding, he and I had a reckoning."

"What happened?"

"He'd been drinking, of course, but wasn't drunk yet, although he was well on his way as usual. He tried to push me around to get his way."

"Oh, Jo."

"Except this time I fought back. He didn't know what hit him. When he figured it out, there was this look in his eye. I think he was actually afraid of me. I was strong enough to stand up for myself, and he was weak. I convinced him trying to even contact my mom or me in the future would be a very bad idea.

"I never thought that would be the end of it, but I wasn't scared of him anymore, and I guess he could see that. A few weeks later, I heard he moved to Arizona." Jo paused and she looked at Rhonda. "I haven't heard from him since, and as far as I know neither has Mom."

"I'm sorry you had to go through that alone."

Jo shrugged. "I handled it."

Yes, you always do, all by yourself. Rhonda hurt for Jo and was sure she wouldn't understand why.

Chapter Eleven

Jo was out of sorts. All because of the call she'd received a few minutes before she left work. Her mom had sounded distraught and worried before she'd broken down crying, and handed the phone off to John. He had reassured her that he was taking care of things and her mom was safe. Apparently, the call was to warn her, in case her father tried to contact her next.

Jo felt some of the tension drain from her body when she walked in the door from the garage into the kitchen. Rhonda's home still felt like her safe harbor. She was still distracted and irritated, and almost walked right by Rhonda without a word.

"Hello? Hey, are you okay?"

Jo stopped walking and turned back. "Hey, Rhonda, sorry just distracted."

"Is everything alright?"

"Sure. Weird day."

Rhonda turned and started gathering items onto the counter. "Want to talk about it?"

"Not really. Would you like any help?"

Rhonda cocked her head. "You want to help me with dinner?" Her voice sounded a bit incredulous.

Jo briefly wondered why. "Yes. Is that okay?"

"Um, sure, how do you feel about chopping vegetables?"

"I live for chopping vegetables. Let me just wash my hands."

As Jo walked to the sink, Rhonda said, "Okay. I need onions and a pepper for the sauce. Then you can work on the veggies for the salad."

"Sounds good." Jo dried her hands, selected a knife, and got to work.

Rhonda watched Jo dice onions for a few moments, appreciating her quick, efficient movements. Then she turned back to her own tasks. Something was off, but if Jo wasn't ready to talk, Rhonda couldn't force her. She'd learned a long time ago that Jo would talk, if she was going to, only when she was ready.

"My mom called me today."

Rhonda looked over to where Jo stood with her head down, focused on dicing onions. The comment had come out of left field.

"How is she?"

"Not good. Apparently, my father is in Florida and he went by the house."

"Oh no, did he hurt her?"

Rhonda noticed Jo's hand tighten on the knife.

"Not physically, but she was pretty shaken up. She couldn't even finish the conversation and handed the phone to John. He said she was safe and he was taking care of her. So, that's good."

"That is good. How are you doing?" Rhonda knew it was risky to ask Jo how she was feeling, especially about anything having to do with her father, but she wanted to help and this was the only way she could think to do that.

Jo blew out a breath and glanced at Rhonda before returning her focus to her task. "I've been better. Mostly, I'm concerned about my mom. I'm pissed at him for reappearing in her life when things are going so well for her. Why can't he just leave us alone?"

Rhonda wanted to go to Jo then, offer some comfort. But she stayed where she was, bound by her own choices. Afraid that if she offered Jo a hug, her secret would come out. So even though it was wholly inadequate, she said, "I don't know. I'm sorry."

"It's okay. I'm tired of trying to figure him out. Mom is safe and that's what really matters. Thank you for listening."

"Any time."

❖

Rhonda wasn't home when Jo returned from work the next evening. She had texted earlier that she had a last minute client meeting that would probably run late. The house seemed so empty without her. Strange that she had never felt lonely in her condo in San Diego, even in the year since Aideen had moved out. Now it felt like something, rather someone, was missing moments after she entered the empty house. She shook her head. She had to get over this crush, if she could even still call it that.

She changed, went downstairs, and rummaged around in the garage and shed until she found what she needed. She had a lot on her mind and doing some yard work seemed like exactly what she needed. Keeping her body busy so her mind could sort through an issue had served her well many times over the years. The crisp, New England October air invigorated her. She set to work, allowing the repetitive nature of her task to soothe away the tension of her day.

With her body occupied, her mind drifted to where it most often went these days. Rhonda. No matter how hard Jo tried to ignore the attraction, it was growing and she was afraid of what she might do. Rhonda was almost constantly on her mind, even when she was at work. If she stopped to breathe for one minute, her thoughts turned to what Rhonda might be doing.

Maybe she needed to get out. She definitely needed a distraction. Maybe she should go out and try to have some harmless fun with someone else. Blow off some steam. It was probably a really good idea. But even the thought left her feeling empty. If it was simply a physical attraction, a distraction might have been the answer. But the more time she spent with Rhonda, the more she shared with her, it was becoming more than physical. Jo didn't know how to deal with that. She couldn't possibly tell Rhonda any of it and risk their renewed friendship, which she treasured.

Rhonda stood on the back deck and watched Jo attack the leaves that had taken over the backyard. Jo was raking her yard. What in the world? She wondered what was on her mind. And why she needed to take it out on the leaves. She had never seen anyone rake with such a vengeance.

Jo had struggled with her temper at an early age. Seeing her father's fury over and over left its mark. But Jo was strong and learned to manage her anger and channel her frustrations in productive ways. As a result, to an outsider Jo appeared calm and relaxed. She kept very tight control on her deepest emotions, never wanting them to be in control of her.

Amazingly, given her past, Jo became one of the kindest, most patient people Rhonda had ever known. Because of this, sometimes figuring out what Jo was truly feeling was difficult. She understood Jo was not hiding her emotions with any malicious intent. It's just how she lived her life. She was an extremely open and honest person in general, but she also kept her most intimate feelings very close to the vest.

Rhonda surveyed the scene from the deck. Jo had amassed quite a pile of bags. She decided it was time to intervene. She walked down to where Jo was furiously raking. "Jo?"

Jo whirled around, clearly surprised. "Hey, I didn't expect you home until later." Jo looked at her watch. "Oh, I guess it is later."

"How long have you been out here?"

Jo leaned on the rake. "Pretty much since I got home."

"That was more than two hours ago."

"Yeah." Jo looked a bit sheepish.

"What's going on?"

"What do you mean?"

"You have more than thirty bags of leaves gathered and you were still raking like someone was chasing you. The only time you used to get into a zone like that was when you had some serious thinking you needed to do. Is that still the case?"

Jo shrugged. "I guess so."

"Do you want to talk about it?"

Jo studied her for several moments. "Thanks, but no."

"Okay. Well, I'm here if you change your mind. Thank you, by the way, for doing all this."

"You're welcome."

"Why don't you come inside and I'll make us some hot chocolate? I'll finish this later."

"Okay. I'll put the tools away and meet you inside."

Jo quickly gathered the tools and put them in the shed. She dusted herself off. Then she took some fortifying breaths, steeling herself to be in close quarters with Rhonda. If she could just remember to breathe, she would get through this. Her mind had been on Rhonda for more than two hours. Her body was still humming from her thoughts. By the time she walked into the kitchen, Rhonda had preparations well underway. Jo walked to the sink and washed her hands. "So, how was your day?" she asked as casually as she could manage.

"Really good. I worked on a design for a business rehab downtown. Then my client meeting this evening was very successful. Did you have a rough day at work?"

"Not especially."

"Did your dad contact you?"

"No, why would you ask that?"

"Well, given our conversation last night, it seemed like a legitimate possibility. I'm just trying to figure out what's wrong."

"I was just working some stuff out in my head. It's as simple as that."

"Jo, you're still radiating tension and that's after raking more than thirty bags of leaves. Maybe it'd help to talk about it." Rhonda said gently.

"No, I definitely don't think that would help."

Rhonda crossed to Jo then and grabbed her hand. "I can be a very good listener."

Jo stared at Rhonda's hand for several moments. Then she lifted her head to meet Rhonda's intense gaze. "I can't do this anymore. I need to go." She pulled her hand away and rushed out of the room.

Jo was shoving clothes into an overnight bag when Rhonda knocked on her open bedroom door. "What are you doing?" Rhonda asked.

"I'm leaving. I'm going to find my own place."

"Why?"

Jo shrugged. "It's just what I need to do." Jo felt bad shutting Rhonda out, but she couldn't tell her the real reason and she hadn't had time to come up with a plausible excuse.

Rhonda looked at Jo in disbelief. "Jo, you have to tell me why. Did I do something?"

"I can't. It's not anything you did. It's me. I just…can't."

"You can't what?"

"Live here."

"So you've said. Now, please tell me why. What's changed since you moved in last month?"

"Everything's changed."

"You know that doesn't tell me anything, right?"

"Rhonda, please, I need to go." Jo zipped the bag and turned. She made a move to walk around her but Rhonda stepped into her path.

"Why, Jo?"

Jo couldn't stand being so close to Rhonda. She tried once more to navigate around her. Her path was blocked again. "Rhonda, I need to go."

"Not until you tell me why you have to leave."

Jo heard buzzing in her ears and her heart hammered in her chest. She was blinded by panic and couldn't find a way out. She reacted. She dropped her bag. She grasped Rhonda's arms and pulled her to her. She crushed Rhonda's mouth with hers. With the first taste she yearned for more. She turned them and followed Rhonda onto the bed. She heard Rhonda whimper, and it snapped her back to reality.

"Oh, my God." Jo pushed herself off of Rhonda and stood. She couldn't look at her, ashamed she'd lost control. "I'm so sorry, Rhonda. Please forgive me." Jo ran from the room.

Rhonda felt the loss immediately. Her body ached for Jo to finish what she'd started.

"Jo, wait!"

The only response she heard was the front door slam. Jo was gone. Once she was sure her legs would hold her, Rhonda stood. She caught her reflection in the mirror above the dresser. Her cheeks were flushed and her hair was mussed. She was damp between her thighs. She needed a drink. She walked downstairs and went directly to the liquor cabinet. She poured two fingers of scotch, neat, and sat in the closest chair. She picked up the phone and called Barbara.

"I need to call in a friend favor. How soon can you get here?"

Ten minutes later, Rhonda let Barbara into the house. "Thank you for coming so quickly."

"It sounded urgent. What's going on?"

Rhonda walked back to top off her drink. "Can I get you anything?"

"I'm okay for now."

"So...Jo's gone."

"Gone where?" Barbara asked.

"I have no idea. She packed a bag and said she couldn't live here anymore."

"Did you two have a fight?"

Rhonda pictured Jo pushing her onto the bed and covering her body. "No, not exactly."

"You're not making a lot of sense. Why don't you tell me what happened."

"Jo kissed me."

"Okay...and then she packed a bag and left?"

"No. I'm sorry. I'm a bit flustered. I don't know why Jo packed a bag. She never got around to telling me why she had to move out. I was asking her why, trying to get her to tell me. She tried to leave and I got in her way. That's when she kissed me."

"Maybe she answered you after all."

"What do you mean?"

"First, tell me exactly what happened, with as much detail as possible."

Rhonda recounted the entire scene in Jo's bedroom as best as she could recall, including Jo's apology as she raced out the door.

When Rhonda finished her story, Barbara nodded. "That's what I thought."

"What is?"

Before Barbara answered, she poured herself a drink and sat on the sofa. "It sounds like Jo realized she couldn't keep fighting her attraction to you while living under the same roof."

"What are you talking about?"

Barbara looked at Rhonda pointedly. "You know exactly what I'm talking about."

"Shit. Yeah, I do. So what am I supposed to do about it?"

"That depends."

"On what?"

"What you want to do about it."

"And if I have no idea?"

"Then you better start figuring it out."

❖

Jo sat in Amy and Randi's basement. Her laptop balanced on her legs which were propped on the coffee table. She glanced up when Amy came into the room.

"Hey."

"What are you doing?"

"Looking for an apartment. I can't crash with you forever."

"You can stay with us as long as you need to, but that's not what I meant. What are you doing?"

Jo didn't have to ask Amy what she meant. She knew. "I'm giving her space."

"Are you just going to leave the rest of your stuff there forever?"

"No. Probably not forever."

"Chicken!"

"Excuse me?"

"You heard me. You've been hiding here for three days. You need to talk to Rhonda."

"What's left to say?"

"I'd wager a whole lot. I've never known you to bury your head in the sand about anything."

"I'm not. I'm just letting things calm back down."

"What needs to calm down?"

"Never mind."

"Look, I don't know exactly what went down since you're not talking. But it's weird that you just up and left. Shouldn't you at least talk to her?"

"I will." Jo knew she owed her at least that much.

CHAPTER TWELVE

Rhonda was nervous. Jo had texted and asked to stop by. There was no reason to be nervous. Jo was her friend. They could talk like reasonable adults and figure out what was going on. When the doorbell rang, Rhonda's pep talk flew out the window. She remembered to breathe. Then she opened the door. She felt herself staring at Jo's lips and mentally shook herself. She stepped back so Jo could enter.

"Hi."

"Hi, this is for you." Jo handed her a bottle.

Rhonda looked at it. "Olive oil?"

Jo shrugged. "I couldn't find an olive branch."

Their shared amusement broke some of the tension.

"How are you?" Rhonda asked.

"I'm okay. You?"

"Fine, I'm fine. Do you want to sit?"

"I'm not sure I'll be here that long. Mostly I wanted to come apologize in person."

Rhonda leaned against the arm of the sofa. "What are you sorry for?"

"You know the answer to that."

"I want you to spell it out for me."

Jo shifted from foot to foot and finally looked at Rhonda. "I'm sorry for losing control and attacking you."

"Attacking me?"

"That's what I did."

"Not even one little bit."

"Still."

Rhonda stepped toward Jo. "And as for you losing control, that part I enjoyed quite a lot."

"What are you saying?"

"Truthfully, I'm not entirely sure. But what I do know is that I liked kissing you."

Jo stood utterly still. "I have no idea what to do with that information."

Rhonda took another step, closing the distance between them. "Maybe we should kiss again."

Jo visibly swallowed. "Why?"

"Mostly because I want to." Rhonda slid her arms around Jo's neck and pulled Jo down to meet her. Rhonda outlined Jo's lips with her tongue. When she pushed for entry, Jo moaned. Then she adjusted the angle of her head and opened her mouth. Her hands were suddenly on Rhonda's hips pulling her closer still. Their tongues met in a clash of heat. Rhonda's knees threatened to buckle and she gripped Jo's shoulders for support. Jo wrenched her mouth away and took a step back, breaking all contact between them. "Jesus."

"Jo?"

"I need to sit down." She collapsed into the closest chair.

Rhonda knelt beside her. "What's wrong?"

"This is not what I expected to happen when I came here today."

"Are you disappointed?"

"No. Confused, yes, but definitely not disappointed."

"What are you confused about?"

"You. This. Rhonda you're straight, aren't you?"

"I always thought so, until recently."

"How recently?"

"Oh, about the time I saw you at the wedding."

Jo stood quickly and crossed the room before turning back to Rhonda. "What are you saying?"

Rhonda stood and tried to go to her, but Jo actively worked to keep the distance between them. It stung. "Look, I'm handling this badly. It seems I have more than a little crush on you. In fact, I'm very attracted to you."

"So the night of the wedding…the kiss…?"

"I wasn't drunk. I knew exactly what I was doing. Dancing with you…I was very turned on."

"You let me think…"

"I know. I'm sorry. I was confused. I acted in the moment and I didn't want things to be weird between us, so I asked you to forget it happened."

Jo finally stopped moving away from her and Rhonda was able to close the distance once more.

"I thought I was going crazy. I thought it was only me."

Rhonda stood directly in front of Jo now. "I'm so sorry. You have to believe me. I was confused at first and I just wanted to give it some time to see if it was something that would pass."

"And now?"

"Now I know it won't."

"What do you want to do about it?"

Rhonda licked her lips and took a risk.

"If you're willing, I would like to explore it with you, slowly. I want you to move back in and we can take our time figuring out what this connection is between us."

"You realize I'm only here for two more months?"

"I know. I'm not asking for a commitment or strings of any kind. I just can't stop thinking about you and all the things I want to do to you. The only thing I think about more is all the things I want you to do to me."

Jo's eyes darkened and finally she smiled. "Well, who in their right mind could turn down an offer like that?"

"Is that a yes?"

Jo bent down until their lips were an inch apart. "Yes." Then she closed the space between them.

❖

Jo walked into Amy and Randi's house whistling. Amy looked over from the couch where she was watching a game. "What has you in such high spirits?"

"I talked to Rhonda."

"Clearly, it went well."

"Much better than expected actually."

"Want to fill me in?"

Jo sat on the chair beside the couch. "So, the reason I've been staying with you is because I couldn't be around Rhonda anymore without wanting her. The day I showed up on your doorstep, I kissed her."

Amy picked up the remote control and turned off the TV. "Are you crazy?"

"I felt like I was."

"Rhonda's straight. You know you're just asking for trouble."

"Well, it turns out, maybe not so much."

"Not so much, what?"

"Rhonda may not be as straight as I always thought."

"Why do you say that?"

"Because today she kissed me and it wasn't the first time."

"Come again?"

"The night of your wedding, after I drove her home, she kissed me. But she blamed that on too much to drink. She apologized for that today. Apparently, she needed time to figure out what was going on."

"And what's going on?"

"She and I are going to explore the attraction we feel for each other."

"At the risk of repeating myself, are you crazy?"

"Maybe. Maybe I am. But when she asked, I couldn't say no. Who could?"

"You're leaving in two months."

"I pointed that out. She said she wanted to explore and didn't expect any commitment."

"Jo, are you actually okay with that arrangement? What about her family?"

"We didn't get that far. But we have some serious chemistry and I'd like to see where that takes us."

Amy shook her head. "I still think you're asking for trouble."

"So noted. Now, I'm going to grab my stuff. Rhonda's making us dinner."

Jo left Amy's feeling a bit deflated. Amy had raised some good points that Jo hadn't thought about in her daze of desire for Rhonda. But when she got back to Rhonda's house, she shook off the mood. They would just take things one day at a time and see where they ended up. She ran upstairs and unpacked her bag in her room. Then she joined Rhonda in the kitchen.

"Hi. It smells great in here."

Rhonda turned. "Hi. Everything go okay?"

"All good. Amy says hello. I literally just this minute realized, I should have asked you first. I told her about our plan. I'm sorry if you didn't want her to know."

Rhonda crossed to Jo then. "It's okay. She's your best friend. I'd be surprised if you hadn't told her." Rhonda put her hands on Jo's shoulders. "But if it's okay with you, I would like to keep the circle small for a while. It's all pretty new to me."

"I understand."

"Don't you want to kiss me?"

Jo's stomach clenched, her throat tightened making her voice hoarse. "Of course I do."

"Then what are you waiting for?"

This kiss was hot and urgent as Jo released some of the pent up desire she held back before. Rhonda moaned and matched the urgency in Jo's embrace. Jo slowed the kiss and lifted her head. "I do enjoy kissing you."

"Likewise. Would you like some wine?"

"I'd love some. I'll get it. Would you like a red to go with the spaghetti?"

"Yes, please."

Dinner with Rhonda was a whole new experience. Not having to hide the desire she felt was refreshing. Jo was able to fully relax and enjoy herself. After they put the kitchen back in order, they moved into the living room with their wine and sat close together on the sofa. Jo's arm lay across the back of the couch and she started playing with the ends of Rhonda's hair.

"Your hair is like silk. I've wanted to touch it again since I kissed you the other day."

"Touch away."

Rhonda turned and leaned into her. She touched her lips to Jo's. The kiss was sweet and tender. Jo restrained herself from taking it deeper, wanting Rhonda to set the pace. Jo didn't have to wait long. Rhonda shifted and sat on Jo's lap. She teased Jo's mouth open and explored with her tongue. Jo joined the dance and when their tongues met with a flash of heat, Rhonda moaned. Jo buried both her hands in Rhonda's hair, trying to hold on. This was Rhonda's show; she would lead the way.

Rhonda broke the kiss and went quickly to kissing Jo's neck from her ear to the open collar of her shirt. Jo moaned. Rhonda returned to Jo's mouth. She guided one of Jo's hands to her breast. Jo ran her thumb over the hard nipple evident through Rhonda's blouse and bra. Rhonda gasped and ground down into Jo's lap. The pressure on Jo's already throbbing clit was almost too much. She slid her hands down to Rhonda's hips. Rhonda whimpered at the loss of contact. Jo broke the kiss. Her breath ragged, she said, "We need to slow down."

"Are you okay?"

"Yes, I'm fine. Incredibly turned on, but fine."

"Then why did you stop?"

"If we kept that up much longer, I would have gotten carried away. You asked that we explore this slowly and that's what I plan to do."

"What if I'm ready?"

"Take a minute and think, when we're not touching."

Rhonda scooted off Jo's lap and broke all contact. She stared into space for a few minutes and took deep breaths.

Jo asked, "Are you?"

Rhonda turned back. "No, not yet."

"Okay."

"I don't know if I should apologize or thank you."

Jo bent and lifted their wine glasses from the coffee table. She handed one to Rhonda. "No reason for either. I like that we're taking our time. I think I've already mentioned I very much enjoy kissing you. We can take this as slowly as you need. When I take you to bed, and to be clear I would like that to happen, I don't want you to have any regrets."

Rhonda leaned over and touched her lips to Jo's. "Thank you."

A short while later, they climbed the stairs to turn in. They both stopped in front of Rhonda's bedroom. Jo bent down and kissed her deeply. "Sweet dreams."

"Sleep well, Jo."

Jo turned and headed for her room as Rhonda went through her door. She quickly stripped naked and climbed between the cool sheets. The soft cotton against her sensitive nipples made her bite her lip to hold back a moan. She clasped her hands behind her head, reluctant to take care of her need even though she had now held Rhonda in her hands. But when she heard sounds from down the hall that were unmistakable, her restraint melted.

She slid her hand down her torso and kept moving down until she could feel her clit. It was hot and swollen as she knew it would be. She moved her free hand to her breast and fondled her nipple while she made long, sweeping strokes up and down her clit. She was already so close. She dipped one finger into her opening and slicked the juices along her labia, then worked her way back to the bundle of twitching nerves at her center. She imagined it was Rhonda touching her. In mere moments, she climaxed so forcefully that her back rose off the bed.

❖

Rhonda woke energized. She'd been honest with Jo. She wasn't ready to go to bed with her, but she was getting very close. When she laid down last night, she'd still been wound up from their heavy make-out session. She'd imagined Jo's hands on her as she brought herself to orgasm. She'd had to stifle her shout of ecstasy behind a pillow. Part of her couldn't wait to have Jo there in person, but she needed time and she owed it to both of them to take that time before they took things further.

She wrapped her silk robe around her and went downstairs. After doctoring her coffee just the way she liked it, she planted herself on a stool and started working the crossword puzzle in the morning paper. She was a bit old school, according to her kids, in that she still preferred to get the paper in paper form, not on a device.

She turned when she heard the front door open. This was one of her favorite parts of the day. Jo walked into the kitchen, hot and sweaty from her run. She saw Jo's gaze dip to her chest before she determinedly looked into her face.

"Good morning." Jo's voice was strained.

"Jo, come here."

When Jo stood before her, Rhonda said, "It's okay."

"What?"

"I like when you look at me. You get this look of hunger in your eyes. That look makes me feel beautiful."

"You're gorgeous."

"And you look yummy when you've been running. You should probably kiss me soon."

Jo bent and touched her lips to Rhonda's, careful to keep the rest of their bodies from making contact. She deepened the kiss briefly and then stepped back. "More coffee?"

"Um, no, I'm good for now." Rhonda watched as Jo went around the bar and pulled down a mug. She watched her pour her coffee. Finally, she asked, "Are you all right?"

"I'm good, why?"

"You seem tense."

Jo blew out a breath and set her coffee down before leaning on her hands on the counter, facing Rhonda. "I seem to be in a perpetual state of arousal whenever you're anywhere close."

"Oh."

"I didn't say that to pressure you, I meant what I said last night. But that's what you're sensing."

"Okay. Have you considered taking care of it yourself?" Rhonda could feel herself blush and knew Jo saw it when she smiled.

"I tried last night, I wasn't going to, but then I heard sounds coming from your room, and they shattered my restraint. It helped for about 2.2 seconds. Like I said, it seems to be perpetual."

Rhonda knew her face was now completely red in her embarrassment. "I'm sorry."

Jo came around the bar then and took her hands. "God, Rhonda, please don't ever be sorry for taking, giving, or getting pleasure."

"I'm not sorry about that. I'm sorry this is hard for you."

"Don't apologize for that either. I have every confidence it will be worth the wait, whenever you're ready."

"How can you be so sure?"

"Because of how turned on I get and how responsive you are when we kiss." Jo kissed her then, slow and deep. "Now I'm going to take a shower. For the record, if you ever want to join me, you'd be welcome." Without another word, Jo grabbed her coffee and left the room.

Rhonda was so tempted to follow Jo upstairs but she refrained. Not fair to Jo, until she was completely ready. Soon, she was sure she would be, very soon.

Chapter Thirteen

By Friday evening, the weather had turned cooler. Rhonda and Jo were enjoying an after work cocktail. Rhonda turned to Jo. "Maybe you can build a fire while I get us refills?"

"Sure."

On Rhonda's way to the kitchen, she stopped at the stereo and selected soft background music.

Jo pulled the screen away from the fireplace. She selected a couple of logs that lay neatly stacked on the side and placed them on the grate. She added kindling from the can beside the logs and was a little in awe that she found the long matches in the same slender box on the mantel where she had always gone for them. She crouched down to arrange the wood and kindling.

She picked up her wine glass and sat close to Rhonda on the sofa. "This is nice."

"Yes, it is."

Jo and Rhonda sat in comfortable silence for a few minutes watching the logs catch, and enjoying the wine and the music. Jo took Rhonda's glass and placed it next to her own on the table. She leaned back and pulled Rhonda close and kissed her.

She kept it simple and light giving Rhonda time to stop her if she wanted.

Rhonda's next words almost stopped her heart and changed her plan to take things between them slowly.

"Jo?"

"Yes?"

"Will you please take me to bed?"

Jo was certain her heart had never beaten so fast. She was sure Rhonda could hear it over the music. She stood and drew Rhonda up with her. She kissed her deeply and then led her to the top of the stairs. Once they were in Rhonda's bedroom, she shut the door behind them, and turned to Rhonda. She saw no hesitation.

Jo moved at a leisurely pace, deepening each kiss a little more. As they reached the bed, Jo stopped and looked at Rhonda wanting and needing her to be sure. "Rhonda?"

"Yes?"

Jo placed her hand on Rhonda's cheek. "You're sure?"

Rhonda placed her hand on top of Jo's and turned to place a kiss on her palm. "I'm sure."

Those were exactly the words Jo needed to hear. She ran her hands down Rhonda's arms and pulled Rhonda's sweater over her head and tossed it aside. "Beautiful," Jo breathed.

Jo stepped back, still holding Rhonda's hand. "Let me look at you."

Rhonda stood there in her bra and jeans and tried not to shy away from Jo's gaze. Jo let her eyes roam over Rhonda in appreciation. "You have an amazing body. You are very sexy."

She ran her hands back up Rhonda's arms as she kissed her. She raised her head to watch Rhonda's reaction when she ran her hand up her stomach to cup her breast. Rhonda's breathing hitched and her mouth parted, but her gaze was steady on Jo's. When Jo flicked her thumb over her hard nipple, Rhonda moaned with pleasure.

Jo wound her hands around Rhonda's back and unhooked her bra. She bent to take a nipple into her mouth and Rhonda gasped. She slid her hands down Rhonda's stomach and unbuttoned her jeans. She drew the jeans down, kissing Rhonda's legs as she exposed them. Jo knelt on one knee as Rhonda gripped her shoulders so she could remove her shoes before finally removing the last of her clothes. Jo paused for a moment and looked up the length of Rhonda's body. Her heart jumped a little at the trust she saw in Rhonda's expression. She stood up and kicked off her shoes and pulled off her jeans and shirt, and moved to Rhonda once more.

Rhonda stared at Jo's body in open appreciation. She tentatively reached out and ran her hands down Jo's strong arms and over the rippled muscles of her stomach. She was thrilled when the muscles quivered under her hand. Then Jo surprised Rhonda by scooping her into her arms. She carried Rhonda the last few steps to the bed. Rhonda felt weightless in Jo's strong embrace. Jo laid her on the bed as though she were precious. Rhonda wrapped her hands behind Jo's head and tugged her down for a searing kiss.

Eventually, Jo raised herself up and shifted to lay the length of her body against Rhonda's. She kissed and tasted while her hand explored, finding the places where Rhonda's body craved to be touched.

Rhonda's skin burned with pleasure, the epicenter of the fire blazing between her legs. She ached for Jo to touch her where she needed it most, but everywhere Jo touched felt so good she didn't want to interrupt. Jo seemed to read her mind, and Rhonda gasped as Jo cupped her center. Rhonda's body arched, pushing into Jo's hand. Jo slid a finger between Rhonda's swollen folds and stroked her clit. Rhonda's hips rose and pushed against her. She needed more and her body writhed with each stroke of Jo's finger. "Oh, Jo, I'm going to come."

"Yes. Yes, come for me, Rhonda." Jo stroked the hard, swollen tissue faster. Rhonda's body clenched as the pleasure all zeroed in on her clit. She climbed fast and crashed down. Before she could catch her breath, Jo slipped two fingers into Rhonda's hot, wet center and drove her up again. The climax left them both breathless. Jo slowed her hand, leaving her fingers inside.

Jo leaned down and kissed her forehead, her cheek, and her mouth. Rhonda struggled to focus. "Wow! That was more than I imagined."

"We're just getting started."

"Sounds promising."

Jo bent down and kissed Rhonda long and deep.

Chapter Fourteen

L ater, Jo kissed Rhonda on the forehead and left her sleeping as she slipped out of bed. She pulled on her jeans and shirt and quietly made her way downstairs. She headed straight for the kitchen to hunt up provisions. She hoped to keep Rhonda occupied for many hours. Refueling was necessary to keep things up. When she opened the refrigerator, she said a silent thank you to Rhonda.

Rhonda had always liked to cook. Jo found the fried chicken she had recently made. She grabbed a big plate and loaded it with chicken and homemade macaroni and cheese. She gathered forks, napkins, and the bottle of wine Rhonda had opened earlier. She put the extra food away and grabbed a bottle of water too. She carefully carried the picnic back upstairs.

Jo set dinner on the bedside table, stripped back down, and climbed into bed. She lay next to Rhonda simply watching her sleep. Before long, she ached to touch Rhonda again.

Lying on her side, Rhonda facing Jo, their bodies inches apart, she started to stroke Rhonda's hip. She moved her hand up her side to her shoulder and down to her hip. Rhonda moaned softly in slumber, as though enjoying a nice dream. On the next upward sweep, Jo grazed Rhonda's breast. Rhonda moaned. The slow seduction and Rhonda's ready response, even in sleep, drove Jo wild. Her own clit pulsed. She had a hard time keeping her hand slow and gentle.

Jo leaned in and touched her lips to Rhonda's. The connection roused Rhonda. She looked dreamily up at Jo, who turned up the heat. She deepened the kiss, and her strokes became fast and fervent. Rhonda's body responded. Jo's restraint was lost. She rolled onto her back pulling Rhonda on top of her. She met Rhonda's lips for a long, burning kiss. She plunged into Rhonda's hot, wet center, driving deep. Rhonda gasped and dug her fingers into Jo's shoulders. Keeping her gaze locked with Jo's, Rhonda rode Jo's fingers fast and hard. As she came, Rhonda took over. She lifted Jo's arms above her head. Then she kissed and sucked Jo's nipples. Jo couldn't catch her breath. Rhonda's hands and mouth were claiming her. No one had ever taken so much pleasure in exploring her body, and it drove her crazy. Rhonda seemed to be everywhere at once. Then she was back for a long, smoldering kiss. Rhonda positioned her body between Jo's legs.

She kissed her way down Jo's body, stopping to explore, spending time nibbling, and caressing her breasts. Her body ached with need, but she wanted Rhonda to do whatever she wanted with her, even if she went insane waiting for the release she needed. Rhonda kissed down her torso and slid her body down so she could explore her center. As Rhonda stroked her clit with her tongue, Jo's body exploded. Rhonda hung on and continued to lick and plunder her to excruciating bliss. Rhonda slowed her tongue and allowed Jo's body to settle. She returned the way she had come, kissing Jo's body on the way back up. She laid her full weight on Jo and placed her mouth to Jo's lips. The kiss was tender and sweet. Rhonda laid her head on Jo's chest and waited until her breathing eased and her heartbeat slowed from the hammer it had been moments before.

Jo didn't have the words to tell Rhonda everything she felt. She raised her head a fraction and found herself looking at the top of Rhonda's gorgeous mane of hair. She kissed the top of her head. Rhonda pushed herself up and shifted so she could straddle Jo's stomach. She raised her arms and stretched them high. Jo watched her. She enjoyed seeing Rhonda so relaxed.

Rhonda expelled a long, deep breath. "I feel amazing."

Rhonda's grin turned into puzzlement as she sniffed the air.

Jo tensed. "What is it?"

Rhonda sighed. "I'm starving."

Jo chuckled in relief. "I can fix that." She turned and looked at the provisions.

Rhonda's eyes widened in anticipation. "Oh yum, how did you manage all this?"

"You, my dear, are a very sound sleeper. I'm not quite ready to leave the bedroom, so I thought I should bring in supplies so we can keep our strength up."

With a devilish grin, Rhonda leaned over and grabbed the plate and, still straddling Jo, bit into a piece of chicken. "Works for me."

Rhonda lifted her hips just enough so Jo could slide up and sit back against the headboard. She handed Jo the plate and leaned back over for the bottle of water. Jo caught herself watching as Rhonda uncapped the bottle and drank from it like she had been in the desert for days. "Hmmm, that's good."

Jo held out her hand.

Rhonda raised the bottle above her head. "For a kiss."

Jo gladly obliged. The kiss lit the embers so near the surface, and she was seconds from setting aside the food and letting the fire consume them. Before she could, Rhonda raised her head. "Food first." Jo fought for control and reined herself in. "I can't get enough of you."

"Nor I you, but we need to eat."

Jo leaned over and grabbed the wine and glasses. She poured and handed one glass to Rhonda and lifted hers in toast. "To slow explorations."

"And to the best picnic I've ever had." They clinked glasses. Rhonda moved to sit beside Jo at the head of the bed, their shoulders touching.

"This chicken is amazing. It may be even better than it was the other night and it was delicious then."

"Thank you."

"How are you feeling?"

"I'm wonderful. Today has been amazing. Part of me still can't believe this is happening."

"I'm right there with you, but I'm sure glad it is."

"Me too."

"Listen, I know we said no strings, but I need you to know while you and I are together I won't be with anyone else. I know I don't have the right to ask, but it would be my preference if you weren't with anyone else either."

"Jo, you have every right. I've never been with more than one person at once and I'm not going to start now. I won't be with anyone else while you and I are together."

"Okay."

Chapter Fifteen

As the first rays of light filtered through the curtains, Rhonda woke and studied Jo's face relaxed in sleep. She was overcome with emotions. A month ago, she never would have expected this to happen, but now that it had, she wasn't sure she wanted it to end. Jo was young and had her whole life ahead of her. Rhonda was determined not to hold her back. She would cherish the time she had with her.

Jo's eyelids started to flutter toward waking. Rhonda returned to the moment, hid her concerns, and smiled brightly. When Jo's eyes opened fully. Rhonda greeted her warmly. "Good morning."

"Hi. How did you sleep?" she said groggily.

"Hard. You?"

Jo snuggled closer to Rhonda. "Better than I have in a long time. How long have you been awake?"

"A little while."

"Why didn't you wake me?"

"I enjoyed watching you sleep. Besides, I thought you could use the rest given the plans I have for you today."

Jo raised her head so she could meet Rhonda's gaze. "Oh, what do you have in mind?"

"Let me show you." Rhonda pushed Jo onto her back and threw her leg over her hips. She leaned down for a scorching kiss.

Quite a while later, Jo lay on her back with Rhonda's head resting on her shoulder. Rhonda had been quiet for a few minutes, but she wasn't sleeping. "What are you thinking about?" Jo asked.

Caught in deep thoughts, Rhonda pulled herself back. "Can I ask you a question?"

"You can ask me anything."

"Are you always so tidy or are you trying to make a good impression?"

"This is what you're actually lying here thinking about?"

"It's been on my mind."

"What do you mean?"

"You never leave anything just lying around. Not your shoes, not a glass, and your room is always immaculate when you leave for work. Even Kona's toys are always put away unless she's actively playing with something. If I didn't know better or see Kona's things around, I wouldn't even be sure you actually live here."

Jo shrugged. "I guess it's a hard habit to break. My father didn't like clutter. It was better to keep things clean. Plus I never want to take advantage of your hospitality."

"And leaving your jacket on the couch or something equally harmless would be taking advantage of my hospitality?"

Jo shrugged. "Why take the risk?"

Rhonda pushed herself up onto her elbow so she could look directly at Jo. "There is no risk. Clearly, you're not a slob, but it won't hurt anything if you wanted to relax your own standards a bit. I meant it when I said I want you to treat my home like your home."

"I'll think about it."

"That's all I can ask. Now come here."

Chapter Sixteen

On Saturday, as they were getting dressed, Rhonda said, "Let's go out tonight."

Jo looked over to where Rhonda was pulling on her slacks. "Sure, where would you like to go?"

"I thought we could get dressed up and go out for dinner and dancing, but I hadn't thought of anywhere specific. How's that sound?"

"It sounds great. I know a place we can go."

"Wonderful. Then it's a date."

As a thought occurred to her, Jo moved closer. "Rhonda?"

Rhonda looked up. "Yes?"

Jo hesitated, trying to find the right words. "This is the first time we'll be 'out' together in public, like on a date. I know we've been out to dinner and stuff before, but this time I'll want to hold your hand and touch you. Is that okay?"

"Of course it's okay, why wouldn't it be?"

"I just don't want you to be uncomfortable."

"I wouldn't have suggested going out if I thought I'd be uncomfortable."

"I just..." Jo paused, wanting Rhonda to know what she might face. "You haven't had to deal with the looks before. There are still people who stare at two women walking down the street holding hands."

"Let them stare."

"Rhonda."

"Jo, I'm not taking this lightly. I understand what you're saying, but I'm grateful to have you in my life. I'm not ashamed of you or what is happening between us. Fear is not going to keep me from showing affection for you, in public or anywhere else." To end the discussion, Rhonda stepped to Jo and pulled her down for a deep, lingering kiss.

"Point taken."

❖

This is crazy, Jo thought as she got ready in the guest bathroom for her first official date with Rhonda. Rhonda insisted on not seeing each other prepare for the evening. She wanted Jo to get the full effect of her outfit, and that wouldn't happen if she watched her dress. Rhonda had been locked in the bedroom for more than two hours. Meanwhile, Jo had run a few errands, fed Kona, and then headed upstairs to get ready.

She finished applying her cologne and slid her shirt on. The tie and jacket followed. She liked the look; glad she'd opted for the dark charcoal gray suit for their evening. With her own preparations done, she went downstairs. Kona followed and lay in her bed by the front window where she could see Jo and the stairs. Moments later, Jo heard the bedroom door open. She turned around at the foot of the stairs and watched as Rhonda approached.

Jo's jaw dropped. She had seen Rhonda in various states of undress and with nothing on at all, but the extra care Rhonda had taken with her appearance tonight had the intended effect. She was awestruck. Her gaze traveled up and down Rhonda's entire body, taking it all in. The emerald green dress was stunning. The plunging neckline and floor length skirt clinging to Rhonda perfectly had Jo's heart racing. As Rhonda stepped down each stair, the long slit in the side of the skirt slipped to reveal a hint of Rhonda's thigh. Jo's heart skipped a beat.

Rhonda's hair was swept into a stylish updo leaving her sleek neck and shoulders exposed. She accented the look with a solitary dangling diamond earring that hung from each ear. Rhonda turned to give Jo a view of the back. The gown was backless, and the fabric rode low on Rhonda's hips. The whole package made Jo melt.

As Rhonda reached the bottom step, she smiled. With three-inch heels, she was a bit taller than Jo. Rhonda could not have been more pleased with her reaction. She reached out and closed Jo's mouth, which brought Jo back from wherever she had gone in her head. She focused on Rhonda. "My God, you're gorgeous, amazing, radiant. I can't tell you how beautiful you look. There are just no words that do you justice."

"Thank you. You're looking pretty handsome yourself. The blue shirt sets off your eyes beautifully," she said, running her hand down Jo's chest.

"Thank you," Jo said automatically.

Rhonda grinned as Jo continued to stare at her. "Jo?"

"Hmmm?"

"Do you think you can take a step back so I can come down this last step?"

"What? Oh, yeah sure." Jo stepped back and Rhonda followed.

"Jo, what's behind your back?"

Jo finally recovered some basic mental functioning ability. She pulled her hand from behind her back. She held out a single white rose. "This is for you."

"Thank you." Rhonda took the rose and kissed Jo lightly on the cheek.

As the kiss ended, Jo breathed deeply. "Your perfume is intoxicating."

"I'm glad you like it."

Rhonda moved to the closet and pulled out her wrap. "Shall we go?"

Jo's brain was finally fully functional again. "Yes, let's. Will you be warm enough with just the wrap?"

"I'm sure if I get a little chilly you'll keep me warm."

Jo held out her arm. Rhonda slipped hers through to walk to the car. Jo escorted her to the passenger side and opened the door. Once she was in, Jo closed the door and walked around to the other side.

She got the heater going quickly and then selected soft background music. Rhonda laid her hand on Jo's leg and left it there. When Jo didn't need her right hand for driving, she covered Rhonda's hand with her own.

While stopped at a red light, Jo said, "Rhonda."

Rhonda turned.

"I'll never question you again if you want to get ready in separate rooms before a night out."

"Good to know."

"One other thing you should know. If anyone stares at you tonight it won't be because you're with me. It will be because you're strikingly gorgeous. Nobody will even see me."

Before long, Jo pulled into the parking lot at the restaurant. Jo walked around to open Rhonda's door and held out her hand to help her. Jo and Rhonda walked hand in hand into the restaurant, and the hostess took them to their table. Jo was full of pride at the heads turning to follow Rhonda. Jo pulled out Rhonda's chair and then moved to her own.

"Wow, everything looks delicious," said Rhonda as she looked at the menu.

"Yes, it does. Are you leaning toward anything yet?"

"I think I might just have to try the seared scallops. How about you?"

"I'm thinking about the prime rib."

Once their order was placed, Jo leaned forward and reached across the table to take Rhonda's hand. "This was a great idea."

Rhonda laced her fingers with Jo's. "It was, wasn't it?"

The entire meal was wonderful. When the check came, they both reached for it.

"Let me," Jo said.

"No, this one's on me. I asked you out after all."

"Well, thank you very much. Dinner was lovely. The next one is my treat, not the company's, mine."

"Fair enough, if you do the asking," Rhonda said slyly.

"In that case, Rhonda, would you like to go out on a date with me next Friday night?"

"I would love to."

Jo decided to leave the car parked, and she took Rhonda's hand to walk down the street to the piano bar. They found a table back a bit from the dance floor. Jo pulled out Rhonda's chair. "Let me get you a drink. Would you like to stick with wine?"

"Actually, I think I'd like a martini, up, three olives."

"Coming right up."

Jo walked over to the bar to place their order, and Rhonda watched the dancers on the floor. She had never seen so many women dancing together. She was enthralled by it.

There was a large crowd at the bar, and it took a couple minutes for Jo to get the bartender's attention. In the meantime, there was a perky little blonde trying to get Jo's attention.

Rhonda looked over to find Jo in the crowd and saw the blonde trying to get closer to her. She couldn't see Jo's expression or hear what was said. The blonde was obviously interested. Rhonda saw that from all the way back here, but Jo must have said something because both of them looked over at Rhonda. She breathed a sigh of relief moments later when she saw Jo shake her head and turn in her direction. The blonde looked after her with the pout of someone used to getting her own way who was just denied.

When Jo saw Rhonda looking in her direction, she smiled broadly. She set their drinks on the table and leaned over to kiss Rhonda on the cheek before sitting down. "Sorry it took so long."

"It's okay. I enjoyed the show." Jo raised an eyebrow in question. "You met a new friend."

"You could say that, although I'm pretty sure she wouldn't call me a friend. I told her I wasn't interested in what she offered because I'm already going home with the hottest woman in the bar."

"You did not!"

"I did. Then she still wanted to give me her number, 'in case I change my mind.' I told her I wasn't interested and walked away."

"She didn't look pleased. I was sitting over here trying not to be jealous as another woman rubbed up against you."

Jo turned to fully face Rhonda. She took her hand and looked sincerely at Rhonda. "You have nothing to be jealous of."

Jo wanted to lighten the mood. She stood and offered her hand to Rhonda. "Now, may I have this dance? I've wanted to get you in my arms all evening."

Rhonda seemed relieved to let the subject drop. "You may."

Jo placed her hand on Rhonda's bare back to guide her to the dance floor. They danced the night away. Jo could fully enjoy the slow dances this time, and she did.

When it was time to head home, the air outside had dropped several degrees. Jo took off her jacket and wrapped it around Rhonda's shoulders. She snuggled into the warmth and breathed in Jo's scent. Rhonda's arm was around Jo's waist and Jo's arm was around her shoulders. Rhonda leaned into Jo. "This whole evening was delightful."

"I'm glad you enjoyed it."

"Did you have a good time?"

"I had an amazing time."

Jo opened Rhonda's door and she slipped inside.

She leaned her head back against the seat and closed her eyes. When Jo got into the car she looked at her and asked, "You okay?"

"I'm amazing. I was just remembering the way I felt in your arms tonight."

"Well, let's get home so you can be there again."

Rhonda took Jo's hand and slipped it through the slit in her skirt and placed it between her legs.

"Oh God, Rhonda." Not only was Rhonda not wearing panties, she was already hot and wet.

"I'm ready. Are you?"

Jo gripped the steering wheel, her knuckles white, as she sought to remain focused. As soon as she threw the car in park, she had her seat belt off. She released Rhonda's restraint and crushed her mouth to hers.

Jo pulled away long enough for them to rush into the house, but as soon as the door closed, Jo pinned Rhonda against it. The kiss was urgent, the need overwhelming. Rhonda matched her intensity in every way. Jo reached through the slit in Rhonda's skirt once more. She was hot, wet, and wanting. Jo hitched up the skirt over

Rhonda's hips and lifted Rhonda who wrapped her legs around Jo's hips opening for her. Holding Rhonda up against the door, Jo plunged into her. The first climax ripped through both of them immediately. Jo kept pumping her fingers into Rhonda.

All Rhonda could do was keep moving her hips to take Jo in again and again and again. As the next wave crashed over them, Rhonda hung on and rode it for all she was worth. Rhonda wasn't sure how Jo managed to keep them upright, but she was beyond thinking right now. Jo was crushed to Rhonda, holding her against the door, and both struggled for breath. Jo recovered first and adjusted so she could lift Rhonda more securely into her arms to walk them over to the couch. With Rhonda's legs still wrapped around her, Jo sat on the couch so Rhonda now straddled her. She placed her lips to Rhonda's and kissed her. "Darling, have I told you how much I like this dress?"

"I think you might have mentioned it." Rhonda looked at their fully clothed bodies. This just won't do, she thought.

Holding Jo's gaze with her own, she removed Jo's tie and threw it aside. Then she unbuttoned Jo's shirt, kissing each bit of skin she exposed. Jo's hands slid enticingly up and down Rhonda's bare back. Once Rhonda had Jo's shirt undone, she pulled it apart over Jo's shoulders, effectively restraining her arms. Rhonda unhooked the strap of cloth around the back of her neck. Then she lifted the entire dress over her head. She was completely naked still straddling Jo who couldn't touch her, her arms still trapped by her shirt. Rhonda ran her nails down Jo's stomach, making her moan in pleasure. Then she unbuttoned Jo's slacks and pulled the zipper down. She reached her hand into Jo's trousers and found what she was looking for. Jo was hot and so wet Rhonda licked her lips in anticipation.

She rose on her knees so she could kiss Jo from above and then she slid off Jo's lap to kneel in front of her. Rhonda put her hands in Jo's waistband, and Jo lifted her hips just enough to allow Rhonda to pull her pants and underwear off. Rhonda pulled Jo's legs so her hips slid forward. When Rhonda spread Jo's legs, she was now in the perfect position for Rhonda to explore her center with her tongue. Jo was at her mercy. There was no place she'd rather be.

Rhonda took her time driving Jo up; there was no hurry. She wanted to give Jo pleasure and wanted it to last. Jo was already so close that the first orgasm shot through her quickly. Rhonda continued to explore, driving Jo up, over and over again.

When Rhonda had her fill, for now, and Jo was sated with pleasure, Rhonda climbed back up. Jo shifted so she was fully lying on the couch and Rhonda snuggled in half beside, half on top of her. Jo managed to pull the throw over them for warmth as she held Rhonda in her arms. After a little while, Rhonda's breathing deepened. She was close to sleep.

Jo stroked her back lightly. "Rhonda, darling, let's get you to bed."

"Uh huh, sleep here."

"I think we'd regret that in the morning. Let me carry you up."

"'Kay."

Jo shifted and stood with Rhonda in her arms. Rhonda wrapped her arms around Jo's neck and burrowed into her shoulder. Jo carried Rhonda up the stairs and into the bedroom. Kona padded after them and curled up on her bed next to the wall. Jo slipped in beside Rhonda who cuddled into her. Jo wrapped her arms around Rhonda and was asleep within minutes.

As the morning light started to peek through the curtains, Jo blinked awake. On her stomach, her head turned toward Rhonda, the first thing she saw was Rhonda, wide-awake, watching her. "Hi." Jo cleared her throat and tried again. "Hi, how long have you been awake?"

"Oh, a little while. I've been lying here debating between waking you up and having my way with you or letting you sleep."

Jo's body instantly reacted. Flames shot to her center. She turned over so her body was open. "Um, I'm awake now."

Rhonda pushed herself up and swung her leg over Jo's hips straddling her. Rhonda's wet center slicked Jo's stomach with her own desire. "Indeed you are."

Later, as Jo and Rhonda snuggled together, Rhonda sighed. "I could get so used to this."

"Me too." Jo stroked her thumb down Rhonda's cheek. "Can we talk for a minute?"

"Of course."

"So, I know when we started this, we agreed that it would be casual, no strings attached."

"Right."

"But it feels like more than that to me. Am I alone in that?"

"You're not, but I don't really know what that means right now."

"We don't have to define it immediately. I just needed to know if it was just me feeling that way."

Chapter Seventeen

Jo was surprised to find the house quiet when she returned from work on Wednesday. Rhonda's car was in the garage. But there was no music playing and Rhonda wasn't in the kitchen where Jo often found her at this time of day. She wandered through the rooms, until she saw Rhonda's office door open. She set her bag down by the stairs and stood on the threshold watching for a few moments. Rhonda was deeply engrossed with something on her drawing table.

She had never had the opportunity to observe Rhonda at work before. She could only see her profile and her long, graceful fingers gripping a pencil. The picture she was sketching took shape before Jo's very eyes. Rhonda was so talented. Jo was impressed by the merest glimpse of her work. She knocked lightly on the open door, once Rhonda's pencil was off the paper.

"Oh, hi. You're home early."

"Actually, I'm not." Jo stepped into the room to get a closer look at Rhonda's drawings. "You are very engrossed in something though."

"I guess I am. I totally lost track of the time."

"Will you walk me through what you're working on?"

Rhonda looked surprised that Jo was interested in her work. "Um, sure." She gestured to the nearest drawings. "I'm working on some rough sketches for a local theater."

"These don't look rough. There is incredible detail," Jo said. "You are amazing."

Rhonda blushed. "Thank you."

"I mean it. I knew you were good or I wouldn't have recommended you to Amy, but you're even better than I remember."

"I like what I do."

"It shows. Do you need to work for a while longer?"

"It would be good if I could get these ideas down."

"Okay. I'll go start dinner. You take all the time you need."

"You don't have to do that."

"I'd like to. You take care of what you need to and I'll make us dinner. Then we can spend the rest of the evening together."

"That I can definitely get on board with, except I need one thing first."

"What's that?"

Rhonda closed the distance between them. She pulled Jo close and stood on her tip toes to kiss her.

"Oh that. There is an endless supply of those."

"Thank goodness."

Jo left Rhonda to her work and went to figure out dinner. She whistled her way into the kitchen. She could definitely get used to this.

❖

As Rhonda climbed into Jo's truck on Friday, she asked, "Are you sure you don't want to tell me where we're going?"

Jo glanced over at Rhonda. "I'm sure. You'll find out soon enough."

Rhonda had no idea where Jo was taking her for their Friday night date. All Jo told her was she should dress warmly but casually. So when Jo arrived at the house after work Rhonda was dressed in jeans, a turtleneck sweater, and boots. Jo made sure Rhonda had her jacket, hat, and gloves before leaving the house.

Rhonda sat beside Jo wondering about their destination. Jo was sweet wanting to surprise her. Wherever Jo was headed, Rhonda knew she was bound to have fun since she'd be with Jo, so she sat back, relaxed, and asked Jo about her day.

Upon arriving, Rhonda looked at Jo. "So this is what you have up your sleeve?"

"If you're up for it."

"Absolutely, this should be fun."

They walked into the building hand in hand. Jo paid their admission and then walked over to the counter to get what the two of them needed. "Jo, what made you think to go ice skating?"

Jo met Rhonda's gaze. "I remember how much you liked to ice skate and I thought it would be something fun for us to do together."

"I'm glad you thought of it. Are you ready to hit the ice?"

Jo stood up and reached for Rhonda's hand. "Sure, let's go."

Neither had been on the ice in years, so it took them some time to find their rhythm. After a while, each glided easily around the rink. At times, Rhonda and Jo skated hand in hand, at others they moved separately, not far from one another. With a sparkle in her eyes Rhonda said, "I'm surprised it all came back so quickly."

"You were always a natural."

They took a break to catch their breath. While Jo headed to the snack bar, Rhonda stood watching the other skaters on the ice.

When Jo returned with the hot chocolate, Rhonda looked lost in thought.

"Everything okay?"

"Hmm, oh yes." Rhonda took the offered hot chocolate. "Thank you."

Jo took a sip from her own cup. "You looked like you were doing some serious thinking."

"I guess I was."

"Care to share?"

Rhonda turned to face her. "I don't know what you like to do for fun."

"What do you mean?"

"I was just standing here thinking if I wanted to plan a surprise date for you, I wouldn't know where to start."

Jo thought for a minute. "Well, you know I enjoy dancing. I also like hiking and climbing rock walls, things like that. I like live performances, like plays and concerts or just about any live sporting event, and I enjoy a good movie. This may sound cheesy, but long walks on the beach and picnics, with the right person, are favorites. I'm sure there are other things, but it's a start. Does that help?"

"Yes, it does, thank you."

Jo held out her hand. "Shall we skate a little more before we head to dinner?"

Rhonda linked her hand with Jo's. "Okay. Where are we going for dinner?"

"It's a surprise."

Rhonda laughed and launched herself back onto the ice.

❖

"I hope you're hungry," Jo quipped later heading back out to her truck.

"Famished actually. I worked up quite an appetite."

"Excellent. My plan is working."

"You're having fun with this aren't you?"

"I am."

A short time later, Jo pulled into the parking lot of Amy's restaurant and ushered Rhonda inside. "I know you've eaten here before."

"Yes, this place is always amazing."

Jo addressed the hostess. "We have a reservation for Adams."

"Adams? Ah, yes, a table for two. Right this way."

As the hostess weaved through table after table without stopping, Rhonda looked back at Jo. "Where is she taking us?"

"To experience something new."

When the hostess walked them into the kitchen, Rhonda was awestruck when she saw the little table for two set with candles. Jo pulled out Rhonda's chair for her and then sat in her own. Rhonda had been in this kitchen many times before; she designed it after all.

But she'd never been in the kitchen in the middle of a service. There was so much going on all at once.

"Jo, what is all this?"

"I thought you might enjoy a chance to see the action."

"This is great. Thank you."

"You're welcome. Would you like a glass of wine?"

"Yes."

Moments later, Amy came over carrying a wine bottle.

"Good evening, ladies. I think you'll enjoy this wine."

Both Rhonda and Jo stood to greet and hug Amy. "How was the honeymoon?"

"Amazing! It's great to see you both."

"You too."

"I'm going to do a tasting menu for you this evening, so you can sample many different dishes," Amy said.

When Amy left to go see to the food, Rhonda turned to Jo. "This is fantastic. What made you think of it?"

"I overheard you say something to Amy at the reception about wanting to see how the magic was done one day. So I touched base with her this week and she put all this into motion. This was more her work than mine."

"Well, then I'll have to thank you both. This is wonderful."

Before Rhonda could say anything more, Amy brought over a couple of dishes. "Careful, the plates are very hot."

Rhonda took a bite. "This is delicious, as usual."

"Amy's always been a great cook. Here, try this." Jo fed Rhonda a bite of the dish in front of her.

Rhonda moaned with pleasure. "Oh yum."

Amy periodically brought over new dishes for them to taste, each surpassing the last. At one point Amy took a few minutes and sat with them. "This is all so wonderful, Amy," Rhonda said. "Thank you for doing this."

"I'm glad you like it. It is great to see you two together."

Later, after saying good-bye to Amy, they headed outside. Rhonda wrapped her arms around Jo's arm and leaned her head on Jo's shoulder. "Tonight was amazing. Thank you."

"You're welcome. I'm glad you enjoyed it."

Climbing into the truck, Rhonda looked over at Jo. "The whole evening was wonderful. I had forgotten how much I like ice skating, and you obviously know my weakness for Italian food, but to be able to watch it all happen, that was great."

"I thought you'd get a kick out of it."

Making their way inside, Rhonda turned to Jo. "Thank you again for a wonderful evening. It made me feel special." Then she pulled Jo down for a tender kiss.

"You are very special." Jo kissed her again before they went upstairs.

Chapter Eighteen

Jo ran downstairs and hurried into the kitchen. She grabbed a bottle of red wine and two glasses. The overhead light flashed on. She whirled around. Christie stood by the door. "Jesus, Christie, you almost gave me a heart attack." Jo didn't bother to try to cover herself even though she was minimally dressed in boxer briefs and a sleeveless T-shirt. This was not good. She had to figure out how to get rid of Christie and fast.

"Sorry, Jo, I didn't know you were going to be here. Mom said you were out of town and she had to go out of town for some business conference. So, I thought I'd check on the place."

"I got back early." Jo held up the wine. "And I'm a little busy."

Christie blushed. "Right. Sorry." She headed for the front door but then stopped. "Out of curiosity, does Mom know you entertain here?"

"She knows."

Christie was almost at the front door when it happened. A voice called from the top of the stairs. "Jo, honey, what's taking so long?"

Christie stopped, her mouth agape. Jo was powerless to stop what occurred next. Rhonda came into view, wearing only her silk robe. When she saw Christie, she was like a deer in headlights, frozen in place not sure whether to retreat or go forward.

Christie found her voice first. "Mom?" She looked between Jo and Rhonda. "What the hell is going on?"

Rhonda said, "Why don't you give Jo and me a few minutes to put on a few more clothes and we'll explain. Perhaps you could pour us all some wine."

Jo was impressed with how calm Rhonda sounded. Before Christie could say any more, she handed her the wine and glasses. "Be right back." Then she hightailed it upstairs and followed Rhonda into the bedroom. As soon as Jo shut the door, Rhonda spun around. "Oh. My. God. What are we going to do?"

"Okay, so clearly this isn't ideal, but we're going to go talk to her. We're all adults. We've done nothing wrong. We can get through this."

They quickly pulled on clothes and returned to the living room. Christie had poured the wine, but it sat untouched on the coffee table as she paced in front of the fireplace.

Rhonda had so many emotions fighting for dominance, she didn't know whether to laugh or cry at the absurdity of the situation. She sank onto the couch and was thrilled when Jo sat beside her, close enough to touch. She didn't, but it was enough to know that Jo was there. Jo supported her, she was with her, and they would get through this.

By the time Christie stopped pacing and turned to her, Rhonda was calm again. "So, Christie, I'm sure you have questions."

"Uh, yeah, you might say that. What the hell is going on?"

"Jo and I are exploring our mutual attraction."

Christie glared at Jo. "Oh, I'm just sure you are."

Rhonda felt Jo bristle beside her. She put her hand briefly on Jo's thigh. "Don't be rude, Christie. This is my home, and you'll treat Jo with the respect she deserves."

"What does she deserve, Mom? She came in here and took advantage of you, and you want me to just stand here and let that go?"

"First of all, that's not what happened. Jo has done nothing but be kind, patient, and honest with me. As for her taking advantage of me, she did no such thing. In fact, if I'd left it up to her, she wouldn't even be living here anymore because she did not want to act on her feelings. She was going to leave rather than do anything that would make me uncomfortable."

"Then how did this happen?" Christie waved her hand between Jo and Rhonda.

"I asked her to stay. I wanted to explore this attraction I felt, and Jo agreed."

"I bet she did. What happens when Jo's contract is up?"

"Then Jo goes back to California and I move forward."

Christie saw it then, the look on Jo's face. Not something her mom could see from where she sat. Jo looked sick with the thought of leaving. She doubted Jo was even aware of how much her face gave away in that moment. That look, more than her mom's words, started to ease her concerns. Christie expelled a heavy breath. She finally picked up one of the wine glasses and sat on one of the chairs flanking the sofa. "So, walk me through this, when did you first realize you were attracted to Jo?"

She listened and watched as the two of them filled her in on how things had progressed from a simple dance at the wedding to what she had virtually walked in on. The more they spoke, the more comfortable they became with her being in the room, and they stopped resisting the urge to touch one another. They were so easy with one another. She wondered if either of them knew how hard it was going to be to let each other go at the end of Jo's time in Massachusetts. She could not remember ever seeing her mom so happy with someone she was with and that included her dad.

Once they closed the door after saying good-bye to Christie, Jo kissed the top of Rhonda's head. "I sense that went better than you expected."

Rhonda tightened her arms around Jo. "Well, it's certainly not how I would have preferred she find out. I'm honestly not sure what I expected, but Christie dealt with the news better than I hoped. One down, two to go. I wasn't sure I was going to tell any of them. But now that Christie knows, I need to tell the others."

Jo kissed Rhonda tenderly. "I wish there was some way I could make this easier for you."

"You being here makes everything easier for me."

Jo turned, and with her hand linked in Rhonda's, she led the way over to the couch. "Okay. Now I want you to sit right here."

Rhonda sat as directed between Jo's legs on the sofa and groaned when Jo's strong hands began massaging her tense shoulders. "Hmmm, that feels wonderful."

"Good. Just relax and enjoy it."

Enjoy it she did. Jo's hands worked magic on her neck and shoulders. The tension soon melted away, and Rhonda was able to concentrate on the feel of Jo's hands on her body. She leaned back, enjoying each soothing touch. Jo must have sensed the change, she gentled her touch to a caress. She leaned over and brushed Rhonda's hair aside to kiss the nape of her neck. Rhonda moaned.

Jo pulled Rhonda close and wrapped her arms around her in a tender embrace. "Rhonda, tell me something I don't know about you."

"Like what?"

"Anything. We have ten years to make up for."

She wasn't sure why Jo's words made her so happy, but she was beyond questioning and enjoyed the moment. "Um, let's see, I'm a sucker for sappy movies. My favorites are romantic comedies. I know life doesn't always happen the way we want it to, but for entertainment I prefer a happy ending."

Jo tightened the embrace and squeezed Rhonda in a quick hug. "Good to know. What else?"

"Uh uh, your turn. Tell me something I don't know about you."

"Well, I love reading mystery novels. I like puzzles and figuring things out. I think that's one reason I like my job so much."

Rhonda realized she hadn't ever asked. "What is it you do?"

"I'm a performance improvement consultant. Basically, it's a fancy title meaning I'm a problem solver. Companies hire me as an independent contractor to determine what's hindering productivity. I show them ways to resolve the issue or issues so the company can increase their bottom line."

Rhonda placed a hand on Jo's leg. "You sound very passionate about your work."

"I enjoy it quite a bit."

"So, as a consultant does that mean you have to move around a lot for your job?" Rhonda asked.

"Sometimes. Sometimes it means I travel to different locations for a few weeks or months. But there are also companies who want to hire people like me full-time."

After a few moments of relaxing into one another, Jo spoke again. "Rhonda, there's another thing I need to know about you."

"What's that?"

"Would you enjoy making love in front of a roaring fire?"

Rhonda laughed in surprise. "Why, yes, I believe I would."

Jo pushed Rhonda playfully. "Then get up, woman. I need to make a fire."

Rhonda started to rise, but she stopped Jo before she could. Rhonda leaned down and kissed her sweetly. As she broke the kiss, she laid a hand on Jo's cheek. "You should also know I really like that you make me laugh."

While Jo built the fire, Rhonda laid a blanket and pillows on the floor in front of the fireplace. She lay appreciating the view. Jo's Henley pulled tightly across her broad shoulders and strong back muscles while she crouched in front of the fireplace. Jo's movements were brisk and efficient. Quickly, she lit the fire then stood and dusted off her hands.

Rhonda had quietly undressed, so when Jo turned to her she was lying in the middle of the makeshift bed waiting for her. Jo removed her own clothing, making a small show of it. Rhonda enjoyed looking at Jo's body, strong and toned, yet soft in all the right places. Jo and Rhonda spent hours in front of the roaring fire tenderly, sweetly, and deliciously exploring each other.

CHAPTER NINETEEN

Rhonda waved to Barbara when she saw her sitting in the restaurant. Barbara stood to embrace her. "You look wonderful."

"Thanks, I feel amazing."

"What's your secret?"

"I have quite a story for you." Rhonda blushed.

"Rhonda, you're killing me here. I need details, woman."

Rhonda told her everything that had happened since she'd seen her last, up to saying good-bye to Jo that morning as she left for work.

Barbara laid her hand across the table. Rhonda took it. "I'm so happy for you. It sounds like you're having a lot of fun."

Rhonda sighed. "I keep pinching myself to make sure this isn't all a great dream. I'm trying to enjoy every moment as it comes. I didn't want this chance to slip by. I'll worry about the aftermath when I need to."

"Are you dreading Jo leaving already?"

Rhonda shrugged. "I am. Everything is going so well, I don't know what to think. Jo has turned into an amazing woman, and I can see us together. But then I wonder if it's too much to hope for or if it's all wishful thinking on my part? So I've decided to enjoy the moments we have."

"Rhonda, you know you will eventually have to have that discussion."

"I know, eventually, but not yet. I want time to see how it goes, to figure things out. I don't want to put too much pressure on us. I want to take it a day at a time. And the deal was no strings or commitments. I promised that. It's not Jo's fault I've started wanting more. I'm not sure I can ask that of her."

Barbara nodded. "Have you told the kids?"

"Only Christie, so far. She came the other night and kind of caught us. It all came out."

"And?"

"She was shocked at first, but she handled it beautifully. I'm still trying to figure out how to bring it up with Julie and Mike. Obviously, I need to tell them soon."

"Your kids love you and want you to be happy. I'm sure it will be fine."

Rhonda sighed. "I wish I was. Oh, before I forget, can you come over Friday night for family dinner?"

"Of course I can."

❖

Rhonda pulled into Julie's driveway and parked. Dylan should be going down for his late morning nap soon. She hoped Julie would have time for a chat. She reached for the pie on the seat beside her and mentally prepared herself for what lay ahead, or at least tried to as best she could. She quietly let herself into the house in case Dylan was already sleeping, and she headed for the kitchen to put the pie down. Julie stood and gave Rhonda a hug. "Hi, Mom."

Dylan was engrossed in whatever he was drawing and only noticed her at that moment. "Gramma!"

Rhonda bent down and was ready for him when he leapt into her arms. She hugged him tightly. "Hey, buddy, what are you doing?"

"Mommy said I could finish my picture before I take my nap."

Dylan loved drawing, and for a four-year-old, he was pretty good.

"Can I see it?"

"Okay."

Rhonda looked at the drawing of a girl with a basketball. "It's for Jamie."

"I think she'll love it."

Rhonda met Julie's gaze over Dylan's head. "Ready for your nap, little man?"

"Okay. Gramma, will you take me?"

"Sure."

As Rhonda carried Dylan to his room, he laid his head on her shoulder. "I love you, Gramma."

Rhonda hugged him a little tighter. "I love you too, Dylan."

After stopping by the bathroom, she got him settled with his favorite Transformer, kissed him on the forehead, and quietly left the room.

Rhonda found Julie in the kitchen. Julie glanced over as she came in. "Thanks."

"You're welcome. You're doing a wonderful job with your kids."

"I had a pretty good teacher."

Rhonda was too distracted by what she needed to say that she ignored Julie's compliment. "Julie, I need to talk to you about something."

"I figured when you called to say you were coming over in the middle of the day. Is everything okay?"

Rhonda tried to reassure her. "Everything's wonderful, at least I think so."

"Okay, what is it you wanted to talk about?"

"Jo and I are dating." Okay not completely accurate, but it was better than telling her they were exploring a sexual relationship due to their mutual attraction. Wasn't it? Technically, they had been on two official dates. Okay, this part so wasn't important right now.

Julie stopped and stared at her in disbelief. "Jo. Jo?"

"Yes."

Julie's face transformed from mild curiosity to outrage. "That's not right, Mom. This is crazy. Jo's my age. How did this happen?"

The anger in Julie's voice shocked Rhonda. She had considered Julie might struggle with this, but she hadn't thought she would be angry.

"Julie, I'll try to answer your questions. But if you don't lower your voice, you'll wake Dylan."

"You want me to be quiet? I'll be as loud as I want to be. You come into my house and tell me you're dating a woman my age and you want me to just take it all in stride?"

"I hoped we could talk about it so you can see how happy she makes me."

"Are you joking? I won't be a part of this. I can't. I refuse to sit here and listen to you say everything is great. Jo makes you so happy."

Rhonda shook her head. "Do you have a problem with Jo specifically or would you have a problem with me dating any woman?"

"You've ruined everything. If you want to ruin your life then leave me out of it. Leave my kids out of it. You need to go."

Rhonda made it to her car before she allowed the first tear to spill out, then she couldn't stop them. She laid her head against the seat in defeat. *Brilliant, Rhonda! That went well, don't you think?* She sat and sobbed, tears streaming down her face. Finally, she wiped away the tears, pulled herself together, and headed home.

CHAPTER TWENTY

Christie was reviewing applications when the phone rang. She glanced at the readout. She pushed her chair back and took her glasses off. If Julie was calling in the middle of the afternoon, it could take a while.

"Hey," Christie managed to say before Julie rushed into why she called.

"Mom was just here and you will never believe what she told me." Before Christie could even guess, Julie continued, "She and Jo are dating."

Hearing Julie's anger, Christie rose and crossed the room to shut her office door. Returning to her chair, she listened to Julie vent.

"She says she's sorry I'm upset, but she can't let that stop her. Can you believe it?"

"Yeah, I can."

"What? You know about this?"

Christie sighed and rubbed the bridge of her nose where a headache was forming. "I do. I stopped in to check on the house the other day because I thought they were both out of town. I saw them together. We all talked. This is about them, and it was strange at first, but then it was good to see them together."

"You're okay with it? You don't think it's wrong?"

Christie didn't hesitate. "I'm fine with it. In fact, I think it's sweet. Mom and Jo have my support and know it."

Julie's next words were incomprehensible.

Christie's efforts to soothe her fell on deaf ears. "Julie, if you'll just listen to me for a minute—"

"This is wrong and I won't stand for it."

Christie raised her voice, only so it would penetrate Julie's rant. "Fine then, you stay mad. I have to get back to work. Call me back when you can talk like a civilized person." And without another word, Christie hung up the phone. She refused to listen to Julie when she was like this. Maybe once she cooled off, they could talk.

❖

Jo was worried as she headed to Rhonda's after work. Rhonda had gone to talk with Julie today, and she hadn't heard from her. She'd tried to call but got Rhonda's voice mail each time. When she walked in the door, the smell of disinfectant was strong. A distant memory surfaced. *Uh oh*! Rhonda went into deep cleaning mode when she was really upset. Jo found her in the kitchen on her hands and knees scrubbing the floor. *This is bad, very bad.*

Jo spoke from the doorway. "Rhonda?"

No response.

Jo crouched down in front of her. "Rhonda."

When Rhonda looked up, Jo saw her eyes were red and bloodshot from crying. Her eyes were dry now but swollen from a long, hard cry. "Talk to me."

Rhonda looked at Jo and shook her head. Jo reached for the brush in Rhonda's hand. She took it and dropped it in the bucket of soapy water on the floor. She grasped Rhonda's hands and pulled her to her feet. Rhonda buried her head in Jo's shoulder and the tears flowed freely again.

Jo gathered Rhonda up and carried her into the living room. She sat on the sofa with Rhonda in her lap. Jo hurt for Rhonda. She felt helpless. She sat holding her, stroking her back until the tears subsided.

Through sniffles, Rhonda finally found her voice. "I'm sorry, Jo. I'm a mess."

"You have nothing to be sorry for." Jo handed Rhonda a tissue from the table next to the couch. "Are you ready to tell me what happened?"

Rhonda mopped up the worst of the tears. "It was horrible. Julie hates me."

After Rhonda got it all out, Jo looked at her. "Rhonda, darling, it doesn't sound like it's you she hates. It's me. I'm the big bad dyke who corrupted her mother."

Rhonda started to protest, but Jo stopped her. "It's okay. I've been called worse. The important thing here is you're hurting. I know we can get through this, but you have to believe it. You already have Christie and Barbara in your corner. Julie will come around eventually."

Rhonda shook her head. "I don't know. She was so angry and nasty. I've never seen her like that."

"She needs time. This is a lot to handle. But she loves you, and once she has time to think it through, I think that's what will be most important to her. How can it not? You raised your kids to be open-minded and kind. Julie was taken by surprise. I think with a little time she will change her mind."

Rhonda dropped her head to Jo's shoulder. "I sure hope you're right. This is so hard."

Jo hated seeing Rhonda in so much pain. She might have to pay Julie a visit. She would have to think about it some more. She didn't want to make the situation any worse. "Rhonda?"

"Hmm?"

"Should we stop?" Jo's gut threatened to revolt at the thought but she needed to give Rhonda a chance to back away.

"What do you mean?"

"Should we, I don't know, push pause on our exploration?"

"Is that what you want to do?"

Jo studied Rhonda for several moments and spoke from the heart. "Not even one little bit but I wanted to give you the opportunity to call it quits if that's what you need to do for you."

"Definitely not. Julie's upset, but I'm not going to let her stop us from being together. Nobody has that right."

"I just want you to be sure."

"Thank you, but I am."

"Okay. You might want to give yourself a day or two before you talk with Mike."

"No, I need to be the one to tell him. He should hear it from me. I'm meeting him for a drink after work tomorrow."

"Do you want me to go with you?"

"Thanks for the offer, to be honest I'd really like you there, but it's something I need to do alone."

"You don't have to do any of this alone."

Rhonda laid her hand on Jo's shoulder. "That's not what I meant. I know you're here and I appreciate you want to protect me, but I want to do this, just Mike and me."

"I respect that. I'll be here when you finish."

"I'm counting on it."

Jo kissed Rhonda's cheek. "Now, why don't you go take a nice long hot bath and I'll make dinner."

Jo made sure Rhonda was settled upstairs then returned to the kitchen. She gathered the cleaning supplies still lying in the middle of the room and took them to the laundry room where she poured the soapy water down the sink. With that done, she pulled out her phone.

When Christie picked up, she was obviously upset. "Jo, thank God. Are you with Mom? Is she all right? I've been trying to call her."

"Hey, Christie, she's okay. She's upset and hurting but calm for the moment. I take it you've talked to Julie."

"Yes, she called ranting and raving after Mom left her place. She wasn't happy when she found out I'm supporting you and Mom."

"I bet. Thanks, Christie. I'm sure that wasn't easy."

"I'm just glad Mom has you there."

"Listen, Christie, you and the family are still coming over on Friday for dinner, right?"

"Yeah, we'll be there. I'm going to try to talk to Julie again after she's had some time to process everything. Maybe it will help."

"Okay, that would be good."

They finished their call and Jo turned her attention to dinner.

When Jo peeked into the bathroom, Rhonda was still in the tub, her head resting on a rolled up towel, her hair pinned up to keep it dry. She appeared peaceful and relaxed. Jo stood still for a moment enjoying the stunning sight of Rhonda in the bathtub. Then she moved farther into the room.

Rhonda didn't look at her but must have heard her approach. "Hmmm. Hi, is dinner ready?"

Jo smiled at the dreamy tone. "Not yet, but I thought you might like a drink first."

Rhonda looked at her then. Jo sat on the rim of the tub. "I would love one." She lifted her hand, and Jo handed her one of the glasses. "Thank you."

"You're welcome."

"Not just for the wine. Thank you for being here and for taking care of me when you came home. I'm not used to having someone take care of me."

"You're welcome."

Rhonda set her glass on the edge of the tub. "Would you hand me a towel?"

Jo set her glass beside Rhonda's and stood to reach for the towel. She held it open for Rhonda to step into and wrapped it around her arms. Jo pulled Rhonda to her and kissed her lightly, pulling out the pins in Rhonda hair so she could run her fingers through the blond, silky waves. Rhonda wrapped her arms around Jo's shoulders and let the towel drop. She leapt into Jo's arms and wrapped her legs around Jo's hips. Jo instinctively cupped Rhonda's bottom to support her. Rhonda crushed Jo's mouth to her own for a hot, urgent kiss. "I need to feel you. I need you now."

The words had Jo's blood pumping, and Rhonda's deep kisses had her head swimming, but somehow she managed to get them into the bedroom and over to the bed. She set Rhonda on the bed and remained standing. She raised one of Rhonda's legs to her shoulder.

This was not the sweet, slow, tender lovemaking of the day before. This was urgent, hot, and frantic. Jo devoured Rhonda, not letting her catch her breath. She found her hot and ready. Her restraint gone, she was thrilled when Rhonda matched her stroke for stroke, pumping her hips to keep up with Jo's fingers thrusting over and over into her center. The first climax was fast and shattering. Jo didn't stop. She drove Rhonda up and crashing down over and over and over again. When Jo finally slowed her hand, Rhonda still quaked from the aftershocks. Jo lay on the bed and settled Rhonda next to her so Rhonda was lying along the length of her with her head on Jo's shoulder. She stroked Rhonda's back from the nape of her neck to her hips.

Wow, was all Rhonda could think as she laid curled into Jo. She had never been so deliciously taken. Gradually, her breathing returned to normal, and she dared to open her eyes. Amused by what she saw, she leaned her head back so she could look at Jo. "Your clothes are all wet."

"Yes, well, I had a sexy, wet, and naked woman jump into my arms. I'm not complaining."

Rhonda rolled onto Jo. She laid her hands on Jo's chest and laid her chin on top of them. "How did I get so lucky you came back into my life?"

"I'm the lucky one." She kissed Rhonda tenderly.

Rhonda looked slyly at Jo. "Didn't you say something about dinner?"

"Yes, I did. I got a little distracted so it will take a little more time. But it's only going to happen at all if you put on some clothes so I don't get distracted again."

"Well then, I better put something on but only because I'm famished. You should know I plan on distracting you again later."

"I look forward to it."

❖

"It smells amazing in here!"

Jo glanced over as Rhonda came into the room. "I hope you like it."

Rhonda poured them more wine. "Can I do anything to help?"

"I'm almost done here. Why don't you pull the bowl from the refrigerator and we can start with salads?"

While Rhonda dished up the salad, Jo moved everything else to the table.

"How are you?" Jo asked.

"I'm okay. It's hard, but I know you're right. Julie needs time to adjust."

"I spoke with Christie earlier. She was worried about you."

"I should call her."

"It can wait until tomorrow. She felt better knowing I was here. She said she tried to talk to Julie."

"Okay."

"Now I want you to try this steak." Jo cut off a bite and fed it to Rhonda.

"Hmmm, that's delicious."

After dinner, Jo carried their wine into the living room and sat on one end of the sofa. Rhonda sat in the middle with her legs under her.

"Dinner was amazing. Where did you learn to cook like that?"

"Oh, here and there. Amy wanted to be a chef, even back in college, and I picked up a few things from her. I don't cook a lot, but someone once told me you should always have a few meals you can do well in case you want to cook for the person you're dating."

Rhonda stared at Jo, her mouth agape. "I can't believe you remember that."

"I try to remember good advice."

Rhonda sat in her car a couple of blocks down from the restaurant where she was supposed to meet Mike. She tried to take deep, cleansing breaths to calm her nerves. It didn't help even a tiny bit. *You can do this. You have to do this. He should hear it from you. Okay, here goes nothing.* She pushed open the car door and stepped out into the chilly afternoon air.

Mike stood as he saw her enter the restaurant and waved her over. He kissed her on the cheek and helped her out of her coat. "Hi, Mom, I ordered you white wine. I hope that's okay."

"It's fine. Thanks."

As Rhonda sat, their drinks arrived. Mike took a sip of his beer and studied her. "Is everything okay?"

Rhonda took a deep, steadying breath that didn't ease any of the concern in Mike's face. "Well, honey, there's something I want to talk to you about, and I think it's wonderful, but it might come as a surprise to you."

"Okay." Mike continued to study her over his beer when she didn't say any more and stared into her wine. "So is it something you want to say fast like ripping off a Band-Aid or do you want me to order an appetizer and we can talk about unimportant things first?"

Rhonda laughed; she couldn't help it. One of the things she liked most about Mike was his ability to put people at ease. "Well, I would like to catch up with you, but I probably should say what I came here to say and get the elephant out of the room."

"Fair enough. You have the floor."

Rhonda took a sip of wine before starting her story.

"Jo and I have started dating. We discovered a mutual attraction. So, we are going to see where things go. And I would like very much for you to be happy for me because I'm the happiest I've been in a very long time."

There. Everything was out now. Now what? Now she would see his reaction. Mike had always been an excellent poker player, and he held all his cards close to the vest on this one.

"Joe who?"

"Jo Adams."

"But she's a woman."

"Yes, she is."

Confusion was etched across Mike's face. "Okay, wow. So what, are you a lesbian now?"

"I haven't put a label on it yet. What I know is that I'm attracted to Jo and she's agreed to explore that."

Mike studied her for several minutes.

Rhonda reached for her drink. "Say something."

"Give me a minute. I'm trying to process all this."

Rhonda sipped her wine, trying to be patient.

Finally, Mike started to speak. "First, I have a question."

"Okay."

"Have you told Christie and Julie?"

"Christie came over the other night and we talked with her about it. She seems fine with everything."

"And Julie?"

Rhonda looked down at the table and then back at Mike. She forced a smile that was more pain than anything. "I have. That conversation did not go very well. Julie is struggling with it and is very angry right now."

"I can understand that." Mike leaned forward and put his hand over hers. "Mom, I love you, but I'm going to need some time with this. I don't know what to do with it. Everything is just spinning around my head and I can't make sense of it."

"That's fair. It's a lot to digest. But I hope you'll realize how happy I am and support me eventually. Are there any questions I can answer for you?"

"No, not right now, I just need to process."

"Okay, if you don't have a date on Friday, we'd love for you to come for dinner. Christie and her family will be there and Barbara. Christie is trying to talk Julie into coming, but I don't know if it'll work."

"I'll think about it."

Chapter Twenty-one

When Christie hadn't heard back from Julie by Wednesday, she decided to take matters into her own hands. After the kids were in bed for the night and Peter was home to keep an eye on them, she headed to Julie's. When Ben opened the front door, he grabbed Christie and pulled her into the house. "Thank God you're here," he said, desperation in his voice.

"Still bad, huh?"

"We've been rehashing the same stuff for two days. She can't tell me why she's so angry. Maybe she'll open up to you."

Christie held up the bottle of tequila she'd brought with her. "Hopefully, this will help. Where is she?"

"In the kitchen. I don't even know what she's doing. She's just sitting at the table."

"You've got the kids covered, so she has no excuses."

"Absolutely. Good luck."

Christie walked into the kitchen. "What are you doing here?" Julie asked with disdain. She might have even snarled a little, but maybe that was Christie's imagination.

Christie simply held up the bottle. She opened the tequila and took down two glasses and poured healthy amounts of the gold liquid. She set one in front of Julie and sat across from her at the table. "Let's talk."

"Why? You're on her side anyway."

"Julie, I don't know why you feel like there need to be sides. You're upset. I get that. I care about you, and I want to understand what's going on."

Julie looked at her warily. "This whole thing is just wrong. I don't understand how you can support them."

Christie raised her glass. Julie reluctantly did the same. Then, in unison, they threw their heads back and downed a shot. The tequila burned Christie's tongue as it went down. "Okay, then let's talk specifics. Do you have an issue with Mom being with a woman or with her being with one our age? Or something else entirely?"

"All of it. I don't know. It's just weird."

"Julie, when was the last time you saw Mom truly happy?"

Julie brushed off the question. "Mom's always happy."

"I know she seems that way, but didn't you ever get the feeling something was missing? That part of her was sad or lonely?"

"I guess I hadn't thought about it much. I mean she seemed different after Dad left, but she never seemed *unhappy*. So, I guess I always thought she was content with her life."

Christie nodded, glad she had started to think things through. "Me too. It's like this spark died when Dad left and she was never the same."

"Right, because she missed Dad so much."

Christie shook her head. "I don't think so. If that was the case, Mom and Dad wouldn't have stayed friends. She wouldn't have been able to go to Dad and Sharon's wedding. She didn't seem especially sad that day. But something has been missing. I think that may be what she has found with Jo."

"How can you say that?"

Christie sighed. "Honestly, Julie, I don't think I would have before the other day. But when I saw them together, they are so comfortable. Mom looked alive for the first time in a long time, like she's whole again. I'm not even sure she's aware of it yet. None of the men she's dated since Dad seemed to inspire the spark that's in her whole demeanor these days."

"It's just all wrong. This isn't how it's supposed to be." Julie sounded sad more than angry now.

"What's all wrong?"

"Everything." Julie finally picked up her glass and drank.

Christie shook her head and sighed. She poured another shot for each of them. Then she held up her glass and grinned at Julie. "Remember the first time we had tequila?"

Despite her anger, the corners of Julie's mouth lifted into a reluctant smile. "How could I forget? Mom and Dad had gone out of town and Mike was staying at a friend's. The three of us had the house to ourselves for the entire weekend."

Christie looked at her. "Do you remember how scared Jo was to drink that first time because she didn't want to hurt us?"

"I remember," Julie said, studying the glass in front of her.

"You know she still doesn't, right?" Christie asked softly. Julie looked into the gold liquid and was silent for a long time.

Once Christie saw Julie start to think things through, she left. Her parting thought to Julie, "You should call Mom. She's hurting too. Come to family dinner Friday, I think it will help if you see them together."

❖

After reading the display and glancing toward the bathroom where Jo was showering, Rhonda answered the phone with trepidation. "Hello?"

"Hi, Mom."

"Hi, Julie, how are you?"

"I don't know. I'm still trying to figure all of this out."

"Of course you are. It's a lot, I know."

"Look, the reason I called is Christie told me about family dinner on Friday. I wanted to let you know Ben and I won't be able to make it. I'm trying, but I can't support this relationship."

Tears burned Rhonda's eyes, but she had to see this through. She had to stand up for herself. "I'm sorry you feel that way, and I hope you'll reconsider. I love you. I hope you'll think about it."

"I will think about it, but no promises."

"I can't ask for more than that."

Jo came into the room drying her hair. "Did I hear the phone?"

Rhonda nodded, her lips shut tight, trying to keep the tears at bay. "Julie called."

Jo sat beside Rhonda. "Oh, are you okay?"

Rhonda breathed forcefully, releasing the tension that had crept into her body during the call. "I think I am. She's still not happy, but at least she doesn't seem quite so angry anymore. She said she would think about coming to dinner on Friday."

"It's a start. It's progress."

"Yes, it is."

CHAPTER TWENTY-TWO

After dinner on Thursday, Jo changed into shorts and a T-shirt and went downstairs to work out. Rhonda followed a few minutes later and watched Jo from the doorway. With the stereo on Jo hadn't heard her yet. The ripple of Jo's muscles under her shirt made Rhonda want to touch her. She moved into the room. "Wow, Jo, this is quite the setup."

"You're welcome to use it. Do you know how the machines work?"

Rhonda looked at all the different equipment. "Mostly, but a refresher wouldn't hurt."

Jo moved from machine to machine explaining how to make the necessary adjustments. Then, she demonstrated the proper technique. Once she showed Rhonda the proper way to use a machine, she moved aside so Rhonda could try it out. Jo made subtle corrections to hand placement and posture. She wrapped her arm around Rhonda's stomach to remind her to keep her stomach tight while working on a machine. The touch was not meant to be seductive, but she had a hard time paying attention to the details of Jo's instructions.

"Jo, I'm going to stop you right there for a minute."

"Okay?"

"Everything I've heard you say is easy to understand. You're a good teacher. The problem is I haven't heard most of what you've said because I'm distracted by how much I want to touch you right now."

"Oh, I see. And how much would that be?"

"Tremendously."

Jo moved closer to Rhonda. "Well, distractions in the gym can be very dangerous. We should take care of it right away."

Rhonda took a step toward Jo. "I think that would be best." Rhonda took a fist full of Jo's shirt, pulled her close, and tugged her down. Their lips met with urgent need.

❖

By Friday evening, Rhonda was a ball of stress.

"Sweetheart, try to relax," Jo said.

"How can I? Christie says both Mike and Julie are coming, and I don't know what to do."

Jo lifted Rhonda's chin. "It's progress that they're willing to come. I'm sure it'll be awkward at first given how you left things with them, but you all love each other, and that has to count for something."

Rhonda took a deep breath. "Part of me knows you're right, but there's this other part of me that just wants to hide under a blanket."

"It will be okay. You're going to have a lot of support here. Remember everyone coming tonight who fully supports you. If you're too stressed to enjoy them, this evening won't be very much fun for anyone."

"I don't know how you can be so calm. Julie is bound to attack you. Figuratively speaking, I hope. Mike is more likely to ignore you or just study every move you make."

"Do you doubt I can handle myself?"

"No doubt at all." Rhonda smiled for the first time all day.

"Then let me worry about it, and you try to just look at it like we are having the whole family over for dinner, which is true."

Rhonda wasn't wholly convinced, but that plan seemed better than worrying herself sick.

"Let's try something." Jo moved her hand to Rhonda's cheek and caressed it. She met Rhonda's gaze, and stroked her thumb across Rhonda's lips. She placed her lips where her thumb had just been and seductively kissed Rhonda. She responded and she wasn't thinking of the dinner party anymore. Jo deepened the kiss.

Jo ended the kiss. "Sweetheart."

Rhonda focused on Jo. "Hmm?"

"If you get nervous again, just remember when everyone leaves we can pick up where we left off."

"Interesting technique. Thanks. Sounds like the first arrivals are here. I'll go see who it is. Will you stir the sauce?"

Mike and Barbara arrived first, followed closely by Christie's family. Soon everyone was hanging out in the kitchen while Rhonda put the finishing touches on dinner.

Mary was talking to Rhonda and Barbara about her new friend from ballet class. Cody sat on Jo's lap at the table with his face close to hers most likely telling her about something that happened at school.

Mike looked from Cody to Christie. "Looks like he's made a friend."

"She was always a good one to have." Christie watched the two of them for a moment longer. Jo and Cody seemed to be in deep conversation about something, as deep as it got with a five-year-old anyway. Then she walked to her mom for a quick hug before greeting Barbara.

Christie finally made her way to Jo and Cody. Cody looked at his mom when she sat beside them. "Guess what?" he asked excitedly.

"What?"

He looked at Jo like he was asking permission to tell. She nodded. "Jo wants to be Grandma's girlfriend."

Christie looked from Jo to her son. "And what do you think about that?"

"It's good. Grandma needs a good girlfriend, like Miss Wells. Her girlfriend makes her happy."

Christie nodded. "Well, I think you're right, Cody. Grandma does need a good girlfriend, and I think Jo will be a great one."

"Me too. I'm gonna go tell Grandma."

As he scooted off Jo's lap, Jo and Christie exchanged a look. Cody made his way through the adults and over to Rhonda. He held out his arms and she lifted him onto her hip. "Hi, sweetheart."

"Hi." Cody then leaned over to whisper into Rhonda's ear. As Rhonda listened, her gaze traveled across the room. Rhonda whispered something into Cody's ear. He nodded enthusiastically and climbed down.

By this time, the others in the room noticed something was happening and conversation stopped. Everyone watched Rhonda as she and Cody walked hand in hand back over to the table. Jo stood to meet them. Christie remained seated with the best view in the house. Cody crawled into her lap after giving Jo a thumbs-up.

"Jo?"

"Yes, Rhonda?"

"I was just told a very interesting secret. Is it true?"

"Not sure what you were told since it was a secret, but if it's that I want you to be my girlfriend, then yes it's true." Everyone in the room chuckled. "Will you?"

Rhonda stepped to Jo. "I would like that very much."

"Yes!" Cody said. Jo and Rhonda looked down to see Cody pumping his fist in celebration. The whole room erupted in laughter and applause. Cody tugged on Jo's pant leg, and she bent down where he said in a loud whisper. "You should kiss her now."

Jo nodded solemnly. "Okay." Jo leaned down and kissed Rhonda tenderly on the cheek.

"Oh, very nice!"

Rhonda whipped around like she had been slapped at Julie's exclamation.

Rhonda hadn't heard Julie and her family arrive with all the commotion in the kitchen the last few minutes. Julie turned back into the living room, and said, "Ben, we're leaving."

Ben said, "No, we're not. We were invited for dinner and you accepted the invitation. The kids want to see their grandma and cousins. We're staying."

"Well, I'm not going in there. I'll wait in the car."

"Suit yourself. Come on, kids. Let's go see everyone." He ushered Jamie and Dylan into the kitchen.

Rhonda turned to Jo with a look of utter distress. "I have to do something. I've got to talk to her."

Jo squeezed Rhonda's hand. "Let me try. You stay with the kids. Jamie and Dylan came to see you."

Without waiting for a response, Jo left the room. By the time she reached the living room, Julie had already stormed out the door. Jo grabbed her coat and followed. Julie sat in the car, her arms crossed over her chest. As Jo approached, Julie rushed out of the car in a fury. "Get away from me. This is all your fault."

Jo tried to reason with her. "I know you're upset, but—"

Julie cut her off. "You don't know anything."

"Then tell me. There's nobody here except you and me. Say whatever you need to or want to."

Julie stopped yelling, but she was far from calm. "It doesn't matter. You've already ruined everything."

"Julie, what are you talking about?"

"My mother comes to me the other day and tells me out of the blue she is dating a woman *my age!*"

Jo wondered briefly if Julie was upset because her mom was attracted to a woman or because she was dating someone her age. "Julie, look—"

"No, you look. I'm not stupid, so it didn't take me very long to figure it all out."

"Figure what out?"

"Don't play dumb. That's the real reason you refused to kiss me back then. You're the real reason my parents got divorced."

Jo was shocked and hadn't seen that coming. She was momentarily speechless. "That's not true," she said finally.

"It all fits," Julie said with a hiss.

Jo struggled for patience. "Julie, nothing happened between Rhonda and me until last month."

Julie crossed her arms and stared hard at Jo.

"First of all, your mom had no interest in me then. As for why I wouldn't kiss you when you asked me to back then, I was honest with you. I knew you were questioning your sexuality, but I wasn't willing to risk our friendship so you could satisfy your curiosity.

What happened or didn't happen between you and me will never go beyond me. There's no reason anyone needs to know about that unless you want them to."

"Whatever. It doesn't matter. I'm tired of talking about this. You should go."

"Come on, Julie. We can figure this out. Tell me what's really going on."

"No." Julie walked to the driver side of the car. She opened the door. "You can tell Ben that I'm leaving with or without him in five minutes." Then she climbed in and slammed the door.

Rhonda tried to enjoy her family, but the situation out front had her on edge. She looked out the front window at one point. Jo and Julie appeared to be having quite an animated conversation but it didn't look like any blood was being shed. Back in the kitchen, as conversation went on around her, her thoughts were outside. One person, then another tried to pull her into conversation, but she was too distracted to utter more than a couple of words.

After what seemed like an eternity, Rhonda was sure she heard the front door open. She wanted to run and see what happened, but she stayed where she was. Jo walked into the kitchen, alone. She looked at Rhonda and shook her head. Then she relayed Julie's message to Ben. He walked to Rhonda, made apologies, and said good-bye. Then he gathered Jamie and Dylan and headed out the door. Dinner was strained and quiet as they just tried to get through it.

Finally, Rhonda closed the door behind Christie, who was the last to leave. She leaned against it and sighed deeply. "Want to tell me what happened?"

"I tried to talk to Julie, but she's still very angry and we didn't get very far. She did manage to blame me for your divorce."

"That's ridiculous."

"I know, but she wasn't hearing that. I'm not sure how to get through to her. Mike was at least mostly civil."

"I'm too tired to try to figure it out tonight," Rhonda said.

"Sounds like we should make it an early night, I should get you into bed immediately."

Rhonda walked into Jo's arms and laid her head on her shoulder. "Sounds nice."

"Let's go then." Jo scooped Rhonda into her arms, and she wrapped her arms around Jo's neck. Jo carried her upstairs and into the bedroom. Jo kissed her softly. "Why don't you roll over and I'll rub your back?"

Rhonda did as instructed. Jo stroked Rhonda's back and hips, lulling her to relax.

Rhonda breathed heavily. "If you're not careful you're going to put me to sleep before I can have my way with you."

Jo smiled behind her. "You sleep, darling. You can have your way with me in the morning."

Jo moved closer, so their bodies touched, spooning her. She protectively wrapped her arm around Rhonda and kissed her back. "Just sleep."

Rhonda's breathing deepened and Jo lay for a long time listening to it before she also drifted off to sleep.

CHAPTER TWENTY-THREE

As the mid-autumn sun started to light the sky, Rhonda woke. Jo's arm was still wrapped around her, and their bodies were tightly pressed together. The arousal hit her hard and fast, but she also felt safe and sheltered in Jo's intimate embrace. *What a wonderful way to wake up.* She carefully turned her body to face Jo, who was barely disturbed by the movement. Rhonda studied her. Jo was so beautiful. With her face relaxed in sleep, she seemed even younger than she was. That wasn't as hard for Rhonda to think about this time. I have to touch her. Rhonda pushed Jo's shoulder so she would roll onto her back and Rhonda climbed on top of her. The movement woke Jo quickly. She had only an instant to look into Rhonda's gorgeous face before Rhonda crushed her mouth to Jo's. Jo's entire body responded. Her heart jackhammered in her chest, her nipples hardened, and her clit swelled and pulsed with need. Rhonda's long hair tumbled down, curtaining them. Jo managed to get her hands up to push back Rhonda's lovely mane. While plundering Jo's mouth, Rhonda slid her body up and down Jo. The contrast of slow dance and urgent kiss lit Jo's body on fire.

Rhonda's hands seemed to be everywhere at once, driving Jo crazy. She wedged her thigh between Jo's legs and rhythmically moved against Jo's center. She straddled Jo's leg and continued the assault on Jo's mouth. She ran a hand down Jo's leg and used her nails on the way back up. Jo writhed under her, crazed with sensations. Jo's hands fell away from Rhonda's hair. She gripped the sheets trying to hold on. Rhonda drove her fingers into Jo and her hips bucked wildly. Rhonda gave Jo no time to think. She was at Rhonda's mercy and gave herself up completely, holding nothing back.

Rhonda left her hand inside but gentled her mouth. She raised her head just an inch or two so she could see Jo fully. What she saw, all the emotion swirling in those darkened blue pools, left her breathless. She continued to watch Jo as she removed her fingers from Jo's center and excruciatingly slowly, ran them over Jo's swollen clit. Jo's hips bucked wildly once more. As Jo's body settled, Rhonda smiled coyly. "Good morning."

"Now that's a great way to wake up."

"You did promise I could have my way with you this morning."

"I'm glad you held me to it."

"Me too."

As Rhonda moved to roll off her, Jo stopped her. "Stay, please."

Rhonda crossed her hands on Jo's chest and rested her chin on them. "If you insist."

Jo brushed the hair back from Rhonda's face. "Good morning, girlfriend."

Rhonda smiled. "Oh yeah, that happened."

"Want to change your mind?"

"Of course not, why would you ask that?"

"Well, I did kind of ask you in front of a lot people. Not exactly a place for careful contemplation."

"Well, you can't take it back now. I'm your girlfriend and you're mine. I have witnesses."

"I don't want to take it back."

"Me either."

"Good." Jo lifted her head to kiss Rhonda. "How did you sleep?"

"Like a log. I was exhausted. But I woke up very refreshed with a lot of energy."

"I'll say. So, since you have all this extra energy, would you like to go for a run with me later?"

Rhonda pondered for only a moment. "Okay, I think I would like that very much. But why later?"

"Because I plan to keep you busy for a little while first." Jo shifted her body and rolled until she had Rhonda pinned to the mattress. Jo lifted Rhonda's hands above her head and held them there lightly. Rhonda could easily move them if she needed, but Jo made it clear she wanted her to keep them there. Then Jo started to seduce Rhonda with her mouth. Jo's movements were as slow as Rhonda's had been fast. Rhonda was breathless from the gentle caresses. She had never felt more alive.

❖

After stretching, Rhonda and Jo started with a slow jog to warm up their muscles. "Take it easy on me. I don't move as fast as you anymore."

"I have no doubt you can keep up with me, but I'll let you set the pace for now." It occurred to Jo that was exactly what she was doing, not only with this run but also in their relationship. She was sure where she wanted to go, but she felt Rhonda needed time to catch up with her. She was a pretty patient person for most things, and if she didn't see doubt on Rhonda's face whenever she talked about their future, it wouldn't be so frustrating to wait. Rhonda needed time to believe in them, so she would try to give her the time she needed. Jo let it go for now and focused on Rhonda.

"You can have the first shower," Jo said when they got home.

Rhonda looked at Jo, a look of desire on her face. "Why don't you join me? You can wash my back."

They raced up the stairs and quickly stripped off their running clothes. Rhonda couldn't wait for the shower. She dragged Jo's mouth down to hers for a smoldering kiss. Then she ended the kiss and turned to go start the shower.

Jo watched her go, for the moment rooted to the spot where she stood. *I'm completely and totally in love with her*. That thought slammed through Jo's head as she watched Rhonda walk away. It didn't scare her. Jo had always been very comfortable with her feelings. Now she just had to figure out when to tell Rhonda she was in love with her. She was pretty sure her feelings would scare Rhonda.

Rhonda peeked back into the bedroom. "Jo? Are you coming?"

"Of course I am." Rhonda may not be ready to hear the words she now ached to tell her, but she could show her how she felt with her touch. Jo stepped into the shower behind Rhonda. She needed to taste her. She moved Rhonda's hair off the nape of her neck and tenderly kissed her neck, then her shoulder.

Rhonda leaned back into Jo. "That feels wonderful."

Jo took her time tasting and touching. Then she poured some of Rhonda's body wash into her hands. She started to wash Rhonda's back. But she didn't stop there. Her hands now covered in suds, she reached around and she pulled Rhonda to her, her soapy back now pressed against Jo. Rhonda braced her hands against the shower wall, giving Jo full access to anything she wanted. Jo ran her hands up and down Rhonda's torso. She cupped Rhonda's breasts and slid over them. She rubbed Rhonda's nipples, making her moan with pleasure. The spray from the shower rinsed Rhonda's body as Jo continued to explore.

Jo washed Rhonda's entire body, enticing and heating it as she went, driving Rhonda up but not giving her that final release. She wanted Rhonda to feel everything. Jo poured her emotion into every touch. She drove them both mad with the slow pace, but she wanted to savor and pleasure Rhonda. Then Jo turned Rhonda to face her. Rhonda's eyes were full of need. Jo poured all she was feeling into a long, tender, passionate kiss. Then, inch by inch, she moved her hand down the front of Rhonda's body.

Jo slipped her fingers between Rhonda's swollen lips and stroked the length of her clit. "Oh, Jo, Oh God, Jo, I'm coming." Rhonda moaned.

Jo watched Rhonda's face as she took her over the edge. As Rhonda was still riding the wave of her first orgasm, Jo slipped her fingers into her. Rhonda grabbed Jo's shoulders trying to hold on as Jo pumped into her, driving her up once more. Rhonda screamed in ecstasy. Jo held Rhonda close as her body settled. Then she kissed her.

Rhonda rested her hands on Jo's shoulders as the water continued to cascade around them. "You can wash my back any time."

CHAPTER TWENTY-FOUR

The following day, Jo stood stretching in front of the house, when Mike pulled up. She said, "I wasn't sure whether you'd show."

Mike shrugged. "I said I'd be here. I honor my commitments."

Jo studied him for a few minutes debating whether to say something about his tone. She decided to let it go and see where the run took them. Sometimes it was easier to hammer things out when you weren't looking at one another.

"Ready?"

"Sure."

They ran easily for a mile, warming up. Then Mike started to challenge her. He kept increasing his speed so he would end up a few yards ahead before she adjusted her pace and caught up. Mike finally spoke. "I'll race you back for her."

Jo stopped immediately. "What?"

Mike slowed his pace and jogged back to where Jo had come to a standstill. "Come on, if you beat me back to the house, I'll consider letting you continue to date my mom."

"Don't be a jerk."

"Scared?"

"Of you beating me in a foot race, not even a little," Jo said matter-of-factly. "Of you being an idiot, yeah, I'm afraid I might be witnessing that."

"What are you talking about?"

"When the hell did you start thinking so little of your mom that you would offer her up as some prize? She is a brilliant, talented, amazing woman who has every right to choose who she wants to be with. When did you decide it was okay to challenge me to some inane duel with Rhonda as the reward?"

Mike looked properly chagrined, but she was just getting warmed up.

"Jesus, Mike. I know she raised you better than that. What the hell are you thinking?"

Mike held up his hands. "Okay, I get it. I'm sorry. That was a stupid thing to say."

"You think?"

"Yeah, I do. Look, this is just a lot to take in. For my entire life, I saw my mom one way, and now all that's changed."

"How does that honestly make one bit of real difference in your life? Can you imagine what it's like for her? Her entire life she saw her life one way. She's twice as old as you and it actually impacts her life in very real ways. Can you stop and think for one minute about her? Give her a break."

Mike seemed to think that over as they started jogging again. "You're right."

"I know."

"You're not going to let me off easy, are you?"

"Should I?"

"No, I was a jerk. I'm sorry."

"Apology accepted, if you start thinking about how your mom is feeling and take that into account before you make any other foolish suggestions."

"I can do that."

"Okay."

They ran on for a while longer before turning around. Mike said, "Did you ever consider becoming a lawyer?"

"Hell no, I hate arguing."

"You're pretty good at it. You made very valid points."

"I was protecting your mom."

"For what it's worth, you're really good at that too."

"I hope so. Now that we have the chatting out of the way and we're warmed up, what do you say we kick this run into high gear?"

"You're on!"

When they got back to the house, Rhonda was in the kitchen. They walked in together. "Hi, you two. How was the run?"

"Good."

"The run was fine, but Jo schooled me."

"What do you mean?"

"She made me realize I've been an idiot and I owe you an apology. I've done a lot of thinking about this situation and what I've figured out is…I want you to be happy."

Rhonda breathed a sigh of relief.

Mike continued. "If Jo makes you happy then so be it."

"Oh, Mike. Thank you."

Mike raised an eyebrow. "For what?"

Rhonda squeezed his hand. "For being you."

"You have a lot to do with who I am, Mom," he said playfully.

"I love you, Mike."

"I love you too, Mom."

❖

Jo finally had a chance to call her mom a few nights later.

"Hello?"

Jo imagined her mom sitting on her screened porch with a cocktail, waiting for John to finish his round of golf. "Hi, Mom, how are you?"

"Hey, I'm good. Same as always. John should be home soon so we can have dinner. How about you?"

"I'm great. Listen, Mom, there's something I'd like to talk to you about."

"Okay, what's up?"

"I told you I'm staying with Rhonda, right?"

"Yes, you did. How is she?"

"She's really good. The thing is…Rhonda and I are dating now."

"What do you mean?"

"We're together."

There was silence on the other end of the line. Jo imagined her mom was thinking of all the reasons she should object to this news, the age difference, the distance, the history. Finally she asked, "Are you happy?"

Jo smiled. It always came down to that one thing for her mom, or at least it had since she had gotten up the courage to leave Jo's father. That was the one thing that was most important to her mom. "Yes, I am. I'm very happy." Jo told her mom what she hadn't yet found a way to tell Rhonda. "I'm in love with her."

"Oh, baby, you've never said that about anyone."

"I know, but I can't imagine life without her. I'm working on making my stay here permanent if I can convince her we can work forever. I'm not sure she's ready to hear how I feel. She has some doubts, which is hard, but given the circumstances it's also understandable."

"Yes, it is. I'm sure she needs time. It might help her if you shared your feelings."

"I'll give her the time she needs if it means we can be together. I'll think about the rest of it."

"I know you will, sweetheart. I sure hope everything works out for you. Keep me posted. I love you, Jo."

"Thanks, I will. I love you too, Mom."

Chapter Twenty-five

While eating breakfast Wednesday morning before work, Rhonda's phone rang. She read the display. "Good morning, Christie."

Jo looked over, curious at the early call.

"We're doing well, thank you. How are you?" Rhonda listened. "Uh huh, let me just make sure." She covered the mouthpiece and explained to Jo, "Peter has to work late and Christie has a meeting this evening. She's asking if we would mind watching the kids after work."

Jo nodded. "I'm game."

"We would be happy to watch the kids. ...Okay, we'll see you then." Rhonda hung up. "Christie will bring them over about five thirty."

"Great. Do you think you'll feel like cooking or would you like me to pick something up on the way home?"

"Let's play it by ear. Will you call me before you head home and I can tell you then?"

"Sure."

Moments later, Jo stood and rinsed her breakfast dishes. Then she turned and wrapped Rhonda in her arms for a passionate kiss. "I hope you have a great day. See you this evening."

"You too, drive safely."

"Always."

❖

Once Jo left for work, Rhonda went for a walk to clear her head before starting her own work for the day. She snapped on Kona's leash and took her out. She had a lot to think about. Having a three-month affair with a woman twenty years younger was one thing. Thinking about a long-term relationship with the same woman was an entirely different story. Jo had hinted that she would be open to that. What was she supposed to do with that? She cared about Jo, a lot, and the sex was amazing, but…was she willing to sign up for something more? That was the big question.

Rhonda had been impressed by Jo, from almost the day they met over a decade ago. As she learned more of her story, her admiration increased. She could have been beaten down by the world she lived in, but instead was a strong, confident, loyal friend who protected those she cared about in any way she could. Jo was much more than a casual sex partner. Rhonda had real feelings for her. But what did they amount to and could she ask Jo to give up her life in California to be with her?

Rhonda felt her thoughts were going in circles and not getting her anywhere, so she headed home and distracted herself with her work. She was in the middle of a couple of fun projects. The winter months were a good time for planning and designing so construction could begin in the spring. Sometime around midday, she stopped for a quick bite and then returned to the plans she was working on. She was so focused that when the phone rang a few hours later, it startled her. She reached for it and answered without looking at the display.

"Hello?"

"Rhonda, sweetheart, are you okay? You sound strange."

"I'm fine. I didn't realize the time and the phone startled me."

"Okay. How's your day going?"

"Really well, I've been very productive. How about you?"

"It's been good. It will be better when I see you."

"Well, then come see me."

"I'm working on that. I wanted to see if you want me to pick up dinner since we have Mary and Cody in a little while."

Rhonda looked at the clock again and calculated. "If you don't mind picking something up that would be great."

"Okay. See you shortly."

Jo arrived at the house at the same time as Christie and the kids. Christie gave her a hug. "Thanks for doing this."

"It's our pleasure." She looked at Mary and Cody. "We're going to have fun aren't we?"

"Yeah," Mary and Cody said excitedly.

"Why don't you all go on in? I just need to grab the food," Jo said.

"Can I help?"

Jo looked at Christie who was already carrying Cody's backpack. "That's okay. I've got it. I'll be right behind you."

As Christie and the kids headed for the door, Jo reached into her truck and pulled out their dinner and quickly followed them into the house. Jo walked through the living room making eye contact with Rhonda before continuing into the kitchen to set down the food. Once Christie said hi to Rhonda and thanked her, she left to get to her meeting on time.

Rhonda turned to Mary and Cody. "Are you two hungry?"

"Yes."

"Yep."

"Okay. Let's go see what Jo brought us for dinner."

In the kitchen, Jo was emptying bags onto the counter. Rhonda pulled out some plates and handed them to Mary. "Will you put these on the table, please?"

"Okay."

Then she pulled out silverware and said the same to Cody. She watched Mary start to help Cody distribute the forks before walking over to Jo. She hugged her tightly from behind. "Hi."

Jo turned so she could gather Rhonda in her arms. "Hi, beautiful. I was right."

Rhonda raised an eyebrow. "About what?"

"My day did get better as soon as I saw you."

"Charmer."

Jo lightly brushed her lips against Rhonda's with tender promises for later. Turning their attention to the kids, Jo and Rhonda carried the food to the table.

Once everyone finished eating, the kids helped clear the table and put things away. Rhonda worked on the last of the dishes when she said to the kids, "Mary, why don't you and Cody go downstairs and pick a movie?"

Mary asked, "Can Jo help us?"

"Of course she can, sweetie. You all go down and I'll be there in just a couple of minutes." Rhonda looked over and saw Mary and Cody each holding one of Jo's hands as the three of them left the room. Jo had certainly won them over Rhonda thought to herself. *I shouldn't be surprised. She's won me over too.*

A short time later, Rhonda went downstairs herself. She stopped at the door of the family room and looked in at the three of them. All of them lay on their stomachs on the floor surrounded by what looked like the entire movie collection from the cabinet.

As she watched she heard Jo say, "No we can't watch this one. It's for adults only." Then she picked up another one. "How about this one?"

"No, we just watched that one."

This went on for a while. Each time one was rejected, it went in a pile next to the cabinet. Finally, they found one everyone could agree on.

"Okay, Cody will you put this on the table so we don't lose it? Mary let's get these picked up."

Jo and Mary lifted themselves up to put the movies away. When Cody turned to put the movie on the table, he saw Rhonda. "Hi, Grandma."

Jo looked over to the door, still down on her knees. "How long have you been standing there?"

"Long enough. That was quite the selection process."

"I know. There were just so many to choose from we didn't know how to decide."

Rhonda glanced at the one finally chosen. "It looks like you made a good choice."

Rhonda dimmed the lights from the switch by the door and everyone sat on the couch to enjoy the movie. Jo and Rhonda were at either end, and the kids were nestled between them. As the movie began, Jo put her hand on the back of the couch and Rhonda did the same, linking their hands behind Mary's and Cody's heads.

Later, Jo glanced over and saw Christie watching them from the doorway. She smiled and squeezed Rhonda's hand and when Rhonda glanced her way she nodded toward Christie.

"Hi," Rhonda said softly. "How was your meeting?"

Christie stepped into the room. "Good."

When Mary heard Christie's voice she woke. "Hi, Mommy."

"Hi, sweetheart, did you like the movie?"

"Umm hmm," Mary said, nodding softly.

"Are you ready to go home?"

Mary rubbed her eyes. "Okay."

Christie looked at Jo and started to reach for Cody. "Let me get him."

Jo stopped her. "I'll carry him up for you."

"Thanks."

Rhonda rounded up the things the children brought with them. Christie deposited the kids' things in the car and then got Mary settled while Jo placed Cody in his car seat. Christie turned to Rhonda and Jo. "Thank you both again. I hope the kids weren't too much trouble."

Rhonda shook her head as she hugged Christie. "No trouble at all."

Jo confirmed. "We had fun."

Christie climbed into the van and waved good night as she backed down the drive.

Rhonda and Jo went upstairs. Rhonda looked at Jo. "Maybe one day you'll tell me where you learned to handle kids so well."

"It's no big secret. I spent my college summers as a camp counselor. I coached soccer and lifeguarded."

"I didn't know that."

"It just hasn't come up yet. It was a fun way to spend my summers, and it helped me be on my own that much faster."

"You must really like kids."

"They're fun to be around."

Rhonda picked imaginary lint off her pants, unable to look Jo in the eye. "Did you ever think about having any of your own?"

"I've thought about it. I've always known I didn't want kids. I mean I never wanted to physically bear a child, and I always figured when I found the woman I wanted to spend the rest of my life with it would be a decision we made together."

"Would you be terribly disappointed if the woman you were with couldn't give you kids of your own?"

"No. Having kids of my own has never been a priority for me. Why all the questions?"

"I was just wondering after watching you with Mary and Cody. You'd make an awesome mom."

"Well, thank you. Coming from you that is a huge compliment. But honestly, being able to play with them for a few hours and then give them back to their parents seems pretty perfect to me. You have a really nice gig, Grandma."

"Oh, please don't call me that."

"Why?"

"Because I want you to see me as sexy."

"You are sexy. A very sexy Grandma."

Rhonda pushed Jo playfully onto the bed. "And don't you forget it."

"No danger of that."

Later, as they lay cuddling, Jo said, "I'd like to try to find a way to stay here when my contract is up. How would you feel about that?"

"It would be great to have more time with you, but is it realistic?"

"There should be some way. I've got some feelers out. Either way, I don't want this to end even if I have to go back to California for a while."

"What are you saying?"

"I love you, Rhonda. I want a real relationship, long-term. I want the strings and the commitment. You don't need to say anything now, but please think about what I've said."

Rhonda studied her for several moments and finally said, "I will."

"You take all the time you want. I'm not going anywhere."

Chapter Twenty-six

R honda, you should come to the reunion with me. You're my girlfriend and I want you there," Jo said.

"No, I shouldn't. We've been over this. This is your high school reunion. It's Julie and Christie's high school reunion, neither one of them need their mom there as one of their friends' date. It would cause too much of a distraction and I'm afraid Christie and Julie wouldn't be able to enjoy themselves. Julie won't want me there."

"I don't want to hide you away."

Rhonda laid her hand on Jo's cheek. "You're not and I know you're disappointed but I don't want to put Julie or Christie in that situation. It's too soon."

Jo reluctantly relented. "I guess you're not going to budge on this."

"No, I'm not."

"Then promise me something."

"If I can." Rhonda smiled at her fondly.

"Promise me you'll go to the twentieth reunion with me."

Her smile faded. "Oh, Jo." Rhonda turned away from Jo and walked to the window wrapping her arms around herself like she was trying to warm herself.

But Jo had seen the look come into Rhonda's eyes before she turned away. She saw fear clouding them. Jo tamped down her own frustration. She hurt for Rhonda. She went to her and put her arms loosely around her waist, seeking only to bring her comfort. Jo leaned down and put her mouth next to Rhonda's ear. "Talk to me. Please don't shut me out."

Rhonda turned in Jo's gentle embrace. She quickly wiped away her tears. She laid her head on Jo's shoulder. "I wish I could have confidence in the future you see for us."

Jo moved Rhonda back so she could look at her. "Why can't you?"

"I'm not sure. A big part of me is scared about being in a long-term relationship with someone, anyone, who is twenty years younger than me."

"I see. So, you're going to blow me off because I'm too young for a real relationship?"

"That's not what I said and it's not what I meant. You're special and I care about you a lot, but let's think for one minute. We are at such different places in our lives. I mean, let's be real. My body will sag long before yours. Are you really going to want to be with me then? I guess part of me thinks you're so young you'll grow tired of me sooner or later. Besides, I'm settled in my life. I love it here and love having all the kids so close. Your life is in California."

Jo kept a steady gaze on her. "Rhonda, you have an incredible body, but that's not the reason I'm with you. Our connection is more than physical. Who says my life has to stay in California? I didn't realize how much I miss this area until I came back for Amy's wedding. I miss having seasons. As for the rest, age is just a number. It has nothing at all to do with feelings. You could just as easily grow tired of me."

Rhonda shook her head and whispered, "I couldn't."

"Then what makes you think I will? Jesus, Rhonda, do you have any idea what you do to me?" Jo moved her hand to caress Rhonda's cheek. With just that simple touch, the pulse in Rhonda's neck started beating wildly. "Do you feel that? That's what I feel every time we touch. It's how I feel when I simply see you across the room. Hell, when I just think about you sometimes my heart starts hammering in my chest. You destroy me, Rhonda. How can you think I could ever walk away from that?"

"Well, when you put it like that," Rhonda began, trying to ease the tension but stopped when she saw the dark emotion still swirling in Jo's eyes. "Once I can actually think, I know I'm being crazy, but it doesn't stop the doubts, not completely. I'm trying to figure this out. I want to believe you when you say you aren't going anywhere."

Jo pulled Rhonda closer. "That's a start."

❖

Jo pulled on her watch and slipped on her blazer. She glanced at Rhonda who was watching her dress and saw the glint in her eyes. "Don't get any ideas. I have to leave soon."

With a mischievous grin, Rhonda walked toward Jo. "I have no idea what you're talking about."

Jo pulled Rhonda into her arms. "Yes, you do." She leaned down and captured Rhonda's mouth and kissed her soundly. "That will have to hold me. Listen, I'm not sure how late I'll be."

"That's okay. Just be safe. Wake me when you get in, if you want."

"Oh, I want."

❖

Jo entered the ballroom. She was quickly surrounded by old friends. Julie pointedly ignored her, but Christie found her and gave her a hug. People were already dancing, and the bar was doing brisk business. They made their way to the bar and then by unspoken agreement headed in separate directions. Jo wandered around for a while taking in the scene. The room was tastefully decorated. The tablecloths were in the school colors, maroon and white. There were easels set up around the room with pictures blown up from their senior yearbook.

Life was a lot different outside of high school, and going back was strange for her. Aside from the time she had spent with Rhonda's family and her time on the sports fields, those years were difficult for her. She finally made her way over to an androgynous woman sitting off by herself watching the action. "Hey, Rooster, how's it hangin'?"

Tamara Diggs looked up in surprise and automatically responded, "Not as good as yours, I imagine." Then she stood and wrapped Jo in a bear hug. "Hi, stud, I didn't know you'd be here."

The exchange brought Jo back to high school. "Indeed I am. In fact, I'm in the area for a while. We should try to get together."

"That would be great. How's life?"

"Really good. I started dating an amazing woman here recently. How about you?"

"Going okay, although nothing new for me on that front in a while. I still have a harder time talking to the ladies than you ever did."

"Don't worry. When you find the right one, it won't be so hard."

"I hope you're right."

Jo took a sip of her beer. "Aren't I always?"

Tam laughed. They talked for a few more minutes before Jo resumed her circuit of the room.

She ran into old teammates and caught up. She was pulled onto the dance floor a number of times by Christie and occasionally others who just remembered how much fun she'd been in high school. She was having a good time. Eventually, she ended up back at the bar.

She turned when she felt a tap on her shoulder and a sensuous voice whisper, "Hi, gorgeous."

Jo studied the stunning blonde with voluptuous curves. She ignored the quick, visceral reaction she had to the beautiful woman in front of her. When her gaze made its way to her face, recognition hit. "Samantha?"

Before the woman responded, she pulled Jo over to the side. She stood so close to Jo, there was no space between them. "I was hoping you'd remember me."

"Of course I do." Samantha had been her first lover, and Jo had fond memories of her.

"Then dance with me. I've been thinking of touching you all night."

Clearly, Sam wanted more than a dance. Jo shook her head. "No, thank you, Sam. I'm flattered, but it wouldn't be a good idea."

Sam's full lips turned down into a frown. "Come on, Jo. It'll be fun."

"I can't, really. I'm involved with someone."

"That's too bad."

Then Jo had an idea. "Listen, Sam, I know someone who would love to dance with you."

"Yeah?" Sam perked up a bit. "Who?"

"Tam." Jo pointed over to where Tam sat watching the crowd.

"She's cute."

"But she's shy." Jo motioned to the bartender. "So, why don't you take these drinks over and see if you can loosen her up just a little? If you do I know she'd love to dance with you."

Sam took the offered drinks. "Great to see you, Jo."

"You too. Have fun."

Jo got water for herself and headed to find her friends. When Jo reached them, Julie glared at her. "What was that?"

"I think it's pretty clear what that was. Sam wanted to get reacquainted. So, that was me redirecting her attention to someone who wouldn't mind."

"It looks like it worked," Christie said trying to ease the tension.

They looked over to where Sam was leading a slightly bewildered Tam onto the dance floor.

Jo dusted off her hands. "My work here is done."

❖

Jo slipped quietly into bed, but Rhonda stirred. "Umm, hi, what time is it?" she asked drowsily.

Jo snuggled close. "A little after midnight."

"Did you have fun?"

"I did."

"Good." Rhonda turned and ran her hand down Jo's lean body. "Did you run into anyone interesting?"

Jo moaned, enjoying the gentle caress. "A couple of people. Tam for one. It was good to see her. We're going to try to catch up soon. And Samantha."

Rhonda's hand stilled. "Samantha? As in the first girl you were ever with, Samantha?"

Jo pushed the hair back from Rhonda's face. "One and the same. She wanted to get reacquainted. I told her I was involved with someone special and wasn't interested. Then I pointed her in Tam's direction. The two of them seemed to hit it off."

Rhonda pushed Jo over and insinuated her thigh between Jo's legs as she climbed on top of her. "You better have told her you weren't interested."

Jo did not miss the hint of jealousy in Rhonda's voice and she did not take it lightly. Rhonda's concerns were one of the reasons she would always be honest with her. Rhonda already had doubts enough about them; there was no reason to give her any more cause for concern. "Rhonda, you are the only woman I want."

"Don't you forget it."

With Rhonda hands driving her system wild, Jo struggled to utter a coherent thought. "You never have to worry about that."

Jo was already pulsing so hot and wet under her leg, Rhonda reached down between their bodies and stroked Jo's swollen folds.

Jo groaned in pleasure, so happy to be home.

CHAPTER TWENTY-SEVEN

Sunday evening, Jo and Rhonda had just finished putting the kitchen back in order after dinner when the doorbell rang. Rhonda opened the door and stepped back so Julie could enter. "Hi, Julie, this is a nice surprise."

Julie stepped through the door but didn't reach out for a hug as she would have in the past. Rhonda didn't extend her arms either, she wasn't sure an offered hug would be welcome. It was hard being this disconnected from Julie. Julie ignored Jo standing less than ten feet away. "Mom, I'd like to talk with you, alone."

Jo started to excuse herself but Rhonda stopped her. "Julie, whatever you have to say to me you can say in front of Jo."

Julie studied Rhonda for several moments. "Fine."

"Would you like to sit down?"

"No. This won't take very long."

"Okay."

"I've been doing a lot of thinking and I came to ask that you consider ending your relationship with Jo."

"That's not going to happen. I'm not going to break up with her just because you are struggling with our relationship."

"I was hoping it wouldn't come to this."

"To what?"

"I won't be coming over here, as long as you two insist on continuing your affair. And I won't bring my children anywhere near it. You are not welcome in my house. And if you try to see them, like at Jamie's games or something, I will pull her from the game and take her home. You will not be around my children while you are carrying on with Jo."

"You can't be serious."

"I am. You don't want to test me on this."

"Julie, I'm very disappointed in your decision. I hope you'll reconsider but I've already told you I'm not going to give Jo up. You should go now."

Julie looked surprised by Rhonda's response, as though she had expected Rhonda to just cave to her demands. "Well, I hope you reconsider. Good-bye." Julie let herself out.

"Rhonda, this changes everything," Jo said

"It doesn't have to change anything. Julie will come around."

"I can't take that risk. I can't be the reason your family falls apart. I just can't do it. Your family has always been there for me, they're all important to you, and I won't be the reason you lose them."

"Jo, you're not. We've done nothing wrong. You said so yourself not that long ago. We're not hurting anybody."

"Clearly we are if Julie won't come in your house as long as I'm here and she refuses to let you see your own grandchildren. Are you willing to risk your family?"

Rhonda was silent. It didn't matter. Jo knew Rhonda couldn't do that. Not when she'd had time to think about it. She looked at her watch. "It's late. I'll call Amy in the morning and stay with her and Randi until I leave."

"So, now you're going to leave? I thought you were trying to figure out a way to stay."

"I was, but I refuse to be the cause of you missing out on your grandchildren growing up. So, I should just leave and let your life go back to normal. I'll sleep in the guest room tonight."

"You don't have to do that."

"I think it would be best. Good night, Rhonda."

Walking out on Rhonda was one of the most difficult things Jo had ever done. Maybe it was better this way. A clean break. She had known it was going to be hard to say good-bye to Rhonda when her time was up, which was why she'd mentioned trying to get another contract in the area or finding another way to stay.

At least this way she wouldn't be dreading it for the next month. It was already done. The fact that it was ripping her heart in two, she would just have to get over that. It was her own fault she'd let feelings get involved, for trying to make it into more than what it was supposed to be. This was never supposed to be long-term. She had only herself to blame for changing the rules in the middle of the game.

Rhonda made her way upstairs. She stared at Jo's closed door for several moments, debating whether to knock and try to change her mind. She went into her own room and sank down on the bed. A tear slid down her face, followed by another. This wasn't the way it was supposed to happen. She and Jo were supposed to have another month, at least. Even that wouldn't have been enough time, but it was more than they'd get now. Damn it. Maybe she could talk to Julie. Maybe there was some way to salvage this. But what was there really to salvage? Clearly it wasn't that hard for Jo to walk away, even after her professions of love and desire for a long-term commitment.

She obviously wasn't as invested in this relationship as Rhonda had become. If she was, she wouldn't have been able to walk away so casually. She would have stayed and talked, so they could have figured out some way to make this work. Rhonda crawled up to the pillows and settled in for a good cry. She had just lost the one person she had never expected to need. She'd better get used to it. Jo had already left in every way that mattered.

❖

The next morning, Rhonda dressed before making her way downstairs. Aside from the change in her attire, she went through her usual routine on autopilot. She sat at the counter staring at the crossword puzzle when she heard the front door open. Jo moved further into the living room and then stopped. She must have changed her mind, because then Rhonda heard her run up the stairs. Soon the shower was running. It stung that Jo didn't come in for coffee before her shower as she had every day for weeks.

She briefly considered going up and seeing if Jo wanted company. She wasn't sure she'd be welcome. So, she stayed where she was and turned back to the puzzle she couldn't concentrate on. She probably should just get on with her day, but she wanted to see Jo before she left. To say what, she wasn't exactly sure, but she couldn't leave it like this.

Jo came into the kitchen a little while later. She went directly to the coffee pot. "Hi."

"Good morning, Jo"

Jo concentrated on her task and didn't turn around until she had her coffee poured and had taken her first sip. Even then, she seemed to be avoiding looking at Rhonda.

"Jo?"

"Hmmm?" Jo responded without raising her head from the paper she was reading.

Rhonda waited her out. Eventually, Jo lifted her head. Rhonda saw it then, the telltale signs of a sleepless night. She also saw the desire Jo could never fully hide when they were together. It lightened her heart to see this wasn't nearly as easy on Jo as her actions last night had made it seem. Her carefully thought out speech flew out the window and she spoke from the heart. "I want to thank you." She held Jo's gaze. "Thank you for the time we spent together, it was some of the most enjoyable time of my life. But I also want you to know how much I appreciate you being willing to take a step back so I don't lose my family. I will miss you very much if you decide to leave."

Rhonda saw Jo about to protest that her decision was already made but she pressed on. "I want you to stay. For very selfish reasons, I want us to have the whole time we were supposed to have together and be able to explore the possibility of more. Part of me would like to tell Julie that she's being immature and she can't dictate to us, but I don't know that I can risk never seeing Jamie and Dylan again. I understand if you stick with your decision, but I wanted you to know that I'm sorry I can't stand up for us."

Jo walked to Rhonda then. She took her hands in hers. "None of this is your fault and you have no reason to be sorry. I can't risk that happening to you. I will miss you too. These last two months have meant so much to me." Jo leaned down and kissed Rhonda on the cheek. "Take care of yourself." She stepped away, turned, and left. Kona followed her and they both walked out of her life.

Rhonda knew she wouldn't be able to concentrate on work. She felt so hollow. She didn't know if she would be able to focus on anything. All she wanted to do was cry. Hell, why shouldn't she? She went upstairs and climbed into bed. She pulled the pillow that still held Jo's scent to her and sobbed.

❖

The roaring thunderstorm outside did nothing to calm Rhonda's frazzled nerves. It had been raining hard for hours, and her mood was as dark as the stormy sky. When she walked into the bedroom this morning and saw Jo's things gone, she felt her heart breaking. After having a good cry, she'd forced herself out of bed, but now she couldn't figure out what to do.

She couldn't shake this dreary mood. She tried working but couldn't concentrate. She thought about baking but she didn't feel like doing that either. Rhonda wandered around the big house thinking about Jo and how empty the house now seemed without her here. Rhonda was amazed how many things had changed since Jo moved in. She hadn't taken everything when she left, saying she'd pick up the rest in a few days. So, there were traces of Jo and Kona all over the house like pieces of the puzzle, like the things belonged there all along and had just waited to be put into place. But now the pieces were all up in the air. When the doorbell rang, she wondered who would come out in this weather. She opened the door to Barbara and saw the rain had stopped.

She welcomed Barbara in with an automatic hug. "Hey, this is a nice surprise."

Barbara raised an eyebrow. "We made plans to go shopping today, which you've obviously forgotten. What's going on?"

"Jo left."

"What are you talking about?"

"Julie told me she wouldn't come to the house and she wouldn't let me see Jamie and Dylan as long as I was seeing Jo. So, Jo moved out. She said she couldn't be the reason my family was ripped apart."

"Why don't we go have some tea and talk for a while?"

Rhonda was relieved to have something to concentrate on. "Sure."

While Rhonda put on the tea kettle, Barbara settled at the bar across from her, watching her in silence for a few moments.

"So," Barbara said with a sigh, "You're just going to let her go?"

"I honestly don't know," Rhonda said gloomily. "What choice do I have?"

"Have the two of you talked about how you feel about each other?"

"She told me she loved me last week and that she wanted to make a commitment to me."

"It's about time," Barbara said, "What did you say?"

"I told her I'd think about it. I should have told her I love her but I was scared. Now, she's left and I don't see her coming back. Julie's ultimatum really freaked her out. She said it changed everything. In a few weeks she's going back to California and I have to let her go."

Jo tossed and turned on the couch in Amy and Randi's basement. Definitely not as comfortable as either of the beds she'd slept in at Rhonda's, but she had to give them credit, they'd welcomed her with open arms and minimal questions. Kona seemed to be holding a grudge though. Jo had never seen her look so sad, even when she and Aideen had broken up and they'd been together two years, not two months. Perhaps she was projecting her feelings onto the dog, but that didn't explain why Kona had practically stopped eating. Not that she had much appetite herself, in fact it was pretty nonexistent. If she didn't have to come home to let Kona out and make sure she was eating something, Jo knew she would have buried herself in work, just so she wouldn't have so much time to think about how much she missed Rhonda. Jo knew from the looks Amy and Randi shot her way they were worried about her, but so far they were giving her space and she appreciated them for that. Jo's phone chimed and she reached for it. Who would be texting her this late?

Christie. "Hey, sorry to bother you so late. Is my mom okay?"

"As far as I know, she's fine. Why, what's up?"

"I called her this morning and she never responded to my voice mail. Very unlike her."

Jo stared at the screen for several moments, not sure what to say. She decided to go with the truth. "I haven't seen her since Monday morning. After Julie's ultimatum, I moved to Amy's."

"Oh, Jo. I'm sorry."

"Yeah."

"I'm going to pop over and check on her."

"Okay."

Jo wanted to ask Christie to let her know how Rhonda was when she got there, but she didn't feel like she had that right any more. An hour later, she breathed a sigh of relief when she got Christie's next message.

"Mom's okay. Misplaced her phone. We managed to find it."

"Thank you for letting me know."

"You're welcome. I know it's not my place to say this but I'm going to anyway because I care about you both. She misses you terribly."

Jo swallowed over the lump in her throat. "It's mutual."

CHAPTER TWENTY-EIGHT

R honda tried to keep herself busy after Jo moved out. She worked hard during the day. She had Christie's family over for dinner. She went out with friends. She tried to tire herself out, so she'd be able to sleep. But every night when she crawled into bed, she missed Jo so much she ached.

There was a big hole that hadn't been there before Jo came back into her life. She missed cuddling with her and talking about their days. She missed Jo's humor and insight. The way Jo would brush the hair off her face and tuck it behind her ear so she could see her more fully. She missed Jo's strength and tenderness.

She tried to rationalize that this was for the best. After all, she still had doubts about maintaining a lasting relationship with Jo. But her heart wouldn't listen to reason. It hurt so badly, she wasn't sure how she'd make it without her.

❖

Rhonda was only at the table for a minute or two when her ex-husband, Bill, walked into the restaurant. They had a standing monthly lunch date, which he'd missed the previous month since he was on vacation with Sharon, his current wife. He scanned the room and waved when he saw her before making his way over. Rhonda stood and embraced Bill in a warm hug. He kissed her cheek. "Rhonda, you look as lovely as ever."

"You're looking pretty good yourself." She and Bill had been saying the same things to each other for nearly a decade. After placing their drink orders, Rhonda asked, "How is Sharon?"

"She's doing well. She said to tell you hi."

"Hello back. How was Hawaii?"

"We had an amazing time. It's beautiful. We're already talking about going back next year. Although Sharon is trying to convince me we should spend some time in Europe."

"Wonderful, I'm glad you had fun. Europe has a lot to offer too, but I don't have to tell you that."

"True."

"Have you talked to any of the kids lately?"

"Not since before I left for Hawaii. Why? What's up?"

Rhonda took another sip of her drink before answering. "Well, I have some news. Do you remember Jo Adams? She was a friend of the girls in high school."

"Sure. How could I not remember her? She practically lived with us for three years."

"Right, well, she's back in town."

"Great. I haven't heard anything about her in years. How's she doing?"

"She's doing well. She was actually staying with me for a while. I have so much room, it just made sense."

Rhonda started to chew her bottom lip.

"What aren't you telling me?"

She blew out a breath and looked directly at him. "Jo and I were dating for a little while."

Bill studied her for several moments. "Okay, that kind of came out of nowhere. I only missed one lunch."

Rhonda let out a deep breath as she looked at him. "I know." Rhonda gave Bill the highlights of the last couple of months. Bill listened intently, occasionally asking a question for clarification.

When Rhonda finished her story, Bill put his hand over hers. "I'm sorry to hear about Jo moving out. It sounds like things were getting pretty serious between you two before Julie interfered."

"They were. It's kind of crazy to think about how quickly things were getting serious. Maybe it's not a totally bad thing this happened when it did. But I have to say I miss her a lot."

"So what are you concerned about?"

Rhonda didn't question how Bill knew she was worried about something. He was always able to see more than most where she was concerned. Only Jo and Barbara could see as much or more.

Rhonda sighed heavily. "I was already having a hard time believing Jo would want to spend her life with me. But now, she's moved out at the first hint of trouble."

"Be fair. She stuck around until Julie declared an ultimatum that you wouldn't get to see her kids any more. She's protecting you. Clearly, she cares. If she didn't, she could have easily finished her contract, continuing to enjoy time with you, and gone back to California. She could have figured, once she left things would go back to normal. Maybe she left so you didn't have to make that decision. She made it easy for you. My guess is, just after hearing you talk about the last couple months, leaving hasn't been easy on her. What else are you worried about?"

"What do you mean?"

"There's something else. Tell me."

Rhonda met Bill's intense gaze. "Even if I can convince her to come back, I'm afraid I'll lose her like I lost you. I'm afraid her passion for me will just be gone one day. I don't think I could stand it."

"I see," Bill said, unfazed by her reference to him. "So, you have no doubt your passion for her will remain?"

"No, none at all."

Bill rubbed his chin and said almost to himself, "Interesting."

"What's interesting?"

"Rhonda, you can't let what happened between us stand in the way of what you have with Jo."

"I'm not."

"Yes, I think you are. Listen. What happened to us was mutual. The passion went out of our marriage for both of us. Nobody was to blame. We were never supposed to be together forever. We tried to make our deep friendship and affection for one another into something more than it was supposed to be. We did a pretty good job of it for a long time. But we owed it to ourselves to be honest with each other."

"I know."

"Obviously, you feel passionately about Jo. I can see it when you talk about her. Why don't you think it can be the same for her?" Bill continued before Rhonda could answer. "I think you feel because of the friendship and affection Jo felt for you all those years ago, this passion she feels for you now has to be temporary because you're clouding the issue with what happened between us."

Rhonda remained silent wondering if what Bill said was true.

"Have you told Jo how you feel?"

"Not completely."

"What are you afraid of?"

Rhonda shook her head as the answer hit her. "I don't want her to feel trapped."

Bill nodded. "You mean like we did in our marriage?"

Rhonda nodded. She and Bill shared a look of understanding. The two of them had dealt with what was between them years ago and there were no hard feelings, no regrets.

"I just wish I was more confident in how she truly feels about all this. I mean, we have talked about it, but you remember Jo has a hard time letting anyone see her deepest feelings. She keeps it all bottled up. So I know what she thinks about it, but I don't truly know how she feels about everything."

"Have you asked her?"

Rhonda shook her head.

"Why? You owe it to yourself to find out how Jo feels. Honestly, knowing Jo's history, I imagine she wouldn't stay any place very long if it's not exactly where she wants to be. She wouldn't consent to staying in a place she isn't happy. I think she's perfectly capable of telling you exactly how she feels. Are you capable of hearing her?"

Rhonda frowned. "I don't want to pressure her."

"Given everything I remember about Jo and all you've told me about your time with her over the last two months, it sounds like she can handle herself pretty well under pressure."

"That's true."

"Let me ask you one more thing?"

"Okay."

"Let's assume Jo left to protect you. What have you done to protect her? How have you stood up for her? How have you fought for your relationship?"

Rhonda couldn't answer, because she'd done none of those things and she needed to figure out why. Bill had certainly given her a lot to think about. There was a reason he was still one of her best friends.

As each of them reached for money to pay the tab, Rhonda's phone rang. "Sorry, Bill, I should get this. Hi, Amy, I'm at lunch, can I call you later?…What's wrong?…Is she…?…Where is she?… I'm leaving right now."

Bill stood with her. "Rhonda?"

"I have to go. Jo's hurt. I have to get to Baystate."

Bill stepped to Rhonda and took her elbow. "Give me your keys. I'll take you. You can't drive while you're upset."

Rhonda wasn't even aware of complying. The next thing she knew, she was in the passenger seat of her car on the interstate. She heard the last part of a phone conversation Bill was having. "Thanks, Sharon. I'll see you there."

Rhonda couldn't think. She could barely breathe. Jo was hurt and she had to get to her.

Bill glanced at Rhonda. He reached out and touched her arm trying to comfort. "Hang on. We'll be there soon."

Rhonda was vaguely aware of the contact but couldn't make sense of what Bill said. She simply stared out the window picturing Jo's face. Beautiful, strong, Jo. *You have to be strong, my love. I can't lose you.*

Traffic slowed as cars crept past flashing lights. A tow truck driver loaded a small SUV onto the flatbed. Comprehension dawned with a rushing wave of nausea. "Oh my God, that's Jo's truck."

The front end was crumpled and the visible side, the passenger side, was so smashed that Rhonda was terrified at how hurt Jo must be having been inside that mangled wreckage.

Chapter Twenty-nine

Bill stopped at the emergency room doors. "Rhonda, you go in and see what you can find out. I'll come find you as soon as I park the car."

Rhonda climbed from the car and ran into the hospital. She made a beeline for the first desk she saw, she asked, "Can you tell me where Jo Adams is? She was just brought in by ambulance. She was in a car accident." Her voice sounded foreign to her own ears.

The young man at the admissions desk looked at Rhonda with an uninterested, glassy stare. "Are you family?"

"No, yes, well, sort of, I'm her girlfriend."

"I'm sorry, ma'am. We can't give out any patient information without the consent of the patient, unless you're family."

"She's unconscious. She can't give her consent. Please, I need to see her. Can't you do something?"

"Do you have medical power of attorney?"

Rhonda was flabbergasted this guy was talking about legalities so clinically when all she wanted to do was get to Jo. "No, but—"

"Ma'am, if you'll take a seat, I'll see if I can find someone to help you."

With no other option, Rhonda collapsed into the nearest chair. Her head spun, her heart raced, and she couldn't focus. She took slow, deep breaths and tried to calm down. Jo was getting the help she needed. But she couldn't believe this guy wouldn't let her back to see her. She was her girlfriend. Even if that was no longer true,

Rhonda still felt it. Who cared what a piece of paper said? Jo needed her. She needed Jo. She began to think about the legalities of it all and wondered if she had any rights at all. Did she?

The anxiety gripped her chest like a vise and threatened to pull her under. She needed to see Jo and make sure she was okay. She was hurt, but Rhonda didn't know how badly. Someone had to tell her something soon or she would go crazy. She marched back up to the admitting desk and addressed the young man. "Did you find someone to help me?" she said more sternly than she intended.

He stared at her blankly. Obviously, that had been a diversion to get her out of his space.

"Look, you need to find somebody right now who can tell me what is going on with Jo Adams or I am going to go back there and find out for myself."

At that moment, Amy stepped up beside Rhonda. "How is she?"

Rhonda looked at Amy. "Nobody will tell me anything."

Amy put her arm around Rhonda's waist in support and looked at the young man behind the desk. "I have medical power of attorney for Jo Adams. Can you please give us an update on her condition?"

Alan, according to his nametag, genuinely looked like he wanted to help at this point, but he still had a job to do. "Can I see your documentation?"

"It will be here shortly. I came straight here, but my wife is bringing it. In the meantime, can you please give us any information, anything at all?"

Alan looked at his computer screen and tapped a few keys on the keyboard in front of him. "All I can tell you at this point is the doctors are running tests."

"Thank you. I'll be back when I have the papers you need to see." Amy steered Rhonda away from the desk and over to some empty chairs. "Rhonda, let's sit down."

Rhonda sat. She grabbed Amy's hand as a lifeline and held on. She was so lost. She had no idea what to do.

Bill rushed in. He sat beside Rhonda and held her other hand. "How is she?"

Rhonda only shook her head.

Amy answered. "Nobody will tell us much yet. The doctors are running tests."

"Okay." Rhonda saw Bill look up as one of the doors by the desk opened. "Sharon, thank God, what's happening?"

Rhonda looked up when she heard Bill's words. "Sharon?"

Sharon crouched in front of Rhonda and put her hand on Rhonda's knee. Sharon said, "Here's what I know so far. The x-rays of Jo's neck and back are clear. The doctor expects she will have quite a bit of bruising from the seat belt. She does not appear to have any other substantial injuries other than the head laceration and a big bruise on her left shoulder. She is still unconscious so she is in CT right now so the doctor can look at her head injury."

Rhonda nodded that she understood. "Thank you, Sharon. When can I see her?"

"I'm working on that. I'll let you know." Sharon then turned to Amy. "Hi, we haven't met. I'm Sharon, Bill's wife and one of the hospital administrators."

Amy shook her hand. "Amy Franklin."

"Alan said you have Jo's power of attorney?"

"Yes, my wife is bringing the paperwork. She should be here soon. But Rhonda is the one who should make any decisions needed and be given any information you have about Jo."

"Okay, that's fine. Listen, I suspect we're going to have quite the crowd here shortly. Knowing the kids are all probably heading this way, why don't I see if I can find someplace more comfortable for all of you to wait?"

Amy nodded. "That would be great."

Sharon quickly found an empty conference room just two doors down from the ER. Once she got the three of them settled, she left a message with the front desk to direct anyone asking about Jo there.

As anticipated, the room started filling quickly. One after another, Randi, Christie, Barbara, and Mike came in and gave Rhonda long, heartfelt hugs. There wasn't anything to do but wait. But when Julie came in looking like she belonged there, it was too much. Rhonda stalked over to her. "What are you doing here? You've made your feelings about me and Jo very clear."

"I came to support you. I may not approve of your relationship, but I still love you."

"You love me? But only if I live my life the way you believe I should, right? You probably should go before I say something I regret. Jo wouldn't even be in the hospital if it wasn't for you."

"What do you mean?" Julie asked, concern lacing her voice. "She was in a car accident."

"She wouldn't have been going that direction if she wasn't staying with Amy and Randi. And she's only staying with them because she moved out the morning after you issued your ultimatum. She wasn't willing to risk our family. Clearly something you aren't concerned about."

"That's not true. That is all I'm concerned about."

"We see that very differently. You should leave."

Julie looked as though she was going to say something more. Then she turned without a word and walked away.

Distantly, Rhonda knew she had been harsh and she would eventually need to apologize to Julie. But right now, she wanted to hold onto her anger a little longer. Even that was better than the cold numbness and despair that had plagued her since Amy had called about the accident. Rhonda knew deep down the person she was actually angry with was herself because she hadn't fought for Jo when she had the chance. Maybe it wasn't too late.

❖

As Christie suspected, Julie hadn't gone very far. She found her in the small chapel. She sat quietly beside Julie and waited. She didn't need to wait long.

"Are you here to blame me too?"

"No."

"Then you're here to try to convince me why I'm wrong about Mom and Jo."

"No."

"Then why?"

"I just have a question, because I want to understand. Why are you so against them?"

"Let's see, the age difference, the fact that Jo is sponging off Mom, Jo taking advantage of Mom, how quickly it all happened, and that's just a few off the top of my head. So, I guess my question back to you is why you are okay with them being together?"

"Well, let's tackle your concerns first and then I'll tell you why. Ben is ten years older than you and yet you fell head over heels in love with him. Would it have made a difference to you if he was ten years older than he is?"

"I doubt it. I didn't even think about his age for more than a few moments."

"Okay. As far as Jo sponging off Mom, I happen to know that Jo offered to pay Mom for staying at the house, but Mom turned her down. They came to some arrangement where Jo took them out for dinner once a week or something. That was Mom's idea. Now, Jo taking advantage of Mom, that was where I got stuck at first too. I mean Jo has so much more experience, at least as far as I know, and also I didn't think Mom had ever been with a woman. But Mom set me right on that one. She's the one who was the aggressor in their relationship. Apparently, Jo was trying to move out so she didn't act on her feelings. She didn't want to disrespect Mom. It took them a month of living in the same house before either of them made a move. I know you and I both moved a lot more quickly with Ben and Peter."

"Okay, I get it. What's your point?"

"I'm simply showing the double standard you seem to be operating under. Why is it okay for you to marry a man older than you, but mom can't even date someone younger than her?"

"So what, Mom's a lesbian now and you're okay with that? What happens when Jo leaves?"

"First of all, I don't know how Mom's identifying these days as I haven't asked. As for Jo leaving, if she hadn't already moved out, I imagine it would have been very difficult for both of them when she left. I think that even more seeing how the last week has affected them both. Mom has been devastated since Jo moved out."

"I thought they were just having fun. Mom said it wasn't anything serious."

"I think neither one of them wanted to admit exactly how serious it already is. I saw it for myself, the night I found out. When I asked the same question about Jo leaving, Jo looked absolutely sick at the thought. Mom was trying to play it off as no big deal, but I could see how much she was hurting just thinking about it. That's part of the reason I'm not against their relationship. I could see how much they already cared about each other, even if they're not admitting it. I couldn't stand in their way. Jo would never hurt any of us intentionally. I mean look at what she is willing to sacrifice, just to protect our family. I think if you would actually look at the situation rather than ignore it, you might see those things too."

"You said that's part of the reason. What's the other part?"

"I've never seen Mom happier than she was with Jo."

"Come on, that can't be true."

"I swear. Even when we were little, I don't remember her ever looking as light and happy as she seems lately, well prior to this last week anyway."

❖

Rhonda alternated between pacing the room and sitting, staring into space. Whenever she sat, there was always at least one person, most often two, flanking her and giving her their silent support. Her family and friends chatted in hushed tones around her, but nobody tried to pull her into conversation. She was grateful for that because her thoughts were on Jo and how she was going to make things right between them. But first, Jo had to be okay.

A woman wearing a State Police uniform came in after a while. Her name tag said Diggs. She walked over to Christie first and chatted with her briefly. Then she walked over to Rhonda. "I don't know if you remember me. I'm Tam Diggs. I went to high school with Jo and your daughters."

"Tam, I didn't recognize you. Jo mentioned she saw you at the reunion."

"She did. She mentioned she was dating someone special, Christie just told me that was you. I'm sorry she's here."

"Thanks. How did you know she was?"

"I was at the scene. I'll need to talk with her when she wakes up."

"Okay. You're welcome to wait with us. I don't know how long it'll be."

"Thanks."

Finally, Sharon came back with a petite brunette who wore a white coat over her scrubs. She introduced the newcomer. "Rhonda, this is Dr. Robbins, the head of neurosurgery."

Rhonda gasped. "Oh God, does Jo need surgery?"

Dr. Robbins answered, "No, not at this point. The head CT was clear other than a subdural hematoma. I suspect Jo will wake up on her own before too long. We will continue to monitor her, and if she hasn't regained consciousness in another four to six hours, we will do another scan. Even if she does wake up within that time, I would like to do another scan to make sure all is still as it should be. But right now, I believe it's just a matter of time."

Rhonda slumped in relief. "Can I see her now?"

Dr. Robbins looked at Rhonda, then around the room. She made eye contact with Sharon before she returned her gaze to Rhonda. "Yes, let me take you up. We've got her in a room upstairs for now."

Rhonda's heart raced as she followed the doctor out of the room.

❖

The lights in Jo's room were dimmed, and the machines that monitored her hummed. After the harsh lights of the hallway, it took a moment for Rhonda to adjust to the lack of light. As soon as she could see, she rushed to Jo's side. Jo looked almost asleep, but this was different. The white bandage across Jo's left temple contrasted sharply with her bronzed skin.

She looked so vulnerable. Rhonda was almost scared to touch her. Afraid she would hurt her somehow, but she had to. She took Jo's right hand in hers, the warmth of it settled her someplace deep inside. She reached up and brushed the hair off Jo's forehead and leaned down and kissed her softly. "I'm here, Jo. Baby, I'm right here. I love you so much. I know I should have told you before now, but I was so scared. Now I'm completely terrified because you're hurt. Please wake up so I can tell you how much I love you."

Jo lay still, too still. Rhonda continued to talk to her. She watched, hopeful that Jo would hear her pleas and come back to her. Eventually, Rhonda pulled over a chair and sat holding Jo's hand in both of hers. She focused on Jo's face and just talked, babbled about everything that came to mind, her lunch with Bill, who all was at the hospital waiting for word on her, and anything else that popped into her head just so Jo could hear her voice.

At some point, Mike came into the room and asked Rhonda if he could get her anything, coffee, something to eat, anything at all. Rhonda just shook her head. He left as quietly as he came, and Rhonda resumed talking to Jo. Several hours after she came into the room, although to Rhonda it seemed so much longer, she thought she felt Jo squeeze her hand.

Rhonda had been staring at Jo's face, but she swiftly looked at their joined hands. She saw as well as felt it this time. When she returned the pressure lightly, Jo definitely squeezed back. Rhonda looked back up to see Jo's eyelids fluttering. Rhonda stood and lightly stroked Jo's head. "You can do it. Open your eyes."

Jo finally managed it and then struggled to focus. "Rhonda?"

Rhonda fought back tears of relief. "Yes, Jo. I'm right here."

"My head…What happened?"

"You were in an accident."

"What day is it?"

"It's Monday. You were only out for a few hours." *The longest hours of my life.* Rhonda couldn't bear to leave Jo's side, but she needed to let someone know Jo had woken up. She leaned over and pushed the button to call the nurse. "Just take it easy. I'm calling the nurse so someone can take a look at you."

"Don't leave."

Jo sounded so weak and scared. Her eyes clouded with pain. Rhonda's heart hurt for her. "Don't worry. I'm not leaving your side." Rhonda would stay but she decided it wasn't fair to Jo to tell her how she felt about her while Jo was in pain. Things were too unsettled between them.

Before Jo could respond, the nurse arrived. When she saw Jo awake and talking, she paged the doctor. Before long, Dr. Robbins strode in. But by then Jo struggled to stay awake. The doctor performed some quick neurological tests and then said, "Don't fight the sleep too hard. It's what you need right now."

"Okay. Can Rhonda stay?"

The doctor looked at Rhonda, who still held Jo's hand. Then she looked back at Jo. "How about I see if someone can bring in a cot so Rhonda can sleep by your side?"

Jo smiled weakly. "That would be great, thank you." Jo quickly faded and fell asleep.

Dr. Robbins looked back at Rhonda and assured her. "Sleep is really what she needs right now. I want to run some more tests, take a look at another CT, and monitor her. The tests I just did looked good. We'll have her back up as soon as we can and by then the cot should be here for you."

"Thank you so much."

Once the orderly took Jo out of the room for the additional tests, Rhonda located her family and filled them in.

Her family also updated her. Bill and Ben had taken her car to the house. Bill had put together some clothes for her. Randi had gone home and brought back a bag of Jo's things. Bill stepped forward and handed her the overnight bags. Randi and Amy would bring Kona over to her house once Jo was settled back there.

She thanked them all and hugged everyone. Then, she returned to Jo's room with Tam.

Rhonda and Tam each took a chair and settled down to wait.

"Tam, we're so lucky you were at the scene. I'm not sure when we would have heard otherwise."

"I'm glad I was there. But, any officer would have done the same as I did and tried to contact the In Case of Emergency number in Jo's phone. You should hold on to this." She handed Rhonda Jo's phone.

"Thanks."

"Sure. I heard everyone talking earlier about how nobody would give you any information when you first got to the hospital. That sucks."

"It did. Clearly, just being someone's girlfriend doesn't mean much when the hospital is protecting patient information. Not being able to find out what was happening with Jo was really difficult. If it hadn't been for Amy and Sharon, I'm not sure what I would have done."

Finally, Jo was wheeled back into the room. She was asleep.

"Since we don't know how long it will be until she wakes up, I'm going to step out to make a call. Do you need anything?" Tam asked.

"No, thank you, Tam. Oh, and thank you for keeping me company."

"You're welcome."

Once the orderly got Jo settled, Rhonda resumed her position by her side.

Before too long, Jo woke.

"Hi, how are you feeling?"

"Not..." Jo cleared her throat. "Not too bad, all things considered."

"Tam was here for a while. She should be back soon. She needs to talk to you about the accident."

At that moment, Tam returned. She stood on the opposite side of the bed from Rhonda. "Hey, Jo. Great to see you awake. How are you?"

"Hey, Tam, I've been better."

"That has to be true. I think that may be the first time since our freshman year you actually used my name."

"I can't very well call you Rooster while you're wearing that uniform and carrying a gun."

"Good point. Can you tell me anything you remember about what happened?"

Jo started to shake her head but stopped when the movement increased the pain. "Sorry, it's not much. I remember hearing metal scrape metal, I felt the truck lurch, and then it's a big blank until I woke up and saw Rhonda standing next to me in this room."

"Okay. I thought you remembering much was probably a long shot, but we have to ask."

"Can you tell me any more than that?"

Tam adopted her professional tone and demeanor and explained. "A young man, traveling at a rate of speed exceeding the posted limit appears to have been distracted by texting, according to witness statements and the timestamp on his phone, when he lost control of his vehicle and pushed your truck into the path of a third vehicle which couldn't stop in time. Both cars pushed you into the concrete divider."

"Ouch. How's my truck?"

Rhonda gripped Jo's hand almost without realizing it, remembering the twisted metal shell she passed on the way to the hospital.

Tam winced, her professional persona vanishing. "Let's just say when you're feeling better you'll need to go car shopping."

"Oh, well, okay." Jo's eyes started to droop as her energy waned. "Thanks for coming by, Tam."

"No problem. I'll touch base with you soon." Before Tam finished saying good-bye to Rhonda, Jo had fallen asleep again.

❖

The next time Jo woke, the darkness outside had enclosed the room. In the faint light of the room, Jo could see Rhonda sleeping on the cot next to her, their hands still clasped through the rail of Jo's bed. She was careful not to move so she didn't wake her. Rhonda had looked worn out when Jo had last been awake. She needed sleep too. She had to convince Rhonda to go. But her heart was arguing with her mind on that point.

Jo lay quietly and evaluated how she felt. Her head still hurt but not as bad as it had earlier. Her left shoulder was very stiff, and her chest felt a bit bruised. Could be a lot worse, given the accident Tam had described. She also noticed that her bladder was full. She suddenly needed to pee very badly. She tried to slip her hand out of Rhonda's smoothly enough not to wake her. It didn't work. Rhonda woke.

"Sorry, I didn't mean to wake you."

Rhonda sat up quickly. "Are you okay? What do you need?"

"I'm fine. I just need to use the bathroom."

Rhonda stood up. "Let me help you."

Jo held up her hand. "It's okay, I've got it."

Rhonda backed off and watched Jo struggle to lower the bed rail for a few moments, her left arm giving her some trouble. "Can I help you with that?"

"Okay, fine," Jo said shortly.

Rhonda easily lowered the rail and stepped aside.

"Thanks," Jo said as she walked gingerly to the bathroom without looking at Rhonda.

Rhonda stared at her back wondering why she was acting so strangely. Oddly, when Jo closed the door, Rhonda felt like she was being shut out of more than just the room. Jo emerged a few minutes later and gingerly climbed back into bed. "I'm sorry. I know I'm grumpy."

"Of course you're grumpy. You probably hurt all over."

"Some. It's not too bad. I'm sorry you were worried."

"You have nothing to apologize for. None of this was your fault."

"How did someone know to call you? My phone is pass-coded."

"Tam was on scene. Apparently, she had Siri call your ICE contact. Luckily, that was Amy and she called me."

"Ah."

"We were lucky Amy had your power of attorney and healthcare proxy or the hospital might not have told us anything."

"You were wrong before. I need to apologize. I'm sorry I left the way I did. I'm glad you were here when I woke up, but you probably should go now."

"Why?"

"Because, if you're with me, you risk losing your grandchildren and ripping your family apart."

Rhonda pressed her lips together, trying to gather her thoughts. "Julie is going to have to come to terms with that on her own. Before anything happened between us, we were friends. And even if all you'll allow me to be is your friend, then I'm going to do that. You're going to need someone with you when they let you out of here. Your head injury was severe enough that they won't let you out of here without someone who can watch for changes. Both Amy and Randi have to work. I'm going to take you home with me and take care of you. Amy and I have already discussed it. You can't fight me on this one."

Jo laid her head back on the pillow and closed her eyes. "I don't want to fight you at all." Then Jo said so softly Rhonda almost missed it, "And I don't only want to be friends." Within moments, Jo's breathing deepened and she drifted off to sleep.

❖

When Barbara and Amy walked in the next morning, Jo was still sleeping. "Hi," Rhonda whispered, hoping to not wake Jo. "What are you doing here?"

Barbara said, "We came to check on you both, and I'm here to take you to breakfast. Don't argue. We all know you haven't eaten anything since lunch yesterday. Amy will stay with Jo."

Rhonda hesitated. She didn't want to leave Jo even though she was out of the woods.

Rhonda hadn't noticed Jo had woken up until she spoke. "Go ahead, Rhonda. Amy can hold down the fort until you get back. We can't have you getting sick."

"Okay, okay. I've been outvoted." She wanted to kiss Jo but settled on squeezing her hand. "I'll be back soon."

"Okay."

Once Rhonda and Barbara left the room, Amy sat lightly on the edge of the bed, facing Jo. "Hi, friend."

"Hey."

"You look like crap."

"Thanks, I noticed."

"So, how do you feel? For real, don't pull any macho crap on me."

"Honestly, not great. You remember when I hit my head on the goal post diving for a ball sophomore year?"

"Of course I remember," Amy said wincing at the memory.

"It's like that, only this time it feels like six defenders trampled my body with their cleats on as I lay on the field unconscious."

"Painful."

"Yeah, pretty much. Don't tell Rhonda, okay?"

Amy looked surprised. "Why on earth not?"

"She'll worry."

"I'm going to let that pass because you're in legitimate pain. Otherwise I'd have to tell you that you're an ass."

"What?"

"Rhonda was terrified yesterday. She's going to worry regardless. If she thinks you're keeping something from her it won't help her. She'll just feel shut out and worry about whether you're pulling away from her."

"I wouldn't do that."

"Does she know that? You did move out."

"I did that so she wouldn't be torn away from her grandkids. Do you think any part of that was easy for me?"

"Don't tell me. I watched your ass mope around missing her. Tell her."

❖

Dr. Robbins strode down the hallway as Rhonda and Barbara approached Jo's room, meeting them at Jo's door. "Good morning, ladies. Jo, it's nice to see you awake."

"Good morning, Doctor. You're here to tell me I can go home, I hope."

"As a matter of fact, I would like to look you over one more time, but if everything checks out, then that is exactly what I will tell you."

Amy stood up. "Barbara and I will wait outside. We'll drive you two home when you're ready."

Jo moved to the side of the bed Amy had just vacated and hung her legs over the side. "What do I need to do?"

Dr. Robbins ran through the exam quickly and efficiently. "Okay, looks like you are good to go. No strenuous activities until you see me for a follow-up in ten days. I don't want to give you anything too strong for the pain because of the head injury. You can take ibuprofen or acetaminophen. If those don't help, let me know and we'll try something else. Also, if you experience any of the symptoms we talked about such as the dizziness, double vision, or your headache gets worse, I want to know about it right away."

"You got it. Just one question, does the ban on strenuous activities include sex?"

Dr. Robbins looked between them. Rhonda blushed. "Gentle lovemaking should be fine in a day or two as long as you listen to your body and don't overdo it."

"That's excellent, thank you, Doctor." Jo stood and shook her hand. "I'll see you in ten days."

The doctor left and Jo turned to Rhonda. But before she could say anything Rhonda beat her to the punch. "What was that?"

Jo didn't pretend to not know what she was talking about. "I just wanted to cover my bases. If you're going to insist on taking me home, I just want to know where I would stand, medically, if I can't keep my hands off you. It seems like forever since I touched you."

"That was the decision you made."

"Rhonda…" Jo looked hurt and Rhonda softened.

"Is this really where you want to have this conversation?"

"Good point. Let's go home."

"Uh, you might want to change first."

Jo looked at herself. She still wore the hospital gown. "Good idea."

Rhonda produced the bag of clothes Randi had put together for Jo while Jo took off the gown. Rhonda gasped when she saw the bruises on Jo's shoulder and chest that the gown had been concealing. "Oh my God, Jo, that must hurt so badly."

Jo shrugged with her good shoulder. "It looks worse than it feels." When she saw tears threatening to spill, she stepped to Rhonda and pulled her close, wrapping her arms around her. "I'm okay. I promise."

Rhonda lay her head on Jo's uninjured shoulder and let her world right itself in Jo's warm embrace. She sighed deeply. "I've missed you, Jo."

Jo pulled back only far enough so she could see Rhonda. "I missed you too." Before Rhonda could say anything more, Jo continued. "Now let's get out of here. I want a real shower and some of your pancakes, if it's not too much trouble."

"As many as you want."

❖

Jo eventually got her pancakes and a bath, but most of Tuesday was a blur. Her energy zapped quickly regardless of what she tried to do. By Wednesday morning though, she started to regain some of her stamina, although the body aches were worse. She never said a word to Rhonda about the pain.

She called her boss and he told her to take her time getting back to work. If she felt up to it, she could work from home but he understood she needed to get her strength back and take care of things like finding a new vehicle. He didn't expect her back to the office until next week at the earliest.

Rhonda could see Jo was in pain by how gingerly she moved, but Jo said nothing. Whenever she asked if Jo wanted anything, meds, an ice pack, or anything, Jo just waved her off saying she was fine. Her frustration grew and finally she couldn't contain it any longer. "Jo, why the hell won't you let me help you?"

"Whoa, what are you talking about?" Jo seemed genuinely confused.

"I can see you're in pain. Why are you trying to hide it? Why won't you let me get you the things that will help take some of the pain away? Why won't you let me take care of you? Damn it, I need you to let me take care of you."

"I didn't want you to worry."

"That might be the dumbest thing you've ever said to me. Of course I'm going to worry. You're hurt and in pain. I worry more when you try to hide that from me because I don't know how bad it really is. I can tell it's worse than you let on. Why are you trying to keep the truth from me?"

Jo looked at Rhonda and then away. Rhonda wasn't sure Jo was going to answer. Then she looked back and met her gaze. "I'm sorry, Rhonda. I'm not used to having to depend on anyone else. I'm not used to having anyone take care of me. It's not something I'm very comfortable with. I never had that luxury except when I stayed with your family as a kid. I didn't want you to ever feel like you had to take care of me again. I need to be strong for you. Forgive me, please."

Rhonda went to her and sat on the couch next to her. "Jo, you are the strongest person I know. Letting me help you, especially when you're hurt or sick, doesn't make you weak. Do you remember the day I talked to Julie about us? You came home and took care of me. I didn't even realize I needed you to. Did that make me weak to you?"

"No, of course not."

"I want and need to know what is happening with you, always. But especially now when there are so many little ways I might be able to help, I need you to tell me what you need. You keep talking about a future together. I don't know if that will happen or not, but what I do know is there won't be a future for us if we're not in this together, equally."

Jo stared at Rhonda. The anger that washed across her face moments before had been replaced by a touch of sadness and calm certainty.

She took Rhonda's hand in hers. "You are absolutely right. What do you want to know?"

"How are you feeling, really?"

"My head is pounding. The body aches aren't too bad." Jo grinned crookedly and continued, "As long as I don't move."

"How about I run you a hot bath with Epsom salts, get you some meds for your headache, and give you a gentle massage after the bath?"

Jo squeezed Rhonda's hand. "That's the best offer I've had all day."

Rhonda settled Jo into the bath. Then she ran downstairs and put the butternut squash lasagna she had prepared that morning in the oven to cook. By the time she got back to Jo, Jo was struggling to wash her hair. Obviously, her shoulder was still giving her trouble. Rhonda took the shampoo out of Jo's hands. "Let me do that for you."

Jo didn't protest. Rhonda used a large cup she had near the sink to wet Jo's hair. She didn't want Jo to have to submerge her bandage. She squirted a small amount of the shampoo into her palm and very gently massaged it into Jo's scalp.

"That feels great."

"Good."

Rhonda covered Jo's bandage with a dry washcloth before rinsing her hair to keep it as dry as possible. Then she wet the washcloth and poured soap into it and washed Jo's neck, back, and shoulders, massaging tenderly as she went. Once Jo was rinsed off, Rhonda helped her out of the tub and toweled her off. As Rhonda knelt in front of Jo, drying her legs, she looked into Jo's eyes. The hunger there was unmistakable. Rhonda was instantly wet. She couldn't deny she was just as famished for Jo's touch, but…"Jo, don't look at me like that. You know what it does to me and it's too soon."

"No, it's not. The doctor said a day or two. It is day two. Tell me you don't want to touch me."

"You know I can't. But remember the rest of what Dr. Robbins said. It needs to be very gentle."

"Works for me."

❖

"Wow, I've missed that."

"Hmm, I could tell, me too."

"Are you okay?" Rhonda asked.

Jo's breathing was ragged as she recovered. "I'm great."

"Really?" Rhonda wasn't convinced. Their lovemaking had been as easy, slow, and gentle as prescribed, but Jo's orgasm had been so intense, Rhonda worried the pain in her head would be worse.

"Truly, this is the best I've felt in days."

"Okay." Rhonda tried hard to take Jo at her word. "I've missed you, Jo."

"I can't begin to tell you how much I've missed you. Please tell me you know I only left to protect you."

"I do know that, but it should have been a conversation. You took away my choice in the matter."

Jo studied Rhonda. "I never looked at it that way, I'm sorry. I thought I was doing what was best for you."

"Next time, you should ask what that is."

"I'll remember. So, are we okay?"

"Yes, we're okay, but we should talk more when you're fully recovered." Rhonda kissed Jo tenderly. "Are you ready for dinner?"

"Sure."

After pulling on robes, they started downstairs. Rhonda was several steps down when she noticed Jo wasn't following her. She looked back and Jo was still at the top of the stairs with her hand braced against the wall. In the space of a heartbeat, Rhonda was at her side. "Jo, what's wrong?"

"Dizzy, need a minute."

"Okay." Rhonda put her arm around Jo's waist to steady her. "Would you like me to help you downstairs or would you rather have a picnic up here?"

Jo seemed to consider the stairs intently. "Actually, a picnic sounds great. Could you help me back to bed?"

"Yes, of course."

Once Rhonda got Jo situated, she went down to put plates together. So consumed by her concern for Jo, Rhonda almost missed the fact that Jo had asked for help. She would keep a close eye on Jo and if she had any more dizziness or additional symptoms, she would call the doctor in the morning. But for the moment, she concentrated on giving Jo what she needed, what they both needed.

Chapter Thirty

Saturday afternoon, Rhonda was busy in the kitchen working on a meatloaf for dinner. Jo had been napping for a little more than two hours. She was surprised when she heard the front door open. She quickly wiped her hands and went to investigate. Julie stood just inside the front door looking uncertain. When she saw Rhonda, she said, "Hi. I didn't want to ring the bell in case Jo was resting."

"Thank you for that, especially since she is. But why are you here?"

"I was hoping we could talk."

"Okay. Let's go into the kitchen so I can finish dinner."

Once they were in the kitchen, Julie launched right in. "Mom, I want to apologize. I'm so sorry for the way I treated you and for the way I behaved."

Rhonda looked at Julie.

"I got this crazy idea in my head when you told me about Jo. It made me angry, and I couldn't let it go. None of this was ever really about Jo and I'm sorry that I made trouble for the two of you."

"What idea?"

"I know this sounds silly, especially since so much time has passed, but I always held out hope that you and Dad would get back together."

"Oh, honey." Rhonda hurt for her little girl.

"I just never understood why you two divorced. I never saw you argue, never saw anything that explained it. All you two ever said was, 'you grew apart.'"

"Julie, let me ask you something."

"Okay."

"Do you and Ben argue, fight, and have heated debates or disagreements?"

"Of course we do. Everyone heard that last month."

"But you know you love each other, and sometimes those fights make you stronger as a couple. Being on opposite sides of an issue is just one more way to figure things out when you're each passionate about your opinion."

"Sure."

"Now given all that, remember what you just said about how you never saw your father and I even argue."

Julie looked at her, comprehension dawning.

"Saying we grew apart made the most sense. How do you explain to three teenagers there has been no passion in your relationship for a very long time? That you're just going through the motions?"

"But you still loved each other."

"Part of me will always love your father, not only because he's a great guy but because he gave me you three kids. But staying in our marriage wasn't fair for either one of us. We each deserved the chance to find someone with whom we were passionate. Your dad found that with Sharon. Don't roll your eyes. You know it's true. I'm happy for him and you should be too."

"I know, Mom. I do like Sharon. But there has always been that teenage part of me that hoped my parents would get back together. Rationally, I know it's a crazy idea, but it's what a tiny part of me always hoped."

"And I pretty much shot that hope to smithereens, didn't I?"

Julie nodded, but she was smiling. "Yes, you did. I want you to be happy, Mom. Really, I do. It will take a little time for me to adjust to this idea of you and Jo but I will try if being with her is what you want. It's not right for me to keep you two apart. I never should have threatened that I wouldn't let you see the kids. I can't believe how mean I was. I am so sorry."

"Thank you for that. I'm sorry this is hard for you, but I care about Jo a lot and I have to see where this goes."

Julie stepped to Rhonda and hugged her. "I know, and she makes you happy. It's already getting easier. I'm glad we talked. I'd like to talk with Jo too. I want to make things right with her also. Do you think she'll be awake soon?"

Rhonda looked at her watch. "I was going to go check on her five minutes ago. Why don't you do that for me?" Julie turned to leave and something occurred to Rhonda. "Wait, Julie."

Julie turned back. "Maybe I should go. It might be too uncomfortable for you."

"What do you mean?"

"Jo's napping in my bed."

"It's okay, Mom. We'll be fine."

"If you're sure."

"I am."

❖

Jo wasn't fully awake, but she smiled when she felt the other side of the bed sink down. "Is it that time already?"

"Way past time, I'd wager."

Jo's eyes popped open in surprise at hearing Julie's voice instead of Rhonda's. "What are you doing here? Where's Rhonda?"

"Relax. She's downstairs fixing your dinner. She sent me up to check on you because I wanted to talk with you."

"Clearly I've missed a lot. How long was I asleep?"

"Very funny. Seriously, though. I've already apologized to Mom, and I owe you an apology too."

"I should sit up for this."

"Obviously, the accident didn't affect your sense of humor."

"Thank goodness for that. But you were saying?"

"You've never been anything but a friend to me and I should have remembered that. I can't believe some of the stuff I said. I was so mad at you and I didn't have a good reason to be."

"I never intended to cause any trouble."

Julie sighed deeply. "I know. When I can think rationally, I know that. You never did like to rock the boat. Even when you 'came out' you were calm and had it all planned out. But all this"—Julie stretched out her arms—"I was so angry and hurt and I couldn't make any sense of it. It was all so…consuming."

"Maybe perspective matters. I'm glad someone thought I was calm. I was a wreck."

Julie's laugh was full of childhood innocence. "You were so serious when you sat us all down to tell us, like we didn't already know."

"Well, how was I supposed to know you did? Nobody ever said anything."

"Mom told us you'd tell us when you were ready. I guess she was right. She's right a lot. I guess I should have remembered that."

"Care to elaborate?"

Julie frowned. "I was so mean to her, but she stood her ground. She said to me, 'I'm getting a chance at something important, and I can't walk away from it. I love you, but I need to do what's best for me.' She was right, but I was so mad at her when she said it. I was being selfish. What had the most weight though was what she said to me at the hospital."

"What was that?"

"She said, 'Jo is too important to me to give up. If I can convince her to come back to me, you're going to have to figure out how to deal with it.' That made me really start to think. If she was willing to stand up against my foolish ultimatum then clearly I needed to start paying attention."

Jo's heart did a little flip when she heard Rhonda's words. But she was curious. "So, what changed your mind?"

"You two have quite the band of supporters. They were coming at me from all sides. But really what made the difference was seeing how distraught and devastated Mom was while you were laying hurt in a hospital bed."

"So, I guess I should be thankful for the accident?"

"I don't know about that. I'm sure I would have come around eventually. I still can't believe what a mess I made of this."

"It was rough on Rhonda and me, but it's nothing that can't be fixed."

Julie looked at her and faced her squarely. "I owe you an apology. I acted badly. I hope you can forgive me."

Jo held out her hand. "Apology accepted."

Julie took the offered hand and pulled Jo into a heartfelt hug. Jo easily returned the warm embrace.

"There's just one more thing."

"What?"

"I need you to know I care a great deal about your mom."

"Haven't we covered that already?"

"There's more."

"Okay?"

"I'm an affectionate person. When I care about someone I show it in different ways. I hold their hand, or put my hand on their leg when I'm sitting next to them, or hug them, or even kiss them, and it doesn't matter who else is in the room. I care about your mom, a lot." Jo looked at Julie. "Are you going to be okay with that? It's not an easy thing for me to turn off, so normally I wouldn't ask. But I know you've had a hard time with this and I wanted to give you a head's up."

Julie considered for a moment and then sighed deeply. "I appreciate it and I'm not going to pretend it will be easy seeing you and Mom together, at first. But that's my issue to deal with. You shouldn't change anything for me. It would just make things awkward and wouldn't help anything."

"Okay. Are you going to stay for dinner?"

"Another time. I should get home to Ben and the kids."

"Maybe we should do a girl's night out soon. Us and Rhonda, Barbara, and Christie, what do you think?"

"I'd like that. It would be nice to have some adult time. And it would be great to really catch up with you. I can't believe how much time I wasted."

"Don't be so hard on yourself. Clearly this whole situation is unusual and you needed time to sort it all out. Nobody is going to fault you for that. We'll just start over with a clean slate."

"I would really appreciate that."

"Let's go downstairs so you can say good-bye to Rhonda before you leave. I'm glad you stopped by."

"Me too. Thanks for taking it easy on me."

"You're welcome. Of course you know that means I owe you double next time you screw up."

"That's a given, my friend."

CHAPTER THIRTY-ONE

The evening of the planned Girl's Night Out finally arrived. As arranged, Christie, Julie, and Barbara came over to the house. Everyone agreed it didn't make sense to take more than one car to go out for the evening and Jo volunteered to drive her new SUV. They soon arrived at the sushi restaurant. The hostess sat them quickly and took their drink orders.

Barbara opened the conversation. "What was the most fun place you ever went on vacation? I'll start. I really enjoyed Austria. There was just something about it that stuck with me."

"I love Bermuda. It's where Ben and I went on our honeymoon," Julie said.

"I think my top so far is Italy," Jo said.

"It's Hawaii for me," Christie said.

When everyone turned to Rhonda, she pondered the question. "I've enjoyed a number of places, but I think the most fun I had was when we'd go to the lake when you all were kids."

Christie said, "That was a lot fun."

"We should all go out to the lake for a couple of weeks next summer," Jo commented casually.

She caught the shadow pass across Rhonda's face. At the first opportunity, she excused herself, claiming she just had to make a quick call she forgot about. She went outside to get some air. She felt like punching the brick wall she was facing. She was frustrated and she needed to get her anger under control before she went back inside. Why couldn't Rhonda trust she wanted a future with her?

"Jo? Are you okay?"

Jo hadn't noticed Julie approaching so she looked at her before she could totally control her temper.

"Jo, what's wrong?"

"Nothing, Julie. Everything's fine."

Julie shook her head. "I think this is the first time in our lives you've ever lied to me. Don't tell me nothing's wrong. I saw the hurt on your face when there was doubt in Mom's when you suggested we all go to the lake. Then I come out here and you look like you want to put your fist through a brick wall. Don't you tell me everything is fine when I can see for myself that is a bald-faced lie!"

Jo scrubbed her hands over her face and ran them through her hair in exasperation. "I'm sorry. I shouldn't have lied to you, but this is between your mom and me."

"It's obvious you two care about each other very much."

"We do."

"So why are you hiding out here?"

"Listen, Julie, your mom is having a hard enough time trusting there's a future for us. I don't want to shove it down her throat."

"Maybe you should."

"What?" Jo asked incredulously.

"Well, you've tried talking about it, right?"

"Every way I can think of, but I can't get her to believe it."

"So, can I give you a piece of advice?"

Jo smiled wryly. "Only if I don't have to follow it if I don't like it."

Julie nodded. "Fair enough. Stop mitigating your emotions. Let her see your frustration."

Jo shook her head. "That will just drive her away."

"I don't think so. I certainly don't want to know details, but think about this, when is sex the best? I'll know you're lying again if you don't answer when it's out of control. When passion takes over and you lose yourselves in each other."

Jo shoved her hands in her pockets. This was not something she wanted to be discussing with Julie. "What's your point?"

"You're always so controlled. You keep a tight rein on your emotions. Knowing you, I understand why, but in a way you're depriving Mom when you don't let her see what you are truly feeling.

I know you think you're protecting her. You've always done that for everyone, but I don't think Mom wants nor needs your protection. I think she wants you, all of you. When you hide this part of yourself, you are robbing her of knowing you—all the parts of you. I know you'd talk until you're blue in the face to try to convince Mom you two have a future together. Obviously, it isn't working. Why don't you try showing her all of you?"

"I don't see how that can help."

"Can it hurt at this point? Let me tell you a little something I learned from my mom recently. She told me sometimes fights make you stronger as a couple. It's just one more way to figure things out when you're each passionate about your side of an issue."

Jo still wasn't totally convinced. "I'll think about what you said. Thanks."

"Any time. I am pulling for you two, I hope you know that."

"Thanks for that too. We should get back. Rhonda will wonder where we wandered off to."

The rest of dinner passed with pleasant conversation and good food. After dinner, they walked to the movie theater. Rhonda and Jo held hands. Everyone enjoyed the movie more than expected.

"This was a great idea," Rhonda said as they exited the theater.

"You're just saying that because you got your happy ending," Jo replied.

"Could be, but I still liked it a lot."

Nobody was ready to go home yet, so Jo suggested they stop for a drink.

Jo sat at a table with Christie, Julie, and Barbara, and watched Rhonda. For the third time tonight, a man had sent Rhonda a drink. Each time, Rhonda politely returned the drink and told them something along the lines of, "Thanks but I'm not interested. I plan to go home with my girlfriend." Then she walked back to the table and gave Jo a kiss.

"Jo, doesn't this bother you at all?" Christie asked.

Jo glanced at Christie. "No. If it doesn't bother Rhonda, why should it bother me? She's an attractive woman with no ring on her finger. It would surprise me if men, and women, for that matter, didn't try to hit on her. She looks like she's having fun, doesn't she?"

"It does, but I don't know how you can be so calm."

"Simple. I know she's coming home with me. Have you actually watched her talk to these men? She's not interested in any of them. She's simply being polite."

As Rhonda returned to the table, Jo stood and she kissed her.

"Hi, gorgeous, would you like to dance?" Rhonda asked.

"It would be my pleasure. Ladies, please excuse us."

When Rhonda and Jo returned to the table after their dance, Rhonda and Barbara headed for the restroom. Jo took the opportunity to chat with both Christie and Julie about an idea she had. A little while later, everyone was ready to call it a night.

Once everyone left, Rhonda and Jo went inside. Jo took Rhonda's coat and hung it in the closet and then her own. "How was your night, sweetheart?" Jo asked.

"Really good. It had been too long since we got together without the kids and had a night of adult conversation."

"I'm glad you enjoyed yourself."

"How about you, Jo? Did you have fun?"

"I did. Catching up with everyone was great. You were quite popular this evening."

"I hope that didn't bother you. I wasn't interested in any of those guys."

Jo pulled Rhonda to her. "You're lucky I'm not the jealous type." When she saw Rhonda was actually concerned, she said, "I'm joking. I know you weren't into any of those guys. I told your daughters as much tonight. Ask them if you want. I could tell by the way you were talking to them you were just being polite. It looked like you were having fun with it though. Rhonda, you're a very attractive woman and I imagine people will hit on you most of our lives. It didn't bother me. I knew you were coming home with me. I don't ever plan to take that for granted, but I knew it was the truth tonight. So I just enjoyed watching you let them down. Okay?"

"If you say so, but will you promise me something?"

"What's that?"

"If it ever does bother you, will you let me know?"

"Deal."

Chapter Thirty-two

Rhonda woke and stretched her whole body. She felt wonderful. She reached for Jo but found the bed beside her empty. She was profoundly disappointed Jo wasn't there. She looked around for Jo's things and breathed a little easier when she saw signs of her all around the room. Then she remembered Mike planned to come over early for a run.

She lay back against the pillows pondering her thoughts in the brief moment before she remembered Jo's morning plans. She would laugh if she weren't so scared this would all end before she was ready. Would she ever be ready for it to be over? As soon as she asked herself the question, the answer was a big fat no.

Jo was doing all she could to allay her fears, but she had a hard time trusting Jo wanted this relationship as much as she did. She smiled, thinking about their time together. The way Jo looked at her, touched her, and craved her touch. Rhonda got hot just thinking about it. Obviously, Jo wanted her physically; that she did not doubt. And Jo always asked about her day and wanted to hear her thoughts on all sorts of things. Jo hadn't flinched at any of the family drama and conflict. *Why can't I just trust Jo wants to be here with me?*

Rhonda suspected when she could answer this question, it would be easier to believe. Tired of thinking about it all, she pushed herself out of bed and pulled on comfy clothes. She went down to the kitchen and pulled what she needed from the refrigerator and cupboards. She turned on the radio and started singing as she worked.

That's how Jo found her when she walked into the kitchen a little while later. Every time she heard Rhonda sing, it took her breath away. She watched from across the room. Kona went to her water bowl and drank, and then she settled by Rhonda's feet. Rhonda turned, looking for Jo.

She smiled shyly. "Hi."

"Hi, yourself. You have a beautiful voice."

Rhonda brushed back a tendril of hair from her face.

"I used to listen to you sing and wish you were singing to me."

Jo caught the wash of emotion cross Rhonda's face as she turned away. She stopped her. "Rhonda?" Jo stepped to her and pushed the stray hair back from Rhonda's face and behind her ear. "What is it?"

"I just missed you." Rhonda pulled Jo close and burrowed her head into her shoulder unfazed that Jo was hot and sweaty from her run.

Jo wasn't fooled. "What aren't you telling me?"

"Can't we just forget it?"

"No, but we can table it for now. Only because Mike is upstairs taking a shower and will probably join us for breakfast once he finds out you're cooking. I'm going to take a quick shower myself, but we will talk about this, whatever it is, later."

Jo was steamed. As she stepped into the shower, she slapped the wall. "Damn it!" She struggled to get herself under control. She stood under the spray trying to even her breathing. Her frustration wouldn't help anyone. Rhonda had given her body to her fully. But Rhonda still guarded pieces of herself. If she gave Rhonda time, she would believe deep down. She would wait as long it took. But waiting wasn't easy. Seeing the doubt creep into Rhonda's eyes whenever she spoke of their future was hard.

She had been as honest as she could with Rhonda. But at the moment she would like to shake some sense into her. Jo shook her head at the thought, glad she had a few minutes to cool off. She wasn't going anywhere, and Rhonda was just going to have to get used to it.

❖

When Mike walked into the kitchen, Rhonda was lost in thought. "Mom, are you okay?"

"What?" Rhonda focused. The sound of Mike's voice brought her back. "Oh hi, honey. Yes, I'm fine. I was just thinking."

"Anything I can help you with?"

"I appreciate it, but no."

"Okay. The bacon smells delicious."

Rhonda was glad she made plenty given Mike's appetite. "Yes, it does. There will also be pancakes and eggs. How would you like your eggs?"

"Scrambled, please."

When Jo walked in a few minutes later, there was no indication that anything was wrong. She walked up to Rhonda and hugged her from behind. "Breakfast smells amazing." Rhonda turned so she could look into Jo's eyes. The heat she had seen as Jo left the room was gone. It seemed for now the storm had calmed. Jo took the opportunity to kiss her lightly. "How can I help?"

"You can tell me how you'd like your eggs and then take these two plates to the table. I think Mike has taken care of everything else."

Jo lifted the indicated plates of pancakes and bacon. "Over easy on the eggs, please."

In minutes, Rhonda had the eggs done and carried them to the table. "How was the run?"

Jo and Mike exchanged a look and said together, "Good."

"You didn't push yourself too hard, did you Jo?"

"No we kept it easy today, I don't have all my stamina back yet, so Mike let me off easy."

"Good."

"So, Mike told me he had a date last night and he's seeing her again today. In fact, he's been seeing quite a lot of her lately."

Rhonda picked up her cue. "Oh really?" She drew out the last word. "Do tell."

Mike laughed at them. "Her name is Sarah. She's in law school too, second year. She's smart, cute, and funny. We are meeting later to watch the game."

"Jamie's game?" Rhonda asked.

"Yes."

"She knows your whole family's going to be there?"

"Yes. When I told her what I was doing this afternoon, she asked if she could tag along."

"It's been a long time since you let us meet one of your women, Mike."

"I like her, but I don't know if it will be serious any time soon, or if I even want it to be. But I did want to see her again today, so she's coming to the game."

"Okay, Mike," Rhonda said, all joking aside. "I look forward to meeting her."

Once breakfast was over, Mike helped put the kitchen back in order then grabbed his bag and headed out saying he'd see them at the game.

Rhonda turned to Jo, nerves dancing in her stomach. "Jo, can we sit down?"

"Sure."

Jo and Rhonda sat on the couch facing each other. Kona lay on the floor nearby. Jo watched Rhonda, waiting for her to say something.

"Jo, I'm sorry about earlier."

"What specifically are you apologizing for?"

"For all of it."

"So, you're sorry you missed me while I was out."

"Of course not."

"Then help me out, because that's all you said when I asked you what was wrong."

Rhonda sighed deeply and took Jo's hand. "I'm sorry I shut you out. That I didn't tell you what was going on."

Jo nodded. "Okay, that's a start."

"It's silly."

"Obviously not to you." Jo laced her fingers through Rhonda's and stroked her thumb over the back of Rhonda's hand. "Tell me, please."

"I had a moment of panic earlier. When I woke up, I didn't remember you went running with Mike and when you weren't there...I jumped to 'she left me again.'"

"I'm sorry you're having difficulty believing I'll stay," Jo said.

"I know. Once my brain kicked in, I knew I was being irrational, but it doesn't alleviate the fear. I'm trying to figure this out. I want to believe you when you say you aren't going anywhere. When we're together, I believe it. But when we're apart, my mind taunts me. I don't know why I can't believe it yet. But I don't want this to come between us cither."

"If that's true you can't keep blowing it off. I want to know what's going on. If we stop talking about these things, issues tend to get bigger, not smaller."

"I'll try. I'm sorry I upset you."

Jo waved it off. "I think there've been enough apologies for one day. Why don't you let me tell you how you can make it up to me?"

Rhonda smiled, glad to be letting it go. "Do tell."

"Well, first I need you to come sit right here." Jo patted her lap. Rhonda obeyed. "Then I need you to kiss me right here." Jo touched her lips. Rhonda did as she asked, and Jo turned up the heat.

Chapter Thirty-three

Rhonda and Jo made their way into the gym holding hands. Jo spotted Julie and Christie first and steered them that way. Rhonda saw people watching them and whispering to each other in the stands. These were people who had known her for years. Jo squeezed her hand in support, and she and Rhonda made it over to the family. Both received warm hugs from the whole gang. All of them were curious to meet Sarah.

"Speak of the devil." Julie had been watching the door, and everyone turned to watch Mike and Sarah walk toward them.

Mike made introductions all around.

Rhonda took Sarah into her arms. "Welcome to the chaos."

Sarah laughed. "Thanks, I think." She turned to Julie. "So it's your daughter who is playing today, right?"

"Yes, Jamie's over there. Number twelve." She pointed to the home bench.

A few minutes after everyone settled, Jo stood up. "I'm going to the snack bar before the game starts. Anyone want anything?" She repeated back the orders and headed down.

Sarah stopped her. "I'll go with you to help carry everything back."

"Thanks."

They walked toward the concession stand. Jo looked at Sarah. "You survived the first round. How do you feel?"

"You mean there's more?"

"No, mostly I'm just giving you a hard time. What movie did you two see last night?"

"What are you, a mind reader?"

"No, Mike told us this morning at breakfast, after our run, that you and he did dinner and a movie last night."

"You're that Jo?"

"As far as I know." Jo nodded.

"So you and Rhonda are dating?"

"Also true," Jo confirmed. "Mike told you?"

"Yes, he did. He thinks it's great. He's very happy for his mom. It was cool to see when he started talking about you two."

"What about the two of you? What's going on there?"

"We're just dating right now, but I like him."

"Okay."

"By the way, it was *Winter Nights*."

Jo raised a brow.

"The movie we saw last night. Good one, I recommend it."

While Jo and Sarah were at the snack bar, a group of ladies Rhonda had been friendly with waved her over. The questions came quickly.

"Who's your friend?"

"Are you two 'together'?"

"I didn't know you were into women."

"Isn't she a little young for you?"

Normally, Rhonda would have ignored these questions, but whatever she said to these women would travel quickly. She thought it would be better to answer them once. "Jo is an old friend. We've known each other for years. We *are* together in every way. I'm very much into Jo. It's a good thing she's young, so she can keep up with me." Rhonda couldn't help herself as their mouths hung agape. "Any more questions, ladies? I'm sure you'll spread the word."

The women were too stunned to speak so Rhonda nodded. "Okay. Well, you have a nice afternoon. I'm going to watch my granddaughter play basketball now that the inquisition is over."

Rhonda made her way back to her seat as Jo and Sarah came back into the gym. All three of them arrived back at the seats at virtually the same time. Christie asked Rhonda, "How did that go?"

"How did what go?" Jo asked.

"Mom was just grilled by the gossip girls."

Jo followed Christie's gaze and saw the four women watching her. Jo sat next to Rhonda. "Sweetheart?"

Rhonda looked at Christie. "I'm fine" Then she said to Jo, "Really. I answered all their questions. And shocked the hell out of them."

Jo leaned in and whispered in her ear, "You seem very pleased with yourself."

"I am, very. I'll tell you all about it later. But right now let's watch the game."

Jo kissed her lightly. "Okay."

Jamie's team won the game easily, and she ran over to her family excited about how well she'd done. She received hugs and congratulations all around.

"Why don't we all go out for pizza to celebrate?" Jo said.

Jamie looked at Julie. "Can we, Mom, please?"

"Pizza sounds good to me."

Everyone agreed and planned on meeting at their favorite pizza joint.

When the twelve of them walked into the restaurant, the staff quickly pulled some tables together.

Rhonda watched Jo across the table interacting with different people. She looked relaxed and seemed to be enjoying herself. Mike said something and Jo laughed heartily. Rhonda's heart tripped in her chest. At that moment, Jo glanced over. Rhonda flushed, glad Jo couldn't see what she was feeling. Jo winked at her.

They both turned to Christie when Julie asked her, "You sure you don't want any wine?"

"I'm sure." Then Christie looked at Peter and reached for his hand. "I won't be having wine for a while, about seven months at least. We found out this week we're expecting again."

There were congratulations and hugs all around. With everyone surrounding Christie and Peter, Jo moved to Rhonda and hugged her from behind. "Congratulations, Grandma. How are you doing?"

Rhonda turned in Jo's arms and hugged her tightly. "I'm happy for them, happy in general. I'm so lucky you came back into my life."

On the way home, Rhonda told Jo about her encounter with the gossip girls. She gave Jo some background so she understood the women were well known gossips but pretty good-hearted in general. Rhonda assured Jo she had always been friendly with them but not close. Then she filled Jo in on the conversation.

"You actually said that?"

"Every word."

"That's great."

When they returned home, Rhonda asked Jo to build a fire. She got them wine and sat back on the couch watching Jo work. Once Jo had the fire roaring, she joined Rhonda on the sofa. Rhonda took a sip of wine and set it down on the side table. She took Jo's glass from her and set it aside as well. She took Jo's hands in hers. "I need to tell you something."

Jo focused intently on her. "Okay."

"I love you. I'm in love with you."

"You've never said that before," Jo said, her voice tight with emotion.

"Actually, I have. You were just unconscious at the time. So probably that doesn't count. I should have said it to you long before now."

"You said it when you were ready, that's all that matters. Well, that and you mean it."

"I do. I love you, Jo. I'm still not sure what the future holds for us, but I didn't want any more time to pass before I told you how I feel.

"I love you, Rhonda."

Rhonda sighed. "You never said it after that one time, so I didn't know if you regretted saying it."

"I don't, I would never regret it. I just didn't want to pressure you by saying it a lot, when you weren't ready or able to say it back. Then with everything with Julie and the accident, I wasn't sure where you were with everything. I never stopped loving you."

"Thank goodness."

Chapter Thirty-four

When Rhonda pulled into the garage it lifted her heart to see that Jo was already home. She grabbed her bag and made her way into the house. All was quiet. She put her work things in her office and hung her coat in the closet. She suspected she knew where Jo was. She walked through the kitchen to make sure she wasn't in there and stopped to grab a bottle of water. As she started to descend the stairs, she could hear Jo's music.

Rhonda watched from the door mesmerized as Jo put her body through its paces. She was sweaty from the exertion and had stripped off her T-shirt. She was focused but occasionally had to adjust or take it slow. Rhonda didn't think she would ever tire of watching the way her muscles moved as she exercised. With Jo in shorts and a sports bra, Rhonda had quite the view of her rippling muscles as she worked the machine.

Rhonda was thrilled Jo was finally recovered enough to resume her normal activities. The doctor had cleared her for all activities two weeks ago, but she had been worn out easily by things that she used to take in stride. Her working out was a hopeful sign. She had been rebuilding her endurance.

Rhonda finally stepped into the room and walked into Jo's line of sight.

Jo finished her reps on the chest press and took her arms from behind the pads and reached for her towel. "Hi."

"I thought you might like some water." Rhonda stepped toward her, effectively blocking her from rising from the machine, and offered the bottle of water.

Jo took the bottle and opened it. She lifted it to her lips and swallowed a good portion of the bottle. She watched Rhonda while she drank. Rhonda licked her lips. Once Jo lowered the bottle and capped it, Rhonda leaned over and kissed her deeply. Rhonda moved closer to Jo and ran a finger over the fading scar on her head. "How are you feeling?"

"Stronger than I have since the accident. Really pretty good, actually."

"Hmmm, that's good." Rhonda lowered herself to straddle her. She pinned her to the machine and kissed her intensely. Rhonda's hands were in Jo's hair. Jo's hands were on Rhonda's hips.

When Rhonda lifted her head a fraction, momentarily breaking the kiss, Jo said, "Rhonda, wait. I'm all sweaty. You'll ruin your suit."

"Does it look like I care? If you're worried about it then you better get it off me." Then Rhonda crushed her mouth to Jo's once more. Jo slipped her hands into Rhonda's jacket and slid it off her shoulders. Then she unbuttoned Rhonda's shirt and tugged it free from her slacks. It followed the jacket to the floor.

Jo unbuttoned Rhonda's slacks, but from their current position, she could not free Rhonda from them. She turned her attention to what she could do. She cupped Rhonda's breast in her hand and rubbed the nipple through her bra. Rhonda moaned and leaned back to give Jo better access. Jo quickly unhooked the bra and took Rhonda's naked breast into her mouth. Rhonda's body moved against Jo's driving them both wild. Jo got her hands under Rhonda's hips and managed to shift her slightly so she could stand up from the machine, Rhonda still in her arms. Then she set Rhonda down in front of her and quickly removed Rhonda's remaining clothes.

Rhonda's nipples were hard. She moved to Jo once more. She ran her fingers down Jo's strong arms. Jo let Rhonda take her time. Rhonda traced Jo's stomach muscles, making them tremble. Rhonda ran her hands up Jo's sides sliding her hands under Jo's sports bra. She freed Jo's breasts and leaned down to taste in one quick movement. Jo removed the sports bra and buried her hands in Rhonda's hair as Rhonda feasted on her breasts. Rhonda moved from Jo's breast to lick down her stomach. She put her hands beneath the band of Jo's shorts and pulled them down exposing Jo's hot wet center.

She stood and wrapped her hands around the back of Jo's neck and pulled her down for a searing kiss. She moved one hand down between Jo's legs and stroked her clit. Jo flung her head back and moved her hands to Rhonda's shoulders to hold on. Rhonda plunged two fingers into Jo.

"Oh God, Rhonda," Jo cried out.

Rhonda took Jo right where she stood. She thrust into Jo again and again. Jo's fingers dug into Rhonda's arms gripping for support. As the orgasm ripped through her, Jo's legs nearly buckled. Rhonda supported her weight. Jo's head was on her shoulder. As her breathing slowed, her lips brushed against Rhonda's neck tenderly. Rhonda removed her fingers and lifted Jo's head to kiss her. Then Rhonda rested her hands on Jo's shoulders. "Jo, have I mentioned how sexy you look when you are working out? Watching you makes me so hot."

Jo smiled down at Rhonda. "Well, that's very good motivation to keep up my exercise routine. So," Jo began in a sultry voice, "just how hot does it make you?" As she finished the question, she cupped Rhonda's center.

Rhonda gasped. Jo moved Rhonda down to the floor and kissed her passionately. Then she moved inch by inch down Rhonda's body. Touching, tasting, and driving Rhonda up. She moved down until she could explore Rhonda's hot, wet center with her mouth. Rhonda writhed under Jo's glorious torture. Jo quickened her tongue and took Rhonda over the edge. Rhonda's hips bucked wildly. Jo wrapped her arms around Rhonda's legs and continued to plunder and send her crashing again and again.

She made her way back up her body kissing here and there as Rhonda's body settled. Jo kissed her deeply. She raised herself up so she could look at Rhonda. "I guess it makes you really, really hot."

Rhonda laughed heartily and nodded. "It does."

Jo shifted so she was lying beside Rhonda and rolled onto her back. Rhonda rolled onto her side and put a leg on Jo and her head on Jo's shoulder. She stroked Jo's stomach, feeling the muscles there. Jo had one hand under her head and her other was softly rubbing Rhonda's back.

Jo and Rhonda lay in silence for a few minutes simply enjoying one another's gentle caresses.

Jo finally broke the silence. "Hi, how was your day?"

Rhonda raised her head and looked at Jo. "Fine, it got better once I got home. How about you?"

"I had a pretty interesting day. I want to talk to you about it, but first I would like a shower."

"I could use one myself. Would you like me to wash your back?"

"I wouldn't say no."

❖

Later, her hair still damp from the shower, Jo walked into the kitchen. She looked through the refrigerator and cabinets to see what she could pull together for dinner. When Rhonda came in a few minutes later, preparations were well under way. She wrapped Jo in a tight hug.

"I hope this is okay," Jo said.

"It's perfect. Would you like a glass of wine?"

"No, thanks, I think I'll just stick with water tonight."

Rhonda filled two glasses with ice water. Within minutes, Jo finished making their meals and dished it up. She carried over the plates and bowls and set them on the island in front of Rhonda.

"Careful. The soup's still hot."

Rhonda sat on the stool beside her. "What inspired this dinner choice?"

"It just sounded good."

They turned their attention to the grilled cheese sandwiches and tomato soup and ate in companionable silence. After a few minutes, Jo stopped eating and turned to Rhonda. "I'd like to talk with you about something."

Rhonda turned and gave Jo her full attention. "What's up?"

"I had a meeting with my manager and his boss today."

"Is everything okay?" Rhonda's brow furrowed with concern.

"Yes, they wanted to tell me how impressed they've been with my work."

"Fantastic."

"It gets better. They offered me a full-time position."

"That's wonderful," Rhonda gushed before she realized Jo hadn't said whether she'd taken the job. "Did you accept?" She asked cautiously.

"Not yet. I told them I needed a day or two to consider their offer. I wanted to discuss it with you first."

"It doesn't matter how I feel about it," Rhonda said.

"Yes it does, it matters a great deal to me. This is a really big decision and I'd like to know what you think."

"I think you should do what is best for you."

"Rhonda, I'm asking for your opinion."

"I don't want to influence your entire future one way or another. It's your life, Jo. What right do I have to weigh in on that?"

"You have every right since I'm asking for your input."

"Would it be a good career move for you?"

Jo thought over the question. "Overall I think, yes. It's basically a lateral position but I wouldn't have to travel as much and the pay is slightly better. Given the cost of living here versus California, it will probably feel like a nice increase."

Rhonda studied Jo intently. "You should do what you want."

Jo was frustrated by Rhonda's response. She rose to put distance between them. Rhonda also stood and put her hand on Jo's arm, to stop her from walking away. "Jo, wait."

Jo turned back. "For how long Rhonda? I've been trying to wait patiently for you to believe in us. To trust we have a future together. How much longer do you want me to wait? When are you going to believe I need you? That I don't want to live without you?"

"I just didn't think it was my place to tell you I think you should take the job, that I want you to take the job, because it would be selfish of me. I don't want you to miss out on anything in life because of me. I don't want you to feel trapped or pressured by me or our relationship."

Jo shook her head. "Don't you get it yet? My life is more with you in it than it ever was without you. You are important to me, and I want your input on a decision that will affect both of us. You have every right in the world to give me your opinion, not only because I asked for it, but also because I need to know it."

"Jo, tell me what you're feeling right now."

"I'm frustrated that you won't believe in a future for us. I don't know how to convince you. I have no idea how to prove to you I need you. Not just your body. I need all of you. You refuse to tell me what you want or need because you don't want me to feel trapped or pressured, right? In case you hadn't noticed, I want to be with you.

"I'm exactly where I want to be, and if you'd stop trying to protect me from you, we might actually get somewhere. I'm completely in love with you, and I'm afraid I won't ever be able to make you believe it deep down inside, that you won't ever trust me the way I need you to. I love you so much it hurts. I know you can't have confidence in the promises I want to make to you, and it hurts because I don't ever want to lose you. I don't know how to make you trust I am all in and here for as long as you'll have me. With or without this job, I want to be with you."

"Oh, Jo." Rhonda rushed into Jo's arms and hugged her tightly. She buried her head in Jo's shoulder.

Jo's frustration started to ease as she wrapped her arms around Rhonda. Jo looked at Rhonda and her stomach dropped when she saw the tears spilling down her face. "Rhonda?"

Before she could say more, Rhonda asked, "Jo? Do you mean it? What you just said, is it true?"

Jo moved her hand to Rhonda's cheek and wiped a tear from Rhonda's face with her thumb. "Every word, this wasn't how I planned to tell you, but I meant everything I said."

Rhonda clung tightly to Jo. She swiped at her own tears. "I had no idea you felt this way."

Jo rested her head on Rhonda's. "Why didn't you ask?"

"I didn't think I had a right to." She rushed on before Jo could respond. "I never wanted to pressure you. You're such a kind and patient person. I didn't want you to feel obligated to stay. I didn't want to hold you back. I couldn't ask that of you. I want it too much. I couldn't ask you for promises because I need you so very badly."

Jo lifted Rhonda's chin with her fingers. "Rhonda, you are the only person who could ever tell when I wasn't telling the whole truth." Rhonda met her gaze, her eyes still damp, and Jo sighed deeply. "I love you. I am completely and totally in love with you. Nobody else has ever even come close to making me feel the way you do. I am yours, always. I want to make a life with you."

Rhonda moved her hand to Jo's cheek. "Jo, my beautiful sweet Jo, I love you with all my heart. I am yours, always. I want nothing more than to make a life with you."

Jo touched her lips to Rhonda's and kissed her passionately.

"Jo?"

"Yeah?"

"You said this wasn't how you planned to tell me. What was your plan?"

"Well, I hadn't worked out all the details yet, but I'm pretty sure there would have been wine and candlelight."

"Sounds nice."

"Are you disappointed you found out this way?"

Rhonda shook her head emphatically. "Not at all, I'm actually a little relieved it happened this way. I saw the passion in your heart. I so very much needed to see how you truly felt. You had said you loved me but I needed to see and hear the passion you just showed me. The words should have been enough, I should have trusted them, but seeing your emotion...I needed that so much." Her face clouded again and she put voice to her last concern. "Jo, I'm twenty years older than you. What happens when I'm gone? I don't want to leave you alone."

Jo held Rhonda's hands in hers. "None of us knows what's going to happen tomorrow, let alone years from now. We both know that more than ever, after what happened last month. I will cherish the time we have together. I will always treasure loving you and being loved by you. I want to share a life with you more than anything in the world. Whether that's for one day or fifty years, being with you makes me happier than I've ever been."

"I believe you. It's the same for me."

"So, I guess I'll take the job."

"I think that's a wonderful idea."

"I have another one, let's go upstairs."

"And the good ideas just keep coming."

❖

Jo waited outside the store until Christie and Julie arrived. "Thank you both for coming. I would appreciate your input."

"Well, we've never been shy about sharing our opinions," Christie said.

Julie looked at Jo. "Thank you for letting us, for wanting us to be a part of this."

"I'm glad you want to be."

They walked into the jewelry store. A woman standing behind a display case greeted them. "Feel free to look around and let me know if I can be of any assistance."

They started to look through the display cases. There were hundreds of choices. "Jo, do you have anything in mind already?"

Jo looked over at Christie. "I'm not sure. But I want it to be special."

Jo gazed down at the solitaires, but nothing felt right and all of them were too flashy. Jo looked over at the woman who had greeted them and made eye contact.

The woman made her way to them. "Hi, my name is Tara. Is there anything I can help you with today?"

"Hi, Tara, I hope you can. I'm looking for a ring for an extraordinary woman and wonder if you might have any suggestions."

Tara didn't miss a step. "Well, let's see. What can you tell me about her?"

Jo looked briefly at Christie and Julie before answering. "She's classy and elegant, beautiful and down-to-earth, strong and intelligent, sexy and warm-hearted."

"That's a good start. Does she work with her hands a lot?"

"Not so much, but I don't think I want a stone that juts out."

"What do you think about a band with stones, maybe emeralds?"

Jo nodded. "That might work. Can I see what you have?"

"Certainly."

Jo followed Tara across the store. Christie and Julie went with her. Tara pulled out the tray covered in the velvet, with many bands with different stones nestled in the folds. Jo hadn't been aware there were so many different types of rings; before today she hadn't had any reason to look for one. Tara offered one to Jo for closer inspection, but Jo shook her head. She pointed to another one she hadn't been able to stop looking at since she spotted it.

"Can I see that one?"

"Of course." Tara took it out and handed it to Jo.

The band was platinum with five small emeralds inlaid, each separated by a diamond. As Jo looked at the ring in her hand, it felt right. But she felt this decision was too important for her to rely solely on her own instincts, which was why she brought along reinforcements. She showed the ring to Julie and Christie. "What do you two think?"

Christie looked closely at the ring. "Jo, it's beautiful. I think it's perfect."

Jo looked over to Julie. Julie looked from the ring to Jo. "I think Mom will love it. It's exactly right."

Jo turned back to Tara. "This is the one."

"Wonderful. Do you know what size she is?"

"Um," Jo started to say she didn't.

Christie jumped in. "She's a size five. Jo, Mom's a size five."

Jo looked at Christie gratefully.

"Would you like me to polish this before I put it in a box for you?"

"That would be great, thank you."

As Tara moved off to prepare the ring, Jo turned to Julie and Christie. "Thank you both so much for coming."

"We wouldn't have missed it," said Julie.

"So, things are coming together better than planned. You won't say anything, will you?"

Christie answered for both of them. "Of course not. We wouldn't want to ruin the surprise. Just let us know what we can do."

"Thanks, I will. Listen, I can handle things from here. Can the two of you do lunch on Friday, the day after Thanksgiving, to discuss details?"

"Of course."

"Sure."

"You two are awesome, thank you." Jo hugged them and said good-bye. Christie and Julie left the store and walked toward their cars.

Just then Tara brought out the box and Jo walked over to her. She opened it to show Jo the newly polished ring. "This is great Tara, thank you. I wonder if I could trouble you to show me one more thing while I'm here."

"Certainly, what would you like to see?"

Chapter Thirty-five

Rhonda had baked for two days. Pies and cakes lined the windowsills. She woke early to get the turkey started. Then she brought coffee up to the bedroom and climbed back into bed with Jo. She had so much to be thankful for this year. She was in love, and Jo loved her too. Her family was happy and healthy; life was good. She cuddled next to Jo.

Jo snuggled in. "Hmmm, good morning, beautiful."

"Happy Thanksgiving, my love."

"Happy Thanksgiving. I smell coffee. Were you already up?"

"Yes, I prepped the turkey so it isn't in the way as everything else is being prepared."

As Jo sat up, Rhonda handed her a cup. "Thank you. Are you excited to have everyone over today?"

"Very, it should be fun."

As Jo sipped her coffee, she casually ran her hand down Rhonda's back. "Yes, it should. How do you see today going?"

"Well, I expect Barbara, Julie, Christie, and I will be in the kitchen for a good part of the day. We have a tradition of preparing dinner together. I imagine Amy will join us. You're welcome to help in there if you want, but I suspect you'd rather hang out with everyone else, watching football or playing with the kids."

"You know me well, but if you need help with anything you'll ask?"

"Sure. There is this one thing I need right now."

"Oh, what's that?"

"You."

❖

Controlled chaos was the only term for it, Jo thought. Those in the kitchen appeared to be performing a scripted dance. Each woman knew when she needed to move and where she needed to be. Every flat surface was covered with food or the ingredients for something being made. Jo shook her head. It looked like everyone knew what needed to be done. She didn't need to understand it. She went in to say a quick hello and wrapped Rhonda in a warm hug. As she left, she grabbed a tray of appetizers and took it to the group watching the game.

The house was full of people. In addition to the gang working in the kitchen, there was a group watching the game, the kids were out back playing with Kona, and there were a couple of quiet conversations going on in various rooms of the house. Jo found herself wandering between the groups, chatting with everyone and offering appetizers around. She could not remember having a better Thanksgiving.

The women in the kitchen were enjoying one another. Soon after Jo left the room, Barbara turned to Rhonda. "Rhonda, you two seem good, but things feel different between you two since a few weeks ago."

"Everything has changed. It started after the accident, but last week Jo and I figured it out. She was frustrated with me because I was tiptoeing around and wouldn't tell her what I thought about a decision she needed to make, because I didn't want to make her do anything she didn't want to do. We finally had it out. We eventually admitted we want to spend our lives together. With the way it all came out, there was no way I could doubt anymore. "It's the most wonderful feeling."

❖

The following day, when Jo arrived to lunch, Amy, Barbara, Julie, and Christie were already seated. Mike soon joined them. After everyone had drinks, Jo said, "This is completely insane, isn't it?"

Christie reached across the table and laid her hand on Jo's. She nodded. "Completely."

Julie joined in. "And totally wonderful."

Barbara said. "It's also exactly right."

Mike shook his head. "I still can't believe how quickly this all came together. That's the insane part."

Jo blew out a relieved breath. "Thank you all for that and for being here to help." Then Jo got down to business and went over the plan with all of them.

Chapter Thirty-six

One Sunday morning in early December, as the first rays of the late fall sun lit the room, Rhonda stretched leisurely. Her gaze fell on Jo's gorgeous face. "Hi, love."

Jo leaned over and kissed Rhonda tenderly. "Good morning, darling."

"What were you lying there thinking?"

Jo shrugged. "Just thinking about how happy I am."

Rhonda wrapped her arm around Jo's waist, threw her leg over Jo's, and moved so their bodies were connected everywhere. "Hmmm, tell me."

"It's still hard to believe, sometimes, how well things turned out. I'm so glad we took the chance on exploring the connection between us. I have never been so content and delightfully happy."

"I feel the same way. We're so lucky."

"It's true."

Jo lazily traced Rhonda's face and her arm, bending down for another lingering kiss as she ran her hand down Rhonda's body. Jo didn't rush. She savored making love with Rhonda.

Later, tangled in one another's arms, Rhonda's head on her shoulder, Jo said, "Why don't we go to brunch this morning?"

"Okay, sounds great."

"I have to run a couple quick errands this morning. I should be back around eleven. We can go then, if that works for you."

"That will work well. I can take a nice long bath and finish easing into the day."

"Now, that sounds like a plan."

Rhonda was ready when Jo came home at eleven. Jo opened the door of her brand new Volvo SUV for Rhonda. Jo stopped her for a smoldering kiss before she climbed into the truck.

❖

Rhonda hadn't bothered to ask where Jo was taking her, so she was pleasantly surprised when she pulled up to the Lord Jeffery Inn. Jo turned to her. "I thought it would be nice to come back to where it all started."

"I think it's a wonderful idea."

Rhonda and Jo were quickly shown to the table, where champagne was already on ice.

"Oh, Jo, this is wonderful."

"I called ahead. I wanted this to be special."

"Being with you is special."

"I feel the same way." Jo reached across the table and took Rhonda's hand in hers. "I love you with all my heart and I want to spend every day of the rest of our lives loving you." Without letting go of Rhonda's hand, Jo stood up and then knelt on one knee.

Rhonda opened her mouth in shock.

"Rhonda, would you make me the happiest woman in the world and marry me?" As Jo talked, she slid her free hand into her pocket and pulled out the ring she had picked out with Julie and Christie. She held it up, looking intently at Rhonda.

Rhonda was stunned and couldn't utter a single word. She looked from Jo to the ring, and back to Jo. Her eyes filled with tears. Finally, she stood and pulled Jo up with her. "Yes, Jo, of course I'll marry you. I love you with all I am."

Jo slipped the ring onto Rhonda's finger. It fit perfectly. She leaned down and kissed Rhonda tenderly. The other patrons in the restaurant broke into applause around them.

Finally, Jo lifted her head. "Rhonda, my love, would you marry me today?"

"Jo, I would marry you today, tomorrow, any day."

"Great, let's do it."

Rhonda looked at Jo, comprehension dawning. "Wait, you want to get married today? We can't possibly."

"We can if you say yes."

"Jo, sweetheart, what have you done?"

"You can find out if you say yes." Jo paused. "Please say yes."

"Yes, Jo, I would love to marry you today."

Jo whispered, "Thank goodness," before capturing Rhonda's lips again.

Jo grabbed Rhonda's hand and the champagne bottle and walked out of the restaurant. "Where are you taking me?" Rhonda asked.

"You'll see."

Jo took her hand and quickly led her to one of the suites. Rhonda had no idea what she expected to find when Jo slid the key card into the lock, but it certainly was not what waited for her. Her entire family was there, her children and their partners, her grandchildren, Barbara, Bill and Sharon, and Jo's mom and stepfather. Jo held up the hand she had slid the ring on mere minutes before. "She said yes. We're on."

There were shouts, cheers, and clapping. Rhonda was overwhelmed and overjoyed. Everyone made their way over to the happy couple for congratulations. When Patty and John reached them, Jo's mom gave Rhonda a long hug and whispered, "Thank you for making my girl so happy."

Rhonda warmly returned the embrace and quietly replied, "It's my pleasure. She makes me happy too."

Once everyone had a chance to chat with them, people started leaving the room. Soon, the only ones left were Rhonda and Jo. Jo wrapped her arms around Rhonda's waist and Rhonda reached up and wound her hands around Jo's neck. "How are you doing?"

"Honestly, I think I'm still in a state of shock, but I'm also blissfully happy. What made you think of this and how did you pull it all off?"

"When I realized I was in love with you and I wanted to spend the rest of my life with you, I couldn't think of any reason to wait. So, I started thinking and planning. As for how it all came together, that was a combination of incredible luck, timing, and fantastic friends. Christie, Julie, Mike, Barbara, Amy, and Randi all pitched in to make today happen. I couldn't have done it without them. Are you disappointed you weren't involved in the planning?'

"No." Rhonda laid her head on Jo's shoulder as emotions overwhelmed her. "There is nothing about this that is disappointing. You make me so happy just being you. I do hope you know I don't need bold gestures like this, as long as I have you, but I am very touched this was something you wanted to do. I still can't believe this is happening."

"Believe it. I love you."

"I love you."

Rhonda pulled Jo down for a long, sweet kiss.

Then Jo walked to the door and let Julie, Christie, and Barbara back into the room. Jo turned to Rhonda. "Sweetheart, these lovely ladies are going to help you get ready. Since I hijacked brunch, I'm having food sent to the room for all of you to enjoy." Jo went to Rhonda once more. "I will see you at two o'clock." Jo bent down for the last kiss before she and Rhonda were married. Then she left without another word.

Rhonda turned to them. "What just happened?"

Barbara was the first to respond. "Well, my friend, I would say Jo took matters into her own hands. Are you ready for this?"

"I'm ready for anything if it means I get to be with Jo."

Just then, Julie managed to uncork the champagne bottle Jo had left behind. She poured it into the plastic flutes stashed nearby. "Let's drink to that."

Christie looked at Rhonda. "Let's get you ready for your wedding."

Rhonda looked at her daughters again. "Oh my God. I don't have a dress."

Christie said, "Of course you do, Mom. Do you have any doubt Jo would think of everything when she decided to throw you a surprise wedding?"

"No, Christie, no doubt at all. Where is it?"

Barbara pulled it from the closet and took off the protective bag.

"Oh," Rhonda whispered softly, "It's incredible."

Julie hugged her. "Of course it is. Christie and I helped pick it out."

❖

In a suite down the hall, Amy punched Jo lightly on the arm. "Don't think I didn't notice that you left no time for me to throw you a send-off party. Pretty smooth how you managed to get around epic send-off payback."

Jo smiled broadly. "I'm a genius."

Amy echoed Jo's question from her own wedding day. "Nervous?"

"Not even a little. The scary part was whether she would agree to do it today. Once she said yes to that, I knew it would all be okay."

"I'm pretty sure Rhonda would do anything you asked of her. She loves you deeply."

"I know. I'm very lucky. I love her so much and I'm so excited to start the rest of our lives together."

"Well then, let's get you ready."

Rhonda watched through the crack of the open doors at the back of the room. She scanned the room filled with family and friends. Like almost two months earlier, Jo and Amy stood at the front of the room dressed in tuxes, their roles reversed. This time, Randi and Mike stood with them. When the music started, Jo blew out a long breath and looked to the back of the aisle. She smiled as Jamie and Mary sprinkled flower petals. She chuckled when Cody and Dylan raced rather than walked down to Amy with the rings. Jo made eye contact and smiled at Christie, Julie, and Barbara as each one walked down the aisle and took their places across from Jo's attendants. Then the music changed and she walked through the doors. She met Jo's eyes and held them as she walked toward her future. In a light-hearted and beautiful ceremony, Rhonda and Jo promised one another forever.

After pictures and toasts, Jo and Rhonda made their way onto the dance floor for their first dance as a married couple. When the music started, Rhonda smiled. "It's our song."

The tune was the only one she and Jo had slow danced to at Amy's wedding, the one that had started it all for them. Jo gazed down at her. "You're a very beautiful woman."

"Is that a problem?"

Jo pulled her closer. "Definitely not."

About the Author

TJ Thomas lives in western Massachusetts where she enjoys a quiet life with her college professor wyf, Elle, and their animals. An IT manager by profession, TJ's passion is writing, and she spends much of her free time in that pursuit. TJ and Elle are equidistant from their two adult children who live in London and San Diego and they enjoy traveling to all points in between and beyond. *A Reunion to Remember* is her first novel.

Books Available from Bold Strokes Books

A Reunion to Remember by TJ Thomas. Reunited after a decade, Jo Adams and Rhonda Black must navigate a significant age difference, family dynamics, and their own desires and fears to explore an opportunity for love. (978-1-62639-534-3)

Built to Last by Aurora Rey. When Professor Olivia Bennett hires contractor Joss Bauer to restore her dilapidated farmhouse, she learns her heart, as much as her house, is in need of a renovation. (978-1-62639-552-7)

Capsized by Julie Cannon. What happens when a woman turns your life completely upside down? (978-1-62639-479-7)

Girls With Guns by Ali Vali, Carsen Taite, and Michelle Grubb. Three stories by three talented crime writers—Carsen Taite, Ali Vali, and Michelle Grubb—each packing her own special brand of heat. (978-1-62639-585-5)

Heartscapes by MJ Williamz. Will Odette ever recover her memory or is Jesse condemned to remember their love alone? (978-1-62639-532-9)

Murder on the Rocks by Clara Nipper. Detective Jill Rogers lives with two things on her mind: sex and murder. While an ice storm cripples Tulsa, two things stand in Jill's way: her lover and the DA. (978-1-62639-600-5)

Necromantia by Sheri Lewis Wohl. When seeing dead people is more than a movie tagline. (978-1-62639-611-1)

Salvation by I. Beacham. Claire's long-term partner now hates her, for all the wrong reasons, and she sees no future until she meets Regan, who challenges her to face the truth and find love. (978-1-62639-548-0)

Trigger by Jessica Webb. Dr. Kate Morrison races to discover how to defuse human bombs while learning to trust her increasingly strong feelings for the lead investigator, Sergeant Andy Wyles. (978-1-62639-669-2)

24/7 by Yolanda Wallace. When the trip of a lifetime becomes a pitched battle between life and death, will anyone survive? (978-1-62639-6-197)

A Return to Arms by Sheree Greer. When a police shooting makes national headlines, activists Folami and Toya struggle to balance their relationship and political allegiances, a struggle intensified after a fiery young artist enters their lives. (978-1-62639-6-814)

After the Fire by Emily Smith. Paramedic Connor Haus is convinced her time for love has come and gone, but when firefighter Logan Curtis comes into town, she learns it may not be too late after all. (978-1-62639-6-524)

Dian's Ghost by Justine Saracen. The road to genocide is paved with good intentions. (978-1-62639-5-947)

Fortunate Sum by M. Ullrich. Financial advisor Catherine Carter lives a calculated life, but after a collision with spunky Imogene Harris (her latest client) and unsolicited predictions, Catherine finds herself facing an unexpected variable: Love. (978-1-62639-5-305)

Soul to Keep by Rebekah Weatherspoon. What *won't* a vampire do for love... (978-1-62639-6-166)

When I Knew You by KE Payne. Eight letters, three friends, two lovers, one secret. Can the past ever be forgiven? (978-1-62639-5-626)

Wild Shores by Radclyffe. Can two women on opposite sides of an oil spill find a way to save both a wildlife sanctuary and their hearts? (978-1-62639-6-456)

Love on Tap by Karis Walsh. Beer and romance are brewing for Tace Lomond when archaeologist Berit Katsaros comes into her life. (987-1-162639-564-0)

Love on the Red Rocks by Lisa Moreau. An unexpected romance at a lesbian resort forces Malley to face her greatest fears where she must choose between playing it safe or taking a chance at true happiness. (987-1-162639-660-9)

Tracker and the Spy by D. Jackson Leigh. There are lessons for all when Captain Tanisha is assigned untried pyro Kyle and a lovesick dragon horse for a mission to track the leader of a dangerous cult. (987-1-162639-448-3)

Whirlwind Romance by Kris Bryant. Will chasing the girl break Tristan's heart or give her something she's never had before? (987-1-162639-581-7)

Whiskey Sunrise by Missouri Vaun. Culture and religion collide when Lovey Porter, daughter of a local Baptist minister, falls for the handsome thrill-seeking moonshine runner, Royal Duval. (987-1-162639-519-0)

Dyre: By Moon's Light by Rachel E. Bailey. A young werewolf, Des, guards the aging leader of all the Packs: the Dyre. Stable employment—nice work, if you can get it...at least until silver bullets start to fly. (978-1-62639-6-623)

Fragile Wings by Rebecca S. Buck. In Roaring Twenties London, can Evelyn Hopkins find love with Jos Singleton or will the scars of the Great War crush her dreams? (978-1-62639-5-466)

Live and Love Again by Jan Gayle. Jessica Whitney could be Sarah Jarret's second chance at love, but their differences and Sarah's grief continue to come between their budding relationship. (978-1-62639-5-176)

Starstruck by Lesley Davis. Actress Cassidy Hayes and writer Aiden Darrow find out the hard way not all life-threatening drama is confined to the TV screen or the pages of a manuscript. (978-1-62639-5-237)

Stealing Sunshine by Tina Michele. Under the Central Florida sun, two women struggle between fear and love as a dangerous plot of deception and revenge threatens to steal priceless art and lives. (978-1-62639-4-452)

The Fifth Gospel by Michelle Grubb. Hiding a Vatican secret is dangerous—sharing the secret suicidal—can Felicity survive a perilous book tour, and will her PR specialist, Anna, be there when it's all over? (978-1-62639-4-476)

Cold to the Touch by Cari Hunter. A drug addict's murder is the start of a dangerous investigation for Detective Sanne Jensen and Dr. Meg Fielding, as they try to stop a killer with no conscience. (978-1-62639-526-8)

Forsaken by Laydin Michaels. The hunt for a killer teaches one woman that she must overcome her fear in order to love, and another that success is meaningless without happiness. (978-1-62639-481-0)

Infiltration by Jackie D. When a CIA breach is imminent, a Marine instructor must stop the attack while protecting her heart from being disarmed by a recruit. (978-1-62639-521-3)

Midnight at the Orpheus by Alyssa Linn Palmer. Two women desperate to make their way in the world, a man hell-bent on revenge, and a cop risking his career: all in a day's work in Capone's Chicago. (978-1-62639-607-4)

Spirit of the Dance by Mardi Alexander. Major Sorla Reardon's return to her family farm to heal threatens Riley Johnson's safe life when small-town secrets are revealed, and love may not conquer all. (978-1-62639-583-1)

Sweet Hearts by Melissa Brayden, Rachel Spangler, and Karis Walsh. Do you ever wonder *Whatever happened to...*? Find out when you reconnect with your favorite characters from Melissa Brayden's *Heart Block*, Rachel Spangler's *LoveLife*, and Karis Walsh's *Worth the Risk*. (978-1-62639-475-9)

Totally Worth It by Maggie Cummings. Who knew there's an all-lesbian condo community in the NYC suburbs? Join twentysomething

BFFs Meg and Lexi at Bay West as they navigate friendships, love, and everything in between. (978-1-62639-512-1)

Illicit Artifacts by Stevie Mikayne. Her foster mother's death cracked open a secret world Jil never wanted to see…and now she has to pick up the stolen pieces. (978-1-62639-472-8)

Pathfinder by Gun Brooke. Heading for their new homeworld, Exodus's chief engineer Adina Vantressa and nurse Briar Lindemay carry game-changing secrets that may well cause them to lose everything when disaster strikes. (978-1-62639-444-5)

Prescription for Love by Radclyffe. Dr. Flannery Rivers finds herself attracted to the new ER chief, city girl Abigail Remy, and the incendiary mix of city and country, fire and ice, tradition and change is combustible. (978-1-62639-570-1)

Ready or Not by Melissa Brayden. Uptight Mallory Spencer finds relinquishing control to bartender Hope Sanders too tall an order in fast-paced New York City. (978-1-62639-443-8)

Summer Passion by MJ Williamz. Women loving women is forbidden in 1946 Hollywood, yet Jean and Maggie strive to keep their love alive and away from prying eyes. (978-1-62639-540-4)

The Princess and the Prix by Nell Stark. "Ugly duckling" Princess Alix of Monaco was resigned to loneliness until she met racecar driver Thalia d'Angelis. (978-1-62639-474-2)

Winter's Harbor by Aurora Rey. Lia Brooks isn't looking for love in Provincetown, but when she discovers chocolate croissants and pastry chef Alex McKinnon, her winter retreat quickly starts heating up. (978-1-62639-498-8)

The Time Before Now by Missouri Vaun. Vivian flees a disastrous affair, embarking on an epic, transformative journey to escape her past, until destiny introduces her to Ida, who helps her rediscover trust, love, and hope. (978-1-62639-446-9)